DARK HOPE

Book cover design by BespokeBookCovers.com

ISBN: 9798745640056

About The Author

R L Stokes was born and raised in South Yorkshire, England. She has a regular 9-5 but her passion is writing, when her nose isn't stuck in a book. Wine drinker and animal lover, she is a born romantic and loves a happy ever after. She lives with her husband and is a slave to her two cats.

For Mum,

whose love of all things Alpha sparked my own obsession.

Acknowledgements

First and foremost, I would like to thank Peter and Caroline from BespokeBookCovers.com. They created the most stunning book cover for Dark Hope, giving me everything I didn't know I wanted or needed. I fell in love with it the moment I saw it and knew it was perfect.

Thank you to my advanced readers, Jacqueline Stokes, Katherine 'Bongo' Bridge, Mel Woodall, Angie Wright and Shaun Stokes. Your feedback and unbelievably kind and supportive words help shape this book into its final incarnation.

I owe a huge thank you to both of my parents for instilling and nurturing my love of reading throughout my childhood. Without those bedtime stories, I would not be the bookworm and writer that I am now. Bigger thanks go to my mum. If you hadn't vehemently insisted I read *This Man,* Rose and Isaac may not exist at all. My love of Alpha males, strong women and fierce love stories comes from you.

My biggest thanks are to my husband. Thank you for allowing me to lose myself in my work for hours at a time. Thank you for letting me talk, at length, about my plans for this book, over and over again. Thank you for keeping our house running while I wrote my heart out, for every meal you've cooked when I was too busy. Thank you for letting me think about another man for the last eight months - you will always be my favourite.

My final thanks are for You. Yes, You. You, holding this book in your hands. I am more grateful to you than I could ever say.

Dark Hope

One man destroyed her.

Another wanted only to save her.

Contents

Chapter One

When I opened my eyes, my body on fire, his was the first face I saw. His mouth was moving but I couldn't hear a word through the ringing in my ears. I tried to inhale but could only wince at the sharp stabbing pain in my chest. I could taste blood at the back of my throat and could feel it dribbling from my mouth when I coughed.

He raised his hand, hesitant and swept it gently across my chin before pulling back, his fingers glistening red. I moved to sit up but my stomach exploded in a symphony of agony. My head was pounding, leaving me no choice but to lay back gasping for the air I needed to help me breathe through the pain.

His hand was trembling when he brought an iPhone up to his ear; his fingers were white as they clenched the casing. His gaze never left mine as he spoke silently into the phone. My eyes searched his face for any hint as to what had happened to me, why I couldn't breathe, why I was choking on my blood in my mouth. Why I could not move without pain. He gave nothing away, only a look of terror that matched my own. Terror and a wave of anger, a terrible fury that made me close my eyes to escape it.

The darkness quickly proved to be more terrifying. I swam on a wave of lancing pain that roiled up from my stomach, scorching a path through my chest and into my mouth. Using all of my strength, I propelled my head to the side as hot vomit threatened to choke me. He dropped the phone and used both hands to gently roll me onto my side, moving my hair from my face before resuming his phone call. I could only lay there continuing to vomit as wave after wave of pain increased my sickness. It was tinged red with my blood.

When my retching had subsided and settled into dull nausea, I was still unable to hear what he was saying. I could only lie there, thinking, w*hat the hell had happened to me?*

I allowed my eyes to drift closed again, feeling more stable now I was laying on my side. I cast my mind back through the mental fog. Everything was black. I didn't know where I was. I didn't know why I was there. I didn't know what had happened. My memory was a black hole. It was difficult to feel too concerned. Maybe I didn't want to know, considering the agony I was feeling.

More shooting pains flew through my neck as my head was carefully lifted from the dirt. *Dirt? I was outside?* I lifted my eyelids to see him kneel in front of me, placing his folded jacket carefully under my head. He was no longer on the phone and kept glancing behind him before turning a concerned gaze back to me. He looked vaguely familiar but I couldn't pull his name from the depths of my memory. But who was I? Could I truly remember nothing? No. I was Rose. Rose Carter. Twenty-nine years old. Only child. Daughter of Phillip and Cassie. Accounts assistant. Except that wasn't right, was it. I wasn't. Not anymore.

A wailing siren broke through the persistent tinnitus still ringing in my ears. I fixed my gaze back to him. He smiled a tight lipped, tense smile and briefly touched his palm to my shoulder before rising to his feet and walking away. I felt suddenly bereft as I watched his retreating back. I opened my mouth to call out to him but only a whimper slipped out. I watched him falter and turn around. He looked back over his shoulder towards the siren then back at me, conflict crossing his features. He jogged back to me, crouching down by my head once again. He put his face close to mine. His voice still sounded like it was coming from a mile away. 'Two minutes. The ambulance will be two minutes. I just need to show them where to come.' Without waiting for me to try to respond, he stood and ran away from me.

Those two minutes felt like an hour. I concentrated on not moving a single muscle. I didn't want to know how badly I was hurt and I wasn't sure whether I wanted to recollect what had happened. My eyelids fluttered closed again, thinking instead about how I knew I was no longer an accounts assistant. I had handed my notice in. I had used a hefty inheritance to set up my own business. Striking out on my own. My colleagues and friends at the accountancy firm I was leaving had organised a surprise party at a club in town to see me off in style. That's where I was before I woke up here.

The memories rushed back with force whilst I lay on the ground, my body stiff and sore, covered in blood and vomit.

I was finishing up my last shift at work when Zara dropped my best dress on my desk with a wink and a smile. 'Get changed, lady,' she said, pulling my hair tie from my head, releasing masses of my waist-length blond hair. 'We're going to celebrate your last day at this shit hole with bottomless cocktails and shots at Shiver.'

'Shiver, wow!' I grinned up at her from my desk, logging off the system for one last time. 'A night spent queuing up outside, hoping for a cancellation while we watch everyone with tickets walk past us to the most exclusive club in town.' I shook my head and grabbed my dress, heading for the loo, trying not to show my lack of enthusiasm.

Zara followed behind me, waving six white cards in front of her face. 'Lucky you handed your notice in six months ago then, isn't it?'

I stopped still with my work blouse halfway open. 'You're joking?' I asked. 'You bought tickets to Shiver six months ago?' Zara nodded, still wafting the sought-after tickets. Shiver was a relatively new club, having only been open just over a year. Insanely popular and undeniably exclusive. You bought a table instead of entry and could stay for an hour or the whole night depending on the price you were willing to pay. Those white tickets being waved in my face were an all-night membership. And Zara had six of them.

Raising her eyebrow, Zara seemed to read my mind. 'This is your leaving present by the way. And you won't have to buy your own drinks either.' Great, I thought to myself. I could definitely expect a hangover tomorrow. I carried on undressing and slipped into my figure hugging black sequinned dress. It sat off the shoulder, accentuating my fuller bust, slim waist and curvy hips. I unclipped the removable straps of my bra and stepped into my black kitten heels, wishing I had a fancier pair of shoes for such a fancy club.

I bent closer to the mirror to freshen up my pink lip gloss, squeezing my cheeks to bring some colour to my pale complexion and finger combed my hair, trying to give the straight strands some volume. 'You look gorgeous,' Zara said, brushing down the front of her own bodysuit. 'Come on, let's go. I've been dying to get into this place since Henry Cavill was seen in there.' I laughed and grabbed her outstretched hand, ready to say goodbye to the nine 'til five life for good.

Still lying on the ground I started to recognise the smell of the river. I must have tumbled down the stairs to the footpath behind the club. That would certainly explain the pain. It must be why he'd had to go and get the paramedics; there was no access for an ambulance down here. I could see them now. Two green-suited paramedics led by him, hurrying down the stone steps. A man and a woman. They were carrying a stretcher between them.

Halfway between me and the three of them were my heels, one closer to me than the other. My bag was on its side, my purse and phone spilling out onto the path. The paramedics dropped to their knees in front of me, fussing around and asking me questions I couldn't quite hear. My eyes were just gazing around blindly now as more memories slammed into my mind. *An abundance of cocktails, laughter and dancing with my team after being greeted at the club with a glass of champagne on the house. I was enjoying my leaving party and was in no rush to leave. It wasn't long before I started to feel tipsy, the drinks mixing on an empty stomach. I remembered heading across to the bar to pick up a bottle of water to rehydrate when I saw Him. The other man.*

It was at that point the male paramedic touched my bare arm and I started screaming.

Chapter Two

The ride to the hospital was a terror filled blur. I remembered everything now, from seeing that man at the bar, avoiding his advances on the dance floor, me stepping outside for some fresh air. A fight breaking out, distracting the bouncers. The man grabbing my arm and pulling me around to the back of the club. Me pulling air into my lungs to scream for help. Him shoving me towards the stone steps. Me losing my footing and tumbling to the bottom, the wind getting knocked out of me and my scream dying in my throat.

I remembered him pulling me by my hair away from the steps, my shoes slipping off. I remembered him thrusting his hand beneath my dress, ripping my underwear from my body. His fist making contact with my face when I tried again to scream for help. Then him pounding my ribs when I tried to fight him off. I remembered his knees spreading my legs apart, his fingers probing. The sound of his belt, his zip, the rustle of his trousers as he yanked them down. I remembered the burning, tearing pain when he thrust himself inside me. The last thing I remembered was him grunting and jerking as he finished and used a fistful of my hair to slam my head into the stone. Then it was black until I woke up, *his* panicked face filling my vision instead.

The memories assaulted me, just as vivid as the attack itself. At some point one of the paramedics gave me something from a syringe. It stopped me screaming and stilled my trembling body but it did nothing to calm my mind.

It was a hive of activity in the hospital. The paramedics pushed my stretcher through the sliding doors of the accident and emergency department, rattling off vitals in too fast a manner for me to keep up with. Once I was deposited in a bay nurses bustled around me, hooking me up to IV tubes, placing an oxygen monitor on my little finger. Some spoke soft words to me while others spoke only between themselves, as though I wasn't there. At one point a very young-looking woman with vivid red hair and a kind face asked if there was anyone she could call for me. I told her my mum and dads numbers were in my phone but the paramedics hadn't thought to pick my bag up. This brought on another irrational round of tears at the thought of losing my possessions but, through my sniffles, I was able to reel off my dads work mobile number; it was the only number beside my own that I could remember.

I was sent for an x-ray and a CT scan to ascertain how severe my injuries were which, remarkably, were only superficial. Bruised ribs, black eye, a small laceration to the back of my head and a sprained ankle from the fall. The pains in my body certainly made it seem worse than it was. I had also regained a more rational mindset by this point and kept trying to catch one of the doctors or nurses to tell them I would need the morning-after-pill and an STI test. The attack had been so hurried; I couldn't imagine he had paused to roll on a condom. No one stopped to listen to me though. Now they knew my injuries were not life threatening or serious, they were buzzing around like wasps. I wanted to trap one under glass to make them listen to me.

Exhaustion soon got the better of me and I drifted into an uneasy snooze, unable to fall into a deep sleep and always constantly aware of where I was. I knew the second my mum and dad arrived because I could hear my mum sniffling before she even rounded the corner into my curtained bay. I contemplated feigning sleep to avoid having to explain what had happened to me but her sniffle turned into a full wail when she took one look at my face. Suppressing a sigh, I opened my eyes and muttered, 'it's not as bad as it looks.'

'Oh, Rose!' My mum rushed to my side, looking for somewhere to fuss and faff over me without hurting, her hands flapping in the air. 'What on earth happened? Your dad got a call from the hospital but nobody really said anything except you'd been found on the embankment in a state.'

I looked towards my dad who looked solid as a rock at the foot of my bed. Nothing ever fazed him except weepy and emotional women. I couldn't fall apart, not yet, not here, not with Dad. I took a second to take a deep breath and gather my thoughts.

'We were all out at a club for my leaving do.' My words flew out of me in a rush. 'I'd only stepped outside to get some air because all the dancing had made me so hot. There was a man in there, trying to talk to me and dance with me. I'd been avoiding him for a while but he was outside when I got out there. He… um…he grabbed me and pulled me away. I tripped or stumbled or something and fell down the steps behind the club. He grabbed me again and dragged me along the river…' I paused, suddenly unable to look at my dad. 'He raped me,' I whispered.

There was the longest silence. It stretched on for hours, or so it felt like. Neither Mum nor Dad spoke and I couldn't bring myself to look at them, shame making my pale cheeks heat. I could feel my heart thudding in my chest. Eventually, to my utter dismay, my dad turned and walked through the curtain without a word. This hurt me in ways I could never have imagined. We had always been close, much closer than me and Mum. Not that we weren't close but I had always been a Daddy's girl. Any problems I had, he was who I went to. He fixed all my problems. Seeing him leave me now when I was facing the biggest problem I'd ever had hurt more than all of my bodily injuries. My lower lip trembled as I struggled to rein in my spiralling emotions. 'Sweetheart?' Mum's soft voice pulled my eyes from the opening in the curtain.

'I'm alright, Mum.'

'Have you told the police?' she asked.

I shook my head. 'No, not yet. I've been for scans to check for broken bones and internal bleeding. There isn't anything,' I added hurriedly when I saw her eyes raise in panic. 'It's just bruising, honestly. I don't think they know the extent of what happened. The nurse who called Dad made it sound like a mugging. I need to speak to someone and get them to come here.'

'Even still, the police should have been here to talk to you about a mugging. Who rang 999? How did the ambulance know where you were?'

'There was a man there when I came round. The man who…he…I passed out after and when I woke up there was someone there. He was the one who called the ambulance. He showed them where I was.' My thoughts drifted back to the man who brought me aid. I still couldn't put my finger on how he seemed so familiar to me. I was just grateful he'd found me. The riverbank was tucked away and I could easily have been missed, especially in the fading daylight. 'I think I've lost my phone as well. And everything in my bag. I'd seen it when I woke up but the paramedics didn't pick it up.' Out of everything I had to be thinking about, this still upset me. My life was in that bag. And there was a picture of me and Nana that I couldn't stand to have lost.

Mum stroked my arm gently, having pulled a visitors chair over to the bed. 'I think there are more things for you to be concerned about than your bag and your phone, sweetheart,' she said. 'Let's concentrate on the next steps here and then we'll start sorting that out.'

'I know. It's just easier to be pissed off about that than everything else.' I was trying not to let my mind drift back to the attack while Mum and I settled into a sort of awkward silence. She held my hand gently, stroking her thumb across my knuckles while I let my eyes fall closed. Neither of us mentioned Dad's abrupt exit, even though neither of us really understood why he'd gone. I just let my mind wander, mulling over all the practical things instead of the more painful memories. Police, tests, home. Police, tests, home. If I thought of nothing but speaking to the police, letting them do their forensic tests and getting home, I didn't feel like I was going to throw up or start screaming again.

We'd been sitting quietly for ten minutes or so when a soft cough disturbed us. We both glanced towards the curtain, expecting to see a doctor or maybe even the police. Instead, it was him. The man who had helped me. My heart started thudding in my chest.

Chapter Three

'Who are you?' Mum stood from her chair, directing all her attention to the man who had just entered the bay. I noticed he was focusing his gaze on me again, just as he had on the embankment. Now my pain had settled into a dull throb, I was able to meet his eye and take a proper look at him. He was tall, around six foot four. He had strong, broad shoulders and a handsome face. Impossibly handsome. His hair was dark and wavy and stylishly messy, his fringe falling into his eyes. His blue eyes. The brightest blue I'd ever seen. Looking into them was like falling into a cerulean lake.

I felt an uncomfortable tug in my belly, a result of my instant attraction to him and the confusion as to why I was experiencing those feelings in the first place. 'My name is Isaac.' He answered my mum but was speaking directly to me, his eyes not leaving mine. 'I found your daughter. And saw who hurt her.' Isaac took a step closer to the bed. His hands were in his trouser pockets, feet spread slightly apart, suit jacket held open by his arms. 'I've been with the police. Your dad is with them now.' He indicated towards the waiting area with a nod of his head. 'I wanted to bring your belongings back,' he said to me now. 'And find out how you were.' He took another step closer to the bed.

I swallowed and tried to clear my throat. 'Thank you,' I said, still unable to break our eye contact.

'Do I know you from somewhere?' Mum asked, forcing him to look away. He removed his hands from his pockets and held his right out towards her in a proper introduction.

'Isaac Yates,' he said, taking her hand in his and shaking gently. 'We've never met. Shiver is my club.' *His club? So that's where I knew him from.* 'I'd seen your daughter being hassled before. I couldn't find her in the bar when I went looking for her.' His responses were short but not brusque. He spoke softly, gently. Isaac turned back to me. 'How are you?' he asked, hands shoved back in his pockets.

I sucked in a breath to give what I sensed would become a standard response. 'I'm okay, thank you.'

Isaac narrowed his eyes. 'You will be.' He nodded, sure of himself. 'I gave your things to your dad.'

'Thank you,' I said again. I was suddenly aware of the state I must have looked. I pulled the thin cotton hospital sheet further up my body and pulled my hair forward in an attempt to hide my bruises. I didn't understand why I felt so ashamed in front of him. My cheeks flushed.

Isaac lowered his gaze, his shoulders lifting in a big sigh. 'I should leave you to recover,' he said, making no move to leave. I opened my mouth to tell him… what? What did I want to say? Stay? Go? Thank you again? What was I even thinking? I felt so confused.

Before I could properly formulate a coherent thought, two women walked around the curtain. One was wearing a uniform, with her shoulder-length brown hair tied in a ponytail, her hat under her arm. The other was in civilian clothes, just a simple pair of black trousers and a white shirt. She had a short blond pixie cut and was holding a notepad and pen. She fixed Isaac with a hard stare. 'Mr Yates, thank you again for your help this evening. Perhaps you could give Miss Carter some privacy while we speak to her.' It was not phrased as a question. Isaac gave her a tight-lipped smile in response.

'Of course,' he said. Isaac turned to Mum. 'Mrs Carter.' He nodded once in her direction before pivoting back to me. 'Miss Carter,' he said, his voice low. My heart stuttered inappropriately. With one last look in my eyes he walked away, leaving me alone with the police. I watched him go, seeing his shoulders flex inside his suit jacket. What was I even thinking? What was wrong with me?

'Where's my dad?' I asked before they could get started. I was only trying to delay telling them the story. I'd have to tell them everything, sparing them no details but, first, I was more concerned with Dad's disappearing act.

The plain-clothed police officer pulled another chair over to my bed and sat, leaving the uniformed officer stood behind. Mum lowered herself back to her chair, seeming slightly shaken herself by Isaac's brief interlude. 'Miss Carter, is it okay if I call you Rose?' I nodded. 'Rose, my name is Detective Constable Susan Neil and this is Police Constable Kate Mcloughlin.' DC Neil indicated the uniformed policewoman who responded with a wave of her hand and a small smile. 'Your dad is waiting in the family room. He thought it would be better to leave you alone for a while, especially while you tell us what happened to you. He was concerned that a male presence may not be a comforting thing for you, at the moment at least.' She cast her gaze toward the spot where Isaac had been stood just moments before.

I had a sudden premonition. This was what the foreseeable future was going to be like. People, men especially, tiptoeing around me, not wanting to upset me, the "Rape Victim". No one would want to cause any distress. I would be labelled. People would now see me as damaged. Broken. I grimaced, the thought leaving a bitter taste in my mouth. I steeled myself before speaking. 'Shall we get started?' I asked, pulling my chin up and squaring my shoulders. I would not give these women a reason to treat me with kid gloves. I would be strong and I would get through this.

DC Neil smiled at me and opened her notepad. I noticed PC Mcloughlin switch on a small handheld recorder. 'If you feel up to it, Rose, would you like to tell us what happened?' *Not really,* I thought to myself. But if I was to be allowed home, I needed to get this over with as quickly as possible. I started from the beginning, telling them the events of that night in as much detail as I could. DC Neil rarely interrupted, only to ask the occasional question to narrow down my statement and pull even more detail from my memory. I spared nothing as I described the assault itself, not wanting to be forced to repeat my recollections at a later date. They would hear it once and only once, so they could have it all. Sideways glances at Mum showed her sat with her hands over her mouth to muffle her sobs, tears running paths down her cheeks. I couldn't waste time being concerned or sparing her feelings. I just needed to get this done and finished. I ended my story as abruptly as I began; with my unconsciousness as a result of my head slamming into the ground. 'I suppose Isaac filled you in on the rest,' I muttered, feeling tired and faintly nauseous again.

After spending a few more moments scribbling the rest of my statement in her notebook, DC Neil looked up at me with something like pity. 'Yes, it appears Mr Yates witnessed the end of your attack. He chased the perpetrator briefly but became more concerned for your wellbeing. He has been kind enough to provide us with CCTV footage from the club and booking information which we hope will lead us to identify him.' This news filled me with a little hope. If I was one of the lucky ones and this case went to trial, at least there was another witness and it wouldn't turn into a "my word against his" sort of situation.

DC Neil cleared her throat, looking uncomfortable for the first time. 'Thank you for sharing that with us, Rose. We do need to ask you now whether you feel up to allowing one of the nurses to take some samples from your body.' I'd known this was coming. It still didn't make it any easier to answer her. I could only press my lips together into a tight line and nod. She stood and gestured to PC Mclaughlin to exit the bay. 'I'll send the nurse in now then. I believe you will be allowed to go home once this part is over.' The detective and officer left, closing the curtain behind them.

I looked at Mum properly now for the first time since I'd started to talk. She had regained some of her earlier composure but was looking very white. Almost sickly. 'I'd like you to wait with Dad please, Mum,' I said before she could offer me any words of comfort. I didn't want them and I wanted my privacy for this next ordeal.

'I'm not sure that's a good idea, sweetheart,' she replied, reaching out for my hand. I wrenched it away, ignoring the look of hurt crossing her features.

I remained firm. 'Please, Mum,' I said again. 'It's bad enough you've had to hear it all, I don't want you exposed to the physical stuff as well.'

'I only want to support you,' she said.

'You can support me from the waiting room,' I spoke more firmly, asserting myself. I could tell Mum wanted to argue but she kept it in and left the bay without another word, passing the nurse as she entered. She introduced herself and told me what she would be doing. I lay back against my pillow and said nothing, silently encouraging her to get on with it.

My clothes had been discarded upon my arrival to A&E, so these were picked up in gloved hands and placed in large clear evidence bags. The nurse took swabs from the inside of my mouth and took scrapings from beneath all of my fingernails. She took pictures of the bruises on both my face and ribs. She had me carefully sitting forward so she could photograph the laceration on the back of my head. Finally she had me lay down on the bed and raise my knees, my legs falling gently apart. She spoke to me throughout, telling me what she was going to do before she did it but no matter how prepared I was, I still cried out when she inserted the speculum. I tried to breathe through the pain and take my mind away but I could feel everything, from the opening of the speculum to each swipe of the swabs. 'One to test for STI's', she said, 'and one to collect his DNA.'

Thankfully, it was over relatively quickly and I was allowed to cover myself with my poorly fitting hospital gown and sheet. The nurse left me alone to gather my thoughts after a gentle pat of my arm and a sympathetic smile. I couldn't remember her name.

The police officers returned soon after to thank me again and to let me know they would be in touch as their investigation progressed. A doctor appeared soon after they left and gave me some painkillers, the morning-after-pill and told me the signs of a concussion I was to watch out for. I was only half listening as I dry swallowed the morning-after-pill straightaway. I told him I would come back if I started to feel unwell. I was also handed a pair of crisp hospital scrubs so when I was alone again, I removed the hospital gown and pulled them on, thoroughly grateful that I would be able to leave with my backside covered.

Mum and Dad were in the waiting room when I shuffled out of the treatment area. My dad was clutching my bag to his chest, his knuckles white. He avoided my eye as I came closer which caused another pang in my heart. I didn't say anything though and just took my bag from him, looping it over my shoulder. 'Can you take me home now, please?' I asked both of them.

'Of course, sweetheart,' my mum replied. 'Your room is ready and you can stay as long as you need.'

'I don't want to come to yours, Mum. I want to go home. To my home.'

Mum and Dad exchanged a glance, communicating silently. 'Okay, if you don't mind stopping at ours first and I can pick some things up. I can stay on your sofa-'

'Alone, Mum,' I interrupted her. 'I want to go home alone.' I looked at my feet, noticing for the first time several scratches across my toes.

'I'm not sure that's the best idea, sweetheart,' my mum countered.

I took a deep breath, fighting to control my growing anger. 'I'm not asking, Mum. I want to be in my flat, on my own.'

'Rose-'

'NO!' I yelled. Silence descended on the waiting room while the other sick and bewildered patients all turned to stare at me. 'Either take me home or I'll ring a taxi.'

The three of us were deadlocked for a moment before my dad said, 'come on, then.' I fought to control my wobbly bottom lip when Mum and Dad turned away from me. I followed them from the hospital toward the car park.

Chapter Four

The journey home didn't take long, despite feeling as though it took forever. Dad drove, his fingers clenched on the steering wheel until his knuckles looked like they would crack. He didn't say one word to me, or to Mum. I knew there was going to have to be a serious conversation between us. I couldn't cope with him not speaking to me, not now. I needed us to be okay and I didn't want him to be uncomfortable around me. Not because of this. He was my rock and always had been. I wasn't going to let this random attack affect our relationship. I didn't care if he thought male company was the last thing I needed. Male or not, I needed and wanted his comfort. Any conversation could wait until tomorrow, though. Tonight, I needed to be by myself.

In sharp contrast to Dad's stoic silence, Mum wouldn't shut up. After some chatter about how she still didn't think it was a good idea for me to go home alone, which I ignored, she then proceeded to fill the silence with utter rubbish. What they were having for tea. Who they were going to meet at the weekend. The continued discussions into whether a dog would fit into their busy lives. None of what she said required a response so I could just sit back and half listen. Thankfully, we pulled up outside of the small bakery which sat beneath my flat in no time at all. I unbuckled my seat belt and opened the door.

'Please don't worry about me,' I told them, one foot already out of the car. 'I just need some time alone to get my head around this. I'll phone you tomorrow, okay?'

'Okay sweetheart. Just promise to ring us tonight if you need anything, please?' Mum looked to be fighting off more tears. I offered her a small smile and a nod before exiting the car. I found I couldn't bear to look at Dad avoiding my eye in the rearview mirror.

I walked down the small alley beside the bakery to where my front door stood about halfway down. It took me a while to find my keys at the bottom of my bag but I eventually fished them out and unlocked my door. I was grateful they hadn't been lost at the riverbank. I limped up the narrow stairs, my ankle really beginning to bother me now. I unlocked the inner door at the top of the stairs and pushed my way into my living room, standing in the middle of the space. I let my bag drop to the rug and my chin dropped to my chest. I felt better already, like I was able to take a full breath again.

My flat was small but very cosy. I loved it here. It had been my home for three years now since I spread my wings and flew the nest, as they say. After spending so many years under Mum and Dad's roof, to have a place I could call my own meant the world to me. I had my living room, which was decorated plainly but furnished with a range of pastel colours. My kitchen was tiny with just enough cupboard space to keep my meagre collection of pots and pans; I was not much of a cook. Pasta and rice just about covered my repertoire. A neat and functional bathroom and my bedroom, which was where I was able to hide my clutter. I liked a tidy living space but my bedroom was another matter. *Floor-drobe* was very apt in my case.

Feeling at a loose end, I hobbled into my kitchen to look for something to eat. The last time I'd eaten was lunchtime at work. After the bellyful of drinks and the hours in between, I thought it would be the best thing to do. I didn't feel particularly hungry but given how strong the painkillers swirling through my system were, I knew I would regret it in the morning if I didn't put something in my stomach.

I peered in my fridge looking for something quick. There was a portion of leftover lasagne so I pulled it out and stuck it in the microwave for three minutes. I gazed out of the window at the quiet shopping street while it nuked, determinedly keeping my mind blank. After the ding of the microwave, I pulled out my food and perched on the end of my dining chair, eating slowly and carefully. There was a spectacular ache blooming in my jaw, probably a result of his fist. I closed my eyes at the memory, one more feeling his fist making contact with my face. I had never been hit before, always wanting to avoid even verbal confrontation at the best of times, let alone any physical kind. I was shocked at how painful it was, how the pain radiated from the point of impact.

It took me by surprise, the way my stomach turned so rapidly. I stayed sat down for the first wave, covering myself with my barely digested lasagne. I had no time to make it to the bathroom for the second wave so I just hauled myself from my chair and leaned over the kitchen sink, powerless to stop my stomach from emptying. I could only wait for the onslaught to be over which, eventually, it was. 'Jesus christ,' I said to myself, using lukewarm tap water to rinse my mouth out and wipe my face.

I was a mess. I stripped in the kitchen, throwing the hospital scrubs straight in the bin. My underwear had been taken into evidence so I lurched naked towards my bathroom where I ran the shower as hot as I could stand it. The water was blissful against my skin, which felt filthy. I stood under the spray, letting it cascade over my body, cleaning the dried blood from my hair. I knew I was running the risk of loosening the glue holding my head wound together but I didn't care. I needed to feel clean.

I grabbed my shower gel, working it into a lather in my hands and rubbing it all over my body. It was my hand gliding over my breast that brought the first choking sob to my throat. I couldn't feel my hand. I could only feel his squeezing roughly, painfully. The water running between my legs stung but I was only aware of his fingers, forcing and scratching before he pushed his way inside, tearing me. It wasn't long before I was right back there, lost in the moment. I relived every single one of his hurried thrusts, felt the pressure of his hand and body holding me against the damp earth. I could still feel the ground rubbing on my bare shoulders and an aching pressure in my hips as he spread my legs further apart. His breath was hot in my ear as he grunted in exertion, groaning his rapid release.

My body folded in on itself; I wrapped my hands around my body as I sank to my knees in the shower cubicle, the hot water creating a curtain of steam around me. I gasped and sucked in a lungful of air, my pain searching for a way to escape. I lifted my head into the stream of water and screamed in one loud wail, unable to stop it all from spilling out. I cried and howled great heaving sobs while I replayed every second of the rape. Agony tore from my throat, ripping violently out of me as I screamed and keened. I did nothing but let it happen, unable to stop it.

Eventually my wracking sobs began to subside, leaving me sniffling under the spray. I returned to my senses and made to stand on shaky legs, using the tiled wall for support. I tried to control my breathing and return my heart rate to something approaching normal but the humidity in the bathroom was making it difficult to breathe. I couldn't seem to get enough oxygen into my lungs. Knowing I needed to get out of here, I lathered my hair with shampoo, skimming over the cut and rinsed quickly. Little moaning cries kept escaping my throat. I wrenched the glass door back and roughly towel dried my hair and body, resisting the urge to rub my skin until it bled. It didn't take long for me to limp into my cluttered bedroom and collapse onto my bed. I curled up into a ball and squeezed my eyes shut, still sobbing quietly to myself until, finally, my brain gave in to the exhaustion my body was feeling and I fell asleep.

It was an uneasy sleep but it did a lot to ease my troubled mind. I knew I could never let anyone see me like that, especially not Mum and Dad. With an inexplicable gulf forming between me and Dad, I had to keep a lid on any outburst like that. Besides, it hadn't even helped. I still felt shit and knew I would continue to do so until I sorted my mind out. I also knew it would take time. Gradually, I was sure I would be able to put this behind me. I thought back to yesterday's realisation that some people were going to tiptoe around me and treat me like a victim. Given that, I wasn't going to start seeing myself that way. I was still me, after all.

Getting out of bed proved more difficult than I'd anticipated. All of my injuries had stiffened up during the night and were reignited the instant I started moving. It took gritted teeth and an audible groan to haul me to my feet. I sounded like an old woman, moved like one too.

The first sight I saw was my reflection in the full-length mirror. I grimaced as I took in my body. Every bruise had bloomed, dark purple and black. My eye looked awful, lids half-closed and puffy. My ribs were a patchwork of bruises and my ankle was swollen but the most surprising injury was on my right forearm. I could trace five distinct marks; fingers by the look of it. He must have grabbed me harder than I'd thought. There were also bruises on my inner thighs that I didn't want to think about.

Unable to stand looking at myself for a moment longer, I grabbed my baby blue fluffy bathrobe and shrugged it on. I padded to my kitchen, ready to make myself a coffee but was instead greeted by the mess I'd made the night before. Wrinkling my nose in distaste, I set about cleaning up. Once I was done, I flicked the kettle on, grimacing as I reached up to the top shelf of my cupboard for a mug before becoming distracted by the chiming of my phone.

On a sigh, I made my way to the living room and scooped my bag up from where I had dropped it last night. There were six missed calls and four texts from Zara, the most recent just dropping a few seconds ago. **Call me bitch. I'm worried.** I wasn't looking forward to this, not sure how I was going to tell her the events of last night. I unlocked my phone, finger hovering over the call button when my gaze fell on a folded piece of paper poking out of my bag. Confused, I dropped to my bum on the rug with a huff to save me having to bend over again and picked up the paper, unfolding it quickly. It was a note.

Please call me when you find this.
I want to know you're okay.
Isaac.

There was a telephone number written at the bottom in an untidy scrawl. My tummy flipped as I stared at it, remembering seeing him in the hospital last night. I still felt as at sea now as I had then. My reaction to his presence was unexpected and, quite frankly, a mystery to me. I couldn't pretend he wasn't an attractive man; any hot-blooded woman could see that. What was confusing me was the pull I felt when I looked at him; when I thought about him now. I felt a heat blossoming across my cheeks as I remembered the way he looked last night in the hospital, his legs slightly spread, hands in his pockets. His eyes, never looking away from mine as I lay in that bed. How could I ever allow myself to think of him that way? Why would I even want to?

Having a decision to make, I pulled up my phonebook and scrolled to Zara's number. I needed to speak to her, considering my vanishing act last night. I didn't know how I would explain why I'd vanished, or even if I would be able to but I knew she needed to know I was okay. *I need to know you're okay.* I thought again of his note. Why would he need to know? Why would he care? Did he feel a sense of obligation? I was one of his patrons, after all.

Sitting on the floor, I contemplated how much worse it could have been. Could Isaac have prevented something worse from occurring? Could I have been killed if he'd been left undisturbed? I shuddered at the thought and knew I owed it to Isaac to call him. At the very least to thank him. Even if I'd already endured the worst of it, I could have been left lying alone by the river for an untold length of time. He got me the help I needed. Decision made, I brought up the keypad and dialled his number.

'Yates.' My call was answered on the second ring and I was unprepared for the abruptness of his greeting.

'Um, hi…Isaac?'

There was a brief pause. I could hear the squeak of a leather chair in the background. 'Miss Carter.' It wasn't a question; he knew it was me.

'Yes,' I whispered, remembering again the way he stared at me in the hospital. 'I found your number in my bag and thought I should call.'

'How are you?' he asked again, an echo of the previous night.

'I'm okay, thank you.' Another echo. 'I'm glad you left your number, I was wanting to find you and tell you thanks. For what you did yesterday.'

There was silence on the other end of the line. I was beginning to clear my throat to ask if he was still there when he said, 'could I buy you a cup of coffee?'

My heart stuttered in my chest. 'Why?' I asked before I had a chance to engage my brain.

'You will forgive me for not believing you when you say you're okay when I can't see any sincerity in your eyes. I'd like to look at you when you say it.' His voice was once again as soft as the night before and left no room for argument. I guessed he wasn't a man used to hearing the word *no.*

There was a part of me that wanted to tell him with a firmness I did not feel that I was okay and he would just have to take my word for it and make him accept my thanks over the phone. But there was another part of me, the part that had screamed herself raw in the shower last night that wanted to be honest. Honesty won. 'I'm not sure you would see any sincerity if you saw me saying it.'

'As I thought,' he said. 'Listen, I know this may sound out of line but I would really like to see you.'

'Why?' I asked again, more curious this time.

'Do I need a reason?' Did he? The pull towards him was growing inexplicably stronger and I did still need to thank him properly. It felt incredibly important to let him know how grateful I was for his quick response.

I thought for a second, chewing on my bottom lip. 'There's a Starbucks in the city if you want to meet there?'

'How soon can you be there?' he asked.

'Half an hour,' I replied.

Chapter Five

Despite my conviction on the phone, thirty minutes was possibly an incredible underestimation of how long it would take to make myself presentable. As it was, I sat on my rug and stared at my phone for several minutes with no thoughts in my head. Just completely blank, gazing at nothing. Then the jolt came and I realised how much of a mess I truly looked. Also, the realisation that I didn't *want* to look like a mess. Not when I was going to walk into a building and sit across a table opposite him.

I hauled myself to my feet, wincing as my stiff and achy ribs complained. I hobbled my way back into my bedroom and stood in front of the mirror again. Top to bottom, I was in an awful state. Having done nothing with my hair the night before, it was a ratty mess of waves with a straw birds nest on top. But not the sexy, tousled kind of wave. Oh no. A beach babe I was not. More the unkempt kind. It would take far too long to straighten or curl properly, what with it being so long so there was nothing for it but to drag my teaser comb through it, being careful not to catch the glue at the back of my head and put it in a long plait, leaving it to hang over my left shoulder.

Clothes weren't a problem. Although I wanted to look nice, I also wanted to cover up my bruises and scrapes as much as possible. As autumn was just around the corner, I figured I wouldn't look out of place in one of my thinner jumper dresses. I pulled on a pair of yellow Snag tights and a loose grey dress. I had a grey pair of Converse in the back of my wardrobe that would suit quite nicely, without having to slip into a pair of boots. It would be warm enough without a jacket, thanks to the long sleeves of the dress.

Having saved the worst till last, I made my way back into the bathroom to clean my teeth and tackle my face. I never really wore much makeup, preferring to stick with the natural look; I was too lazy to bother with it most days in all honesty. The makeup I did have was relatively good stuff though, so I was hoping my Bare Minerals was going to do a good job of covering up the worst of the bruises. Zara would have been able to cover them up, no problem. Her makeup skills were second to none. I also knew she would be round like a shot to help me out but I still didn't know what to tell her, which reminded me; I still had to call her back. Unable to face her inquisition, I settled instead for a text. **Just woke up now, got a raging hangover. Had to call it quits. Too much to drink on an empty stomach. Serves me right :-) I'll give you a ring later on. Sorry for worrying you.** I felt terrible about lying to her but it was the only thing I could think of to tell her that would give me some breathing space for a while. Sure enough, it was only a couple of minutes before her reply pinged my phone. **Haha, lightweight. Thought you'd copped off, should have known better, lol!** I grimaced at her choice of words, wishing for all the world it had been that way. Or even that I had indeed had too much to drink and needed to pack in early. Shaking my head, I pushed the memories out of my mind and picked up my foundation and brush and got to work.

It took a good twenty minutes to cake enough foundation on my face to cover up the worst of the bruises. I'd been hoping for airbrushed but looked instead like a teenage girl trying out her mum's makeup for the first time. Mascara was a no go considering the level of swelling on my left eye, making it pointless using it on the other. I just used a little bronzer to break up the foundation and a touch of blusher in an attempt to take attention away from the shiner. I looked nothing like myself and I wasn't really hiding anything, but at least I wasn't presenting Isaac with the same face he saw yesterday. Without knowing why, I didn't want to be the battered and broken woman in front of him.

After faffing with some loose tendrils of hair that were escaping from my plait, I gave up in the end and, in a huff with myself, grabbed my phone, stuffed it in my bag and headed out the door.

I didn't live far from the city centre and would usually walk there via the picturesque river paths. I immediately turned left at the side of the bakery to head towards the steps leading down to the river but felt a bubble of panic rising from my stomach. I faltered in my steps, unable to continue. I couldn't do it. I couldn't put myself back on that path. What if it wasn't a random attack? What if my rapist had planned it all and knew where I lived? If he was stalking me and knew I walked the river path when I headed into the city? What if he was waiting there for me, ready to continue what he'd started? Fighting back tears, I turned and headed towards the main road instead, my heart beating furiously in my chest.

It took a little longer to reach the city centre on the main road and I was running seriously late by the time I reached the Starbucks. I'd become more and more frazzled the closer I got. It was busy; Saturday always brought more people out and I was getting jostled with every step I took. I couldn't seem to focus and my breath was coming quicker and harder. I knew I'd left Isaac waiting for so long, he would most likely have left now. I should have just told him no. Being here wasn't doing me any favours. But I pressed on, thinking I could at least get a coffee. I never did manage to have one before I left the house.

I pushed my way into the Starbucks, the noise of all the customers talking and laughing assaulting my ears. I was practically gasping for air, ready to run back out the door when movement in my peripheral vision caught my eye. I turned my head towards the rear sitting area and there he was, standing in the doorway. The moment I locked eyes with him, all sound stopped. It was like there was only him and me in an empty room, until someone bumped into my shoulder on their way to the counter queue, that was. I flinched away and looked around me before swinging my eyes back to Isaac. My breath flew from my lungs on a shaky sigh and a single tear fell from my eye as I took a hesitant step towards him.

His eyes narrowed in concern and he moved towards me, meeting me in the middle of the room. He raised his arm towards me and circled it around my shoulders as I entered his orbit. With only the gentlest of pressures, Isaac steered me towards the sitting area which was, thankfully, much quieter. The conversations in here were more muted, even though the room was full. Without the hissing of the coffee machine and the baristas shouting out orders to each other, with more people working on laptops or tapping away on their phones, there was an eerie stillness to the area.

There was only one small table available in the corner, an empty coffee cup on one side. I headed to the empty side of the table but Isaac guided me to the other so I could seat myself in the corner, away from all the other customers. He sat opposite me and lifted his hand to gently wipe my tear away. My breath hitched as I followed his hand's progress as he rolled the little dewdrop between his thumb and middle finger. 'I'm sorry,' I said. 'I don't know what's wrong with me. I feel a bit overwhelmed.'

Isaac nudged his chair closer to the table, leaning close to me. He took in my face, lingering at my swollen eye. The intensity of his gaze brought a blush to my cheeks, not that he would have been able to see it under the layers of makeup. 'Not to worry,' he said, his breath blowing across my face. It smelled fresh and minty with only a slight undertone of coffee. 'I was going to ask how you are again, but I feel like that's becoming redundant.' I smiled a little as I matched his scrutiny with my own. I couldn't remember ever having seen a more attractive man. Those eyes. And his mouth, half curled up in a small smile of his own. I couldn't bring myself to look away. 'I'm glad you came. I was beginning to think you weren't.'

'I'm sorry, I didn't mean to be so late,' I told him. 'It took me longer than I thought it would to get ready.' I vaguely indicated my made-up face. 'I didn't want the bruises to show up so much.'

'Why?'

Taken aback by the forcefulness of his question, I stuttered. 'What?'

'Why hide?' Isaac narrowed his eyes as he stared at me. He looked frustrated.

'I didn't want to look quite so damaged,' I told him truthfully. He sighed and shook his head. 'I thought it would make me feel a bit better.'

'And did it?'

I nearly laughed aloud at his abruptness. 'Not really, no.' We shared a small smile. 'I guess I just didn't want you to see me like that again.'

'Like what?' he asked.

I thought for a second and just shrugged, gesturing again at my face. 'A mess,' I said, looking down at the table.

Isaac made a noise of disgust. 'You look nothing like a mess,' he said. 'You're beautiful,' he added under his breath, so softly I wasn't sure I was supposed to have heard. My eyes shot back to his. He gave his head another shake and leaned back in his chair. 'I'm sorry,' he said. 'I'll get us some drinks. What would you like?'

'A latte, please?'

'Of course. I won't be a minute.' Isaac rose from his chair and moved with purpose to the counter, leaving me alone with my thoughts. I really was confused with myself. There I was, just about to hyperventilate my way out of the coffee shop until I clapped eyes on him. What on earth was that about? What was I hoping was going to happen here? I'd agreed to meet him for coffee to thank him for calling an ambulance, so why did I spend so much time getting ready? To look nice? And the makeup. Why? Why would I even need to try to make myself up for him, as though we're meeting for a date? And what about his comment? Beautiful? That thrilled me more than it should. I looked up through my eyelashes, through the archway towards the counter where he stood, hands in his grey trouser pockets, just like last night. He was wearing a pale blue fitted shirt that clung to his broad chest and lean stomach. I needed to give my head a shake. I was unsure why I wasn't more uncomfortable with the way my thoughts were going. Was this normal after a traumatic event?

When I saw Isaac walking back towards me with our coffees, I pulled myself together and smiled as he placed my latte in front of me and slid his empty away at the same time. 'Thank you,' I told him, wrapping my hands tightly around the mug, enjoying the warmth.

'Welcome,' he said, taking a sip of his coffee, drizzled in what looked to be a caramel sauce. He caught me looking as he put it down and grinned. 'Caramel macchiato. I know. I look like an espresso sort of guy, but my sweet tooth rules my heart.' I couldn't help but smile until his expression became serious. 'Listen, I need to say this now, get it out of the way.' I gulped. 'I spoke to the police again this morning. They wanted to go over my statement. They also wanted me to flesh out my description of him.' I noticed Isaac's hands were clenched into tight fists on the tabletop. 'I took them to the club so they could see the CCTV footage for themselves.'

'So they know what he looks like? Do they know who he is?' I asked.

'Yes. And no. They have his picture now so I imagine that's been circulated. But they didn't recognise him, either. I pulled up the booking records for last night too. His ticket belonged to a John Smith.'

'Popular name,' I commented sarcastically.

Isaac cocked his head. 'We take card information at booking, to secure the tickets. His was paid for by a gift voucher, purchased by a woman, a Nicola Simpson. I gave the police her name too. She should give them the bastards real name.' He practically snarled the last sentence, his teeth gritted. I was quite surprised by his apparent fury.

'Thank you,' I said again. 'For your help. Today, and last night.'

'You don't need to thank me, Miss Carter.'

'Rose,' I interjected. 'Just Rose.' Miss Carter sounded far too formal coming out of his mouth.

Isaac nodded his head slightly in my direction. 'Rose. You really don't need to thank me,' he said again.

'I do. I kept thinking last night how much worse it could have been and I want you to know how grateful I am that you came when you did.' I looked him right in his cerulean blue eyes. I needed him to know how serious I was. 'You might have saved my life last night.'

Isaac was shaking his head. 'Anyone would have done the same.'

'Would they? There were a lot of people on that street last night. Surely someone heard the commotion or saw him grab me. I know there was that stupid fight but still, someone must have seen.' I took a long sip of my latte, not wanting Isaac to see how much it hurt me that other people might have seen something but just stood by, leaving me to be violated. A thought popped into my mind, then. 'Why were you there, though? You said you'd seen me being hassled?'

'Hmm,' he said around another mouthful of his macchiato. 'I often go into the security suite and take a look at the cameras, make sure everything's alright.' I had to rein in a grin of my own at the thought of him surveying his empire. 'I'd gone in to find him on the cameras after hearing he'd got handsy with one of my waitresses. I saw him on there with you. Pestering. I left the suite to find him and have him removed but by the time I'd made it up to the dance floor, I'd lost sight of him. I couldn't see you either and it scared me.' *Scared him?* 'I headed outside to take a look around when I couldn't find you in the club.' He looked right at me now. 'I just wish I'd come looking sooner.'

I wanted to speak, to respond to him, to assuage what sounded like his guilt, but something had stolen my voice and the breath from my lungs right along with it. We stayed like that for several minutes before Isaac was the first to break our eye contact, blinking slowly before leaning closer to me again. 'Why were you at my club last night, Rose?' he asked me softly. 'Were you celebrating something?'

I nodded, pleased to have something more pleasant to discuss. 'It was my leaving party with work friends. They'd bought me the ticket as a leaving gift. Drinks on them all night. It was great. I'm just sorry my night was cut short.' I tried hard to disguise the bitterness in my tone.

'Me too,' he said. 'I'd be very glad to have you back there, sometime.'

I chuckled. 'I'm not sure I'll have many more reasons to go somewhere so exclusive again,' I said. I wouldn't mention the cost of the place; I didn't want to risk insulting him.

'Not even one reason?' Isaac asked me, raising his eyebrow ever so slightly. *Was he flirting with me?* Before my mind could form a proper response amongst my scattering wits, he saved me by asking, 'so, a leaving party? Moving on to pastures new?'

'Yes, sort of,' I replied. 'I've actually started my own business.'

'Oh?'

'Yeah, I've bought some unused land from one of the farmers over at the end of Fulford, near the A64 and had a cattery built there.' Isaac raised his eyebrows in encouragement, wanting me to continue. 'The builders have finished, I have electricity now and it's all been plumbed. I just have to get in there and decorate and get the wifi connected and then I'll be good to go. I get my first cat in a fortnight,' I said, pride making me sit up a little taller. 'That's why I finished work yesterday, so I would have time to get everything sorted.' I caught a glimpse of the time on his watch as I finished; a stainless steel Patek Phillipe. *Fancy,* I thought to myself. 'Which reminds me,' I said, pushing my now empty mug away from me. 'I really should be going and getting to work. Thank you, again, for the coffee,' I told him as I stood up.

Isaac rose with me. 'You're more than welcome, Rose,' he said as he extended his arm to allow me to leave first. I could feel him fall into step behind me as we walked towards the exit.

It was still busy outside and as I turned to say goodbye to Isaac, I found I had to step closer to him to keep clear of an errant pushchair. I wasn't expecting to find myself quite so close to him and I swayed a little as I bumped into his chest. He steadied me gently by placing his hands on the tops of my arms. My breath caught in my throat at his touch, tingles now running through my body. 'Would you let me take you out to dinner?' he asked me, not letting go of my arms.

I was caught off guard by the question. 'Like a date?' Isaac nodded, trying and failing to hide a smile. 'I'm not sure,' I answered honestly. 'I don't know what sort of company I'll be.'

He caught a loose length of my hair that was blowing in the breeze and tenderly tucked it behind my ear. 'I'd really like to see you again,' he told me, seemingly oblivious to the crowds weaving around us. 'Would you at least think about it?'

I swallowed, far too loudly. 'Can I call you?' I whispered.

'Please,' he replied.

I gave him a shy smile and turned to leave, feeling strangely sad to lose his gentle touch on my arm. I walked to the end of the street, to the pedestrian crossing before I turned back around. He was still stood there, an immovable rock in a river of people. He held his hand up in a wave before turning and walking in the opposite direction, towards the heart of the city.

Chapter Six

On the way to work, I stopped off briefly at my flat to change into a pair of leggings and an oversized t-shirt; I just needed something scruffy to wear that I wouldn't mind splashing paint all over. I left my Converse on because they had seen better days. Once I was suitably dressed for a day of painting, I headed back to the main road and made the twenty-minute walk through Fulford to my new premises.

When I arrived I was pleasantly surprised to see my sign had been delivered and fitted up at the entrance. It was beautiful; the silhouette of a sleeping cat done in white on a pale purple background. The name of the business, *Carter's Cattery*, was alongside the website information. I couldn't help smiling as I walked up to the front door and let myself in.

The builders had done a great job with my large L shaped building. I had twelve rooms, all with individual underfloor heating so I only had to warm up whichever of the rooms were in use. Each room had a separate sleeping area with a window for views of the outdoors and enough room for the kitty to have a play with their toys and a little run about in their mad moments. All of my rooms were large enough to house three cats comfortably. I'd asked for sturdy wall shelves placed in all of the pods so there were plenty of high spots for the tree dwellers. Each room also had two remote cameras; one in the main area and one in the sleeping box so the owners could tune in to a live stream of their fur-babies while they were staying with me.

At the end of the building, in the short arm of the L was my office and storeroom, with shelves in place for all of my cat safe cleaning products and various foods that I wanted to keep in stock so the owners would have a choice of their favourites. I'd already been and bought all of my decorating supplies and dropped them off in the storeroom. A soft light grey for the office and storeroom to offset the cream marble effect tiles and magnolia for each of the rooms to work with the pale grey tile I'd chosen for them. Eager to crack on and get started, I quickly undid my plait and shoved my hair on top of my head in a messy bun, grabbed my headphones from my bag and plugged them in to my phone, tuning into my favourite playlist and got to work.

Having started with the magnolia in the individual rooms first, figuring the office and storeroom could wait if I ran behind, I managed the first coats in four of the rooms before I broke off for a drink. While I was waiting for the kettle to boil, I noticed I'd missed a call and had a voicemail from DC Neil. I poured the hot water into my mug and let my tea brew as I returned her call. It was quite unproductive really; she asked how I was, I told her fine, as was my new mantra. She told me she was exhausting every avenue to find my attacker and that I was to call her if I needed anything. I told her I would and thanked her. I sipped my tea and perched on the edge of my desk, contemplating the idea of dinner with Isaac. I have to say, I was very tempted, although I wasn't sure why. I mean, he was gorgeous and seemed like a good guy and it was flattering to know he wanted to spend more time with me. I'd like to get to know him better. There was definitely an attraction there, a pull I'd never felt before. But where could it go, really? A date here and there, leading to what? A relationship? A sexual relationship at that? That's what I'd meant when I told him I wasn't sure what sort of company I'd be. I shuddered at the thought of being intimate with someone. That's not to say I didn't find him attractive enough to want to sleep with him but right now? I felt queasy thinking about it. But how did I know he wouldn't wait, if one date led to another and another, until I felt in a better place? Could I trust him to take things slowly with me while I worked through the shit in my head?

I slammed my mug down on the desk and picked up my phone. I needed advice here, real advice before I thought myself up in knots. I picked up my phone and called Zara, bracing myself for a difficult conversation.

'Feeling better?' she asked instead of hello.

'Not bad,' I told her. I paused briefly. 'Are you doing anything today?' I asked.

I could hear her stifling a yawn. 'Not a thing, why?'

'Do you want to come up to the cattery for a bit? I could do with a chat.'

'You don't want me to paint, do you?' she asked warily.

I laughed. If she wasn't keeping her house spick and span, she was possibly one of the laziest people I knew but I loved her to death. I'd not been working at the accountancy firm for long before she claimed me as her friend. We'd been close ever since and I had no worries at all that we wouldn't stay that way now I'd left the company. 'No, I'm not roping you in to help out, I could just do with talking something out with you.'

'Something like?' she asked, her curiosity piqued. Before I had a chance to reply, she gasped down the phone. 'Did you meet someone? Last night? Rose Carter, you little fibber. Too much to drink, my arse!'

'No, Zara, listen.' I needed to rein her in before she got too excited. 'It's complicated. Could you come and meet me, please?'

'Course I will,' she said. 'I'm already on my way.'

I wanted to forewarn her about the state of my face but she'd already hung up. She didn't live in the city so I knew she'd be around twenty minutes so, to keep myself busy, I grabbed my roller and headed into the next room.

I could hear Zara arrive before I could see her, tripping over her own feet coming through the door. I could also smell something tasty, which made me realise I hadn't eaten anything I hadn't thrown straight back up since yesterday lunchtime. My stomach was growling. I popped my head out of the room I was working in, ready to call out to her to warn her, but she was already in the corridor. She stopped dead when she saw me, her mouth falling open into a shocked O.

'What the hell happened to you last night?' I took her by the hand and led her into my office where I told my sad little story again, hopefully for the last time. 'Jesus christ, Rose,' she said when I'd finished. 'The police were there last night, speaking to the barman and owner of the place. We heard about a rape behind the building but you were long gone by this point. We didn't think it could have been you.' She looked pale, her hands clutching her cheeks. 'I'm so sorry.'

'Don't worry,' I said. 'I just want to try and forget the whole thing. I'm alright, really. Just some scrapes and bruises.' Zara opened her mouth to probe further but I wasn't having any of it. 'Honestly,' I told her firmly. 'I'm alright. I don't want to keep going on about it.' And now I was getting to the reason I'd asked her here. 'The owner was the one who found me, he called the ambulance yesterday. He wanted to meet me this morning, to see how I was.' My stomach grumbled loudly so I dived in the box and grabbed a slice of pizza. Cheese and tomato, that was my Zara. A vivacious wildcard except in her choice of pizza toppings. I ate a big bite, chewing quickly. "I met him for coffee.'

Zara raised her eyebrow, for once in her life saying absolutely nothing. 'He wants to take me out for dinner.'

'Right?'

Right? I swallowed another bite of pizza. 'Right. And I don't know what to do.'

'Why?' She pulled a slice of pizza out for herself, taking a nibble from the crust first, the weirdo.

'Why?'

'Is there an echo in here?' She rolled her eyes.

I shot her a glare. 'I don't know what you mean by why.' I was growing frustrated.

'Well, do you like him, or not? Do you want to see him again, or not?' It was always so black and white with her.

'Does it matter if I like him? If I want to see him again? I was just raped, Zara. What am I going to be like on a date? Hardly the best company.'

'I thought you didn't want to keep going on about it,' she said, blunt as ever.

I stopped short, my next bite halfway to my mouth. She was sat on the edge of my desk, her mouth twisting up into a sly little smirk. She certainly had me there. I lowered my slice back to the box. "So,' she said. 'Do you like him, or not?'

Could it really be that simple? As black and white as all that? Was I overcomplicating things? I certainly knew the answer to her question. 'Yes, I do. He's magnetic. I can't keep my eyes off him when I'm with him.' I thought back to when he appeared in the hospital yesterday. It was like my eyes were glued to him.

'I guess that should tell you all you need to know, then. You didn't need me at all.' Zara shrugged and rolled her remaining slice into a pizza swiss roll before polishing it off in two bites. 'I couldn't really see him last night, they weren't at the bar long before they moved into a private area. What's his name?' She pulled her phone out of her bag. I knew what was coming and would be powerless to stop her. She could give MI5 a run for their money when it came to tracking people down on the internet. So I told her and it wasn't long before she whistled and spun the phone round to me. 'Is that him?'

I felt familiar butterflies swoop through my stomach as I took in his Facebook profile picture. It looked like a candid shot of him and his bartender behind the bar at Shiver. His bartender had just launched a cocktail shaker across the space towards Isaac and his arms were outstretched in an apparent attempt to catch it, the still picture capturing the most beautiful open-mouthed smile I had ever seen. His messy hair was long and falling in his eyes which were gorgeously crinkled in laughter. I'd thought he was stunning before, all serious and a little playful, but this? What I wouldn't give to hear what that laugh sounded like. Men shouldn't look that good. It was criminal.

Zara's laughter snapped me out of my fixation. "Fucking hell, Rose, I wish you could see your face.' She grabbed her stomach as she bent double. 'If you don't date the guy, I will.'

As an unexpected pang of jealousy ripped through me, I passed her phone back. 'What if he wants things to go further than just a date or two?'

Sobering up in an instant, she said, 'so what if he does?'

'I can't even think about that.'

'Maybe you won't feel ready or able for a while. Maybe you will. But if you don't and if it's working out, he'll wait.' Zara crossed her arms across her chest and gazed out the window. 'That being said, if it were me, I'd fuck him into next week without batting an eyelid.'

Now it was my turn to burst out laughing, feeling a hysteria bubbling through me. "You're such a filthy slut!' I choked out through my laughter.

'I know,' she said on a shrug.

After finishing the pizza and chatting away for another hour, Zara left to go back home, leaving me feeling better than I'd ever expected to. I felt positive and hopeful. I actually felt good. I spent the rest of the afternoon doing the first coats in the rest of my rooms and then started to walk home. Pulling my phone out of my pocket, I considered calling Isaac. Was it too soon to take him up on his offer of dinner? Would I seem too eager? As I was pondering my decision, a now-familiar number flashed up on my screen. 'I was just thinking about you,' I answered, by way of hello.

'I thought you might be,' he said softly, his deep voice causing a thrill to shoot through me. 'Still hard at work?'

'Not anymore, I'm just heading home.'

'That's why I was calling actually, to see if you needed a lift home.' I smiled to myself as my feet pounded the pavement. 'Are you outside?'

'Yeah, I'm just walking home.' I was confused by his sudden change in tone. 'It's not too far.'

'It's dark.'

'I'm on the main road. Twenty minutes tops. More like fifteen, actually.'

I could hear hurried movement on his end of the line. 'I'm coming to get you.' *Was he panicking?* 'Stay where you are,' he barked.

'Isaac, I don't know where you're coming from but I'll be home by the time you get here. Don't worry.'

'I don't want you on your own,' he said. Yep, he was panicking. I could still hear him moving around.

'Please don't worry. I'll be home before you know it.' I felt oddly touched by his concern. 'If I was going to wait for you, I'd still be on my own.'

'Go back to the cattery then. I know where it is, I'll get you from there.'

'No!' I spoke loudly, pulling him up short as a shot of adrenaline burst through me. I needed him to listen to me, to not overrule my decision. 'I'm nearly halfway home now.' I could almost feel him bristling down the phone. 'What are you so worried about?'

'You.' He was firm. Abrupt. Furious. Tension radiated through the airwaves. 'I want you safe.'

I hesitated for a split second before my earlier concerns flooded back. I'd avoided a river walk for the same reason. I, too, wanted to be safe. But I knew I wasn't putting myself in any overt danger; it was only just turning dark and the streets were well lit. Plus, I didn't want to become too afraid. I was an independent woman before and I was determined not to let that change. But still, hearing him voice my same concerns made me pick up the pace. I was more grateful than ever that I lived close to my new base of operations. 'How about you talk to me until I get home?' I asked him. 'Then you'll know I'm safe.'

'I'd feel better seeing you through your front door.' Isaac sounded stubborn. His protective urge gave me a little thrill.

'Will this do?'

'I suppose it'll have to,' he replied, sulking now. I could imagine his brow furrowed and his lip sticking out in a pout. I wished I could be seeing it in person. Which made me all the more determined to see him again.

'So, I was thinking about your offer,' I began, wanting him to get back to his earlier playful tone of voice.

'Yeah?' I smiled, still hearing him sulk.

'Ycah,' I said. 'How does Friday sound?'

I heard him sigh. 'Friday?' What was wrong with Friday? 'You'd make me wait that long to see you again?'

'Yes I would,' I replied. 'It'll increase the anticipation.' Was I flirting? Plus it would give my swollen eye and other bruises some time to subside.

'My anticipation is already running high,' he said. 'Patience is not my strong suit.'

I chuckled. 'So I've noticed,' I muttered, mostly under my breath. 'Where were you thinking of taking me?' I asked.

Isaac thought for a minute. 'Meltons,' he said. 'You been before?'

I told him I hadn't. I knew of it, though. Very fine dining. Intimate. I'd need to dress well, which reminded me I'd need to go shopping. I had one good dress and there was no way I'd be able to wear it again, even if I did get it back from the police. It would give me another chance to meet Zara; she could help me find something appropriate.

While I walked, Isaac told me about the restaurant and his day preparing the new wine menu in the club. I found I loved listening to him speak about his work. He was incredibly passionate. Much too soon, I was unlocking my front door and trudging up the stairs, my ankle protesting with the effort. 'Thank you for keeping me company,' I told him. 'You can relax now,' I teased.

'I'm not sure relaxing is the right word,' he said. 'It's going to be a long week.'

'I hope you have a good one,' I said, throwing myself onto my sofa.

'I suspect my weekend will be better,' he breathed before I said goodbye, causing a delicious shiver to run down my spine. I wasn't wrong about the increased anticipation.

Chapter Seven

Time had a frustrating habit of slowing down when there was something to look forward to. Isaac was right, it was going to be a long week. I decided to take Sunday off, figuring I could do with a rest. I hadn't taken time off after leaving the firm and knew I was going to be busy in the run-up to the opening. I made the most of the day off by taking my mum up on her offer of a roast dinner.

I turned up at twelve, knowing dinner would be on the table at half-past on the dot. Creatures of habit, my parents. Mum opened the door, taking in my bruises with a sad pout of her lips. She wrapped me in her arms in a big hug which I returned, gladly. 'Don't fuss,' I whispered in her ear. 'I'm okay.' She sniffled as she released me, capturing my face in her hands, placing a gentle kiss on the tip of my nose.

'I just want things to be normal,' I told her which, for the most part, they were. Mum had made my favourite; roast lamb with roast potatoes, mash, Yorkshire puddings and a ridiculous selection of veg, for just the three of us. The ancient table in the corner of their living room was groaning under the weight of it all. Mum poured me a large glass of wine from the already open bottle of red while Dad stuck to his traditional can of Boddingtons and then we all dug in, helping ourselves to whatever we fancied. I swerved the majority of the carbs, knowing there would be either a homemade pie or crumble and custard for dessert.

I'd been concerned about how Dad would be around me before I arrived. None of those concerns were really assuaged throughout the afternoon. He spoke normally, both to me and Mum, filling me in on the team troubles in the warehouse he managed. He listened to me ramble on about my excitement of the cattery opening and the work still left to complete and even agreed to come and help me fit the cameras for the boarding rooms. It would have been like normal times, except he didn't look at me. Not once. His head turned in my direction whenever I required his attention but his gaze was always just off to the side, staring into the distance behind me. I tried not to let it bother me, realising it could very well be my battered face that made him uncomfortable. I could only hope our relationship would fall back onto an even keel by the time I'd healed. I decided not to push it for now. I would give him his time.

After I'd helped with the dishes, to many protests from Mum, I jumped in a taxi home laden with enough leftovers to feed me for a week. Mum was always concerned my general lack of cooking skills would lead me to waste away. I'd lost count of how many times I'd told her it wasn't a "can't cook" scenario, but more a "won't cook" one. I had neither the inclination nor the patience to slave over a hot hob to feed myself, unless absolutely necessary.

The remainder of my afternoon and evening was spent alternately reading and watching Netflix. My film choice was poor. Although brilliant, *Five Feet Apart* managed to tear my heart out, rip it into pieces and stuff it back inside my chest. I think I used a whole box of tissues and god knows what my neighbours in the flat next to mine must have thought, listening to me sobbing for an hour, even after the film was over.

I kept myself busy at the cattery during the week, making good progress in there. By the end of Tuesday, I had completed the walls and ceilings of all twelve rooms. I spent Wednesday morning dressing them all, making sure they all contained their litter boxes, beds, blankets, bowls and toys. At lunchtime, I hopped on the number seven bus to the designer outlet so I could meet Zara for some retail therapy. I didn't like shopping, always seeming to struggle to find something to flatter my shape. Cursed with a fuller bust and wide hips (child birthing hips, my Nana insisted on telling me, taking great pleasure in my wrinkled nose whenever she said it), I grew more and more frustrated with every outfit I tried on. Zara, on the other hand, could flit through the shelves and racks, zeroing in on the best choice for me. My favourite clothes had all been picked by her in recent years. I'd grown accustomed to trusting her. It saved me a lot of arse-ache.

As I approached the entrance to the outlet, I could see her waiting there, munching on her sandwich. Her face lit up when she saw me walking over before casting a glance down at my paint-spattered leggings. She shook her head on a sigh and tossed her sandwich wrapper in the bin. 'Swelling's going down,' she said as I reached her, her mouth full. The swelling might have gone down but the bruise was still a violent shade of purple in the middle. Luckily, the edges were beginning to fade to a soft yellow, so I was hoping I'd be able to disguise it better without using quite as much makeup by the time I got ready on Friday.

'Thanks for helping me,' I said as we moved into the centre.

'Anytime, you know I love any excuse to spend money. Even yours.' She pulled me towards Ralph Lauren but I shook my head. My sequinned number was from there and I wanted nothing at all to remind me of last Friday while I was spending time with Isaac. 'So, where's he taking you?' Zara asked as we wandered through the outlet.

I told her about Meltons. Like me, she had heard of it but had never been before. 'I want to look feminine. Classy. He's always been dressed well, both times I've seen him. I want to make a good impression.'

She scoffed. 'You're not going on a blind date with him, Rose. The impression has already been made.' She looked at me out of the corner of her eye as I pursed my lips together. 'He wouldn't have asked you to dinner if it wasn't a good impression.'

'Well, I want to change his impression, then,' I said firmly, determined to make him see me differently. His first real look was me lying on the ground being violated by a violent thug. He'd seen me vomit. I paled as I realised he would have seen me in a state of semi undress, with my dress pushed up to my waist. All of that was bad enough but I didn't want those images to be the only things he thought of when he looked at me. I wanted and needed him to see me for me. The woman I really was. Not that. Never that. I caught Zara's eye and silently dared her to contradict my thoughts before a mannequin in a window in Cath Kidston behind her stole my gaze.

I moved past her, drawn to one of the most beautiful dresses I'd ever seen. It was everything I didn't know I wanted. It was a vintage 1950's style with a mid-calf length, full skirt and a scooped boat neckline. Its narrow waist was cinched in with a bow tie. The dress was black with red and pink roses blown up in a large print all over. It was stunning. 'Wow,' Zara breathed beside me. 'I hope they have your size.'

Thankfully, they did have my size. I might have wept if not. I took it straight into the dressing room. It fitted like a dream, hugging my curves, clinging in all the right places, the full skirt falling from my hips perfectly. I shook my hair loose from its ponytail and arranged it over one shoulder before heading out of the cubicle to show Zara.

I found her scrolling through her phone. She lifted her head, her mouth dropping open. 'You're gonna blow his mind in that,' she said, making me blush. I'd never been very good at taking a compliment. 'Shoes?'

'I think it might be time to give the hand-me-downs a test drive,' I told her, looking down at my bare feet, imagining how they would look with the dress.

Before my Nana passed away, while she was still well enough to live at home, she took me to her bedroom and pulled a gold box from the bottom of her wardrobe, placing it delicately on the end of her bed.

I knew what was in that box; I had been looking inside it with wonder for several years. 'You know I've only worn these three times,' she told me as I lifted the lid of the box, marvelling again at the bright red inside and the stunning pair of black heels resting at the bottom. I had smiled at her, consumed by such love for her. Nana had been quite the glamour-puss in her time and had enough sass to render even the most powerful person speechless. The love for glamour and fashion had never left her and, despite becoming more and more unsteady on her feet as she'd aged, she still had to purchase this pair of killer heels. Her cancer had grown quickly, viciously spreading through her organs. By the time the doctors found it, it was too late to do anything. 'I'd like you to have them.'

'I thought you were being buried in these?' I had joked, trying to ignore the sadness that filled me at the thought of her no longer being here.

'Those Louboutins should be worn, baby girl. Enjoyed. They're much too good to be rotting on the end of my feet.'

'Nana,' I reprimanded her sadly.

'I want you to promise me something, Rosslyn.' Nana was the only person to ever call me by my full name; she was also the only person I would ever allow to call me it. 'I want you to promise me that you will wear those shoes. Wear them and live your life.'

'I am living my life, Nana.'

'I mean *really* live it. Get out there. Meet people. Make friends. Love.' She knelt beside me on the floor, taking my hand. 'I love the bones of you, Rose, but you frighten me. I was hoping to have seen you in love before I go, to have seen that light fill your eyes.'

'We're not all as lucky as you, Nana,' I said, squeezing her hand in return, knowing how much she missed my grandad. He had passed away four years previously, a sudden stroke taking him from us.

'Rubbish. You're just not out there enough to find him.'

I sighed. 'You know I'm just busy with work,' I told her.

'Work you don't even like.'

'I like it just fine. It pays my mortgage.'

Nana scoffed. 'Work should do more than pay the mortgage. It should be something you're passionate about. I don't want you to be as unhappy as your father. I don't mean to say he's not happy with Cassie,' she hurried on before I could interject. 'And he worships the ground you walk on, but he isn't as fulfilled in other areas of his life and you well know it.' I couldn't disagree with her there. Dad had been working at the same company for years. 'But forget about your job. I know you'll soon be able to follow that dream of yours. Then I need you to concentrate on becoming passionate in other areas of your life. You have to promise me, Rose.'

I sighed. 'I can't promise that, Nana. You know I haven't been interested enough to make a real go of it with someone.'

Nana looked at me thoughtfully. 'Real love isn't always something you look for, baby girl. Sometimes you can find it in the most unexpected of places when you least expect it. Will you at least promise you'll be open to it when it comes along?'

I had told her I would, if only to make her happy at the time. Those Louboutins had been in the bottom of my wardrobe since she had passed because I had never seemed to find a reason to pull them out. Zara thought I was stupid and had admitted many times that she would have worn them every day if they were hers. As it was, her eyes were sparkling at the mention of the hand-me-downs.

'Nana's "fuck me" shoes?' She clapped her hands together and did a little jig. I really hated it when she called them that. 'He's not going to be able to keep his tongue in his head when he sees you!'

The rest of the week passed agonisingly slowly as well. My bruising continued to go down, which left me confident I would be able to hide the worst of it without making myself up like Pennywise the clown. My ankle started to feel much better so I felt comfortable wearing my high heels. I spoke to Isaac very briefly on Thursday when he called asking for my address so he could come and pick me up for our dinner. I could hear plenty of hustle and bustle behind him so, not wanting to distract him for long, I settled for letting him know I was looking forward to it. His low voice told me he was too which filled me with more delight than I cared to admit.

I was pretty much done with all of my decorating now, with only my office and storeroom to do. Isaac was coming to pick me up at six so we could enjoy a drink before dinner, so I was going to give myself until half three before heading home and getting myself showered and ready. I was tempted to enjoy a glass of wine before he got there to settle my nerves. My stomach was full of butterflies and I kept breaking out in a grin. But I knew I needed to keep busy, at the very least to stop myself from going crazy.

My hair was pulled into a high ponytail after I'd nearly dipped it in paint and I was cutting in the second coat of grey on one of the office walls, listening to my music on shuffle. By three o'clock, I knew I would only have time to finish this wall before packing up for the day so when Sam Fender started singing about losing his mind if Saturday didn't come soon, I couldn't help singing along and dancing around. By the time I was pulling the masking tape up, I was swaying my arse and flicking my hair all over the place, lost in the lyrics and the rhythm. I turned to drop my scrunched up ball of tape with the rest of my rubbish when I stopped dead, wanting the ground to swallow me whole.

Stood in the doorway, leaning his shoulder against the frame with one foot crossed over the other ankle, was Isaac. I drank him in in an instant, my cheeks flaming red with embarrassment. His hair was, as usual, sexily mussed, just falling into his eyes. Those eyes were narrowed, blazing as he looked at me and his mouth was curved up in an amused smile. 'And here I was thinking tonight would be the best part of your weekend,' he said. 'Yet I find you looking forward to Saturday instead.'

'How long have you been stood there?' I squeaked, absolutely mortified.

'Long enough.' Isaac shrugged himself off the door frame and walked slowly over to me, coming close enough that I had to lift my head to look him in the eye. His hands were back in his pockets, fitted navy jacket pushed open revealing a black shirt tucked into navy blue slim-fitting trousers. My breath caught in my throat as I swept my gaze up his body. What a way to play it cool. I might as well have been drooling at the sight of him.

I jumped when he took his hand from his pocket and brought it to my cheek, smearing a splash of paint across my skin. 'You are far too early,' I told him as he rubbed his middle finger and thumb together again, just like he had with my tear in the coffee shop.

'I know,' he replied simply. 'I just couldn't wait another minute.' Good grief. Desire unexpectedly pooled low in my belly as he held my eye. He was attractive without trying, but now? When he spoke in that seductive tone? He was becoming something else.

'I'm not exactly looking my best,' I said, pulling my baggy t-shirt lower to make sure it covered my bum.

'I disagree.' I held my breath as he lowered his mouth to my cheek and placed a gentle kiss. 'It's good to see you again.' Isaac took a step back before I could lose my mind and turn my mouth to meet his. 'Would you like to show me the place?' he asked, moving towards the hallway to take a look around.

I frowned as I followed him. 'Have you really shown up here nearly three hours early to have a look around my cattery?'

'No.' He stopped, causing me to bump into his back. I reached out to steady myself, surprised by how firm his forearm was. He turned to face me again. 'I've got to be honest, I have an ulterior motive.'

'Oh?' I didn't trust my voice to say any more.

'I've driven myself crazy this week, worrying about you walking home alone.' I kept a straight face, despite wanting to laugh out loud at his expression. He looked so on edge. 'I was hoping you wouldn't mind me taking you back tonight, so I can finally relax.'

'How very selfish of you,' I said, my sarcasm evident.

'Indeed,' he said, a smirk teasing the corners of his mouth.

'And what will you do while I get myself ready?' I asked him, letting him take a peek into a couple of my finished rooms.

Isaac nodded appreciatively at my hard work, making me glow with pride as he answered. 'I had been hoping to watch but if that makes you uncomfortable, I can just wait on the sofa.' My face flamed red once again as he turned to look at me. 'Only joking,' he teased, giving me a cute boyish wink.

I coughed some sense into myself and smiled. 'I should hope so,' I teased back, feeling relieved to see him smile in return. 'Shall we?'

He held his arm out to indicate I should walk ahead of him. Parked in front of the building was a very lovely car. 'Wow, very nice.'

Isaac fixed me with a look. 'You know what it is?' Pure snark. Two could play at that game.

'Of course I do. It's a Mercedes. A blue one.'

He barked out a laugh. It was a gorgeous sound. 'Very good. It's actually anthracite blue, but never mind.' I rolled my eyes. *Boys and their toys.* 'Just get in the car, woman.'

Chapter Eight

What was normally a twenty-minute walk took only a good fifteen in the car - which I learned was a Mercedes S 560 Grand edition - thanks to the traffic. It really was a lovely car. All white leather interior. Loads of space. Heated seats. It felt like it wanted to be off like a bullet from a gun. Very luxurious and very expensive, no doubt.

There was tension in the air as I sat next to Isaac, the powerful car thrumming beneath me. It wasn't awkward but the air felt charged. He kept his hand on the gear stick as he stopped and started through the rush hour traffic. My knees were angled towards the middle of the car and I kept glancing down at his hand, pinky finger resting so close to my thigh. I couldn't stop thinking about the feel of his lips brushing against my cheek. About how much I'd wanted to turn and press my lips to his. How much I still did. He was quiet now, his snark and playfulness gone. He appeared deep in thought, which frustrated me. I wanted more than anything to know what he was thinking.

We'd been in the car for five minutes when I settled back in my seat, listening to the music pumping softly through the speakers. I was comforted to hear the familiarity of Royal Blood's *Figure It Out*. I relaxed with my head against the headrest. It was only when we stopped at a red light and Isaac turned his head to stare at me that I realised I'd been singing quietly to myself. I flushed *again* and said, 'I like this song.'

His mouth curved upwards in a sweet smile. 'Me too,' he said. 'Have you seen them live?'

'No, I haven't. I'd like to, though.'

'They're playing in Manchester next year. Supporting The Killers.'

I turned to him, mouth open. 'They're my favourite!' I shook my head sadly. 'Bet that's sold out already.'

'Maybe,' he said with a nod. 'I could probably get tickets, though.' I looked at him from the corner of my eye, eyebrow raised. 'Perks of the job,' he shrugged.

'You need to take the next left,' I told him, pointing out my turning. He flicked the indicator down and smoothly steered onto the tree-lined street.

Scanning the street, he asked, 'you got a parking space?'

'It's all residents parking here so just go anywhere. There's always a few spaces free.' Isaac nodded and spotted a gap further down the street. Driving ahead of the space, he put his left arm on the seat back behind me, turning in his seat to look out the rear window before performing one of the most perfect parallel parking manoeuvres I had ever seen. Isaac winked at me as he switched off the engine, making me laugh out loud. *Smug bastard*, I thought.

We exited the car and I led him past the bakery and down the side to my front door. I rummaged in my bag for the keys and Isaac looked around the little alley. 'Could do with a light here,' he said. 'Motion sensor.'

I agreed with him. 'I usually have to juggle my phone for the torch when it's dark,' I told him. 'I always plan on buying one but never seem to get round to it.' After extricating my keys from my bottomless pit, I unlocked the door, scooped up the small pile of post and headed up the stairs, opening the door into my flat. I held the door for Isaac to pass me, chucking the letters on my small corner table. He stood in the middle of my living room, filling the space. It was the first time I had appreciated how tall he was. His presence was dominating as he turned around, taking in my cosy home. I gulped as he stopped to face me, those stunning blue eyes hooded and piercing. I was so attracted to him and there was no point in me trying to deny that to myself anymore. 'Can I get you a drink?' I'd aimed for courteous, the good little hostess but what slipped from my mouth was a sultry tone that took me by surprise.

Instead of answering, Isaac stalked across the space towards me, taking my face in his hands. I was completely immobile as he lowered his soft, full lips to mine. I responded without thought, my mouth moving in time with his, parting slightly to make space for his tongue. He wasted no time and accepted my silent invitation, his tongue swirling and dancing with mine for several moments. I could feel my legs getting weak with the force of his kiss and I knew I'd not taken a breath for several seconds. I was in danger of going dizzy. He tasted amazing, all minty and fresh and the smell of his aftershave filled my nostrils. I leaned my body into his, shocked to feel his erection pressing against my lower stomach. It took me by surprise and I stiffened in his grip. Isaac noticed but broke our kiss gently. 'I'm sorry,' he breathed, planting a gentle peck on my lips. 'I've wanted to do that since I first saw you on my security cameras.' He took a slight step back, trying to subtly arrange himself in his trousers.

I'd been rendered completely speechless. I'd never been kissed like that in my life and I found I didn't want to lose his touch. Yes, I'd been shocked to feel his arousal but, maybe strangely, I didn't mind. I took a step towards him, wanting to feel him close to me again. He put his hands on my shoulders to hold me in place. 'That's not why I came here,' he said, maintaining eye contact with me.

'You don't want to?' The words tumbled out of my mouth in a rush.

Isaac shook his head, paused, nodded, sighed and looked torn. 'Yes, but not...not...like this. The first date. Especially...well.' He broke off, now avoiding my eyes. And I got it. Completely understood. A range of emotions flew through me. Lust. Relief that he didn't want to put me under pressure. Sadness that he wasn't. And then anger. Anger that he was taking the choice away from me. Just like *he* did.

I narrowed my eyes and pulled away from his grip. 'I'm not broken,' I told him. I looked him in those beautiful eyes and saw them fill with sorrow and the one thing I didn't want to see; pity. 'Isaac, I'm not broken.'

'I don't think you are,' he said, although his next step back told a different story.

I could feel my anger bubbling, ready to spill out. I had a feeling he might be behaving differently if I was someone else. 'I need to know something.' He didn't say anything, just waited for me to continue. 'If you hadn't found me how you did last week, if you'd approached me in the club instead, what would have happened?' He still didn't say anything but I could see his jaw tensing as he gritted his teeth. 'I get the feeling you're not always such a gentleman when you find someone you like,' I shot out.

'Honestly?' he asked. I nodded, wanting to hear it. 'No, I'm not. It's not coming easily to me, being patient. I see it, I take it. But considering what happened to you, I don't feel like that's the best approach.'

'And if you'd found me in the club?'

'I wouldn't have let you leave without fucking you first.'

I tried not to show how affected I was by his words, I really did. But my heart started racing and I felt the colour drain from my face. I wanted him. I knew it as sure as I knew my name. 'Do you still want to fuck me?' I asked him, taking another step towards him, feeling bolder than I'd ever felt before.

'Yes.' I was further emboldened by his response and took another step, then another. He caught my arms again, stopping me in my tracks. 'Rose, I can't.' I just looked at him. I could feel myself getting lost in my want, growing more frustrated and angry as he denied me. 'I can't. I'm sorry, I just can't.' He sank to my sofa, putting his head in his hands.

I dropped to my knees in front of him, placing my hands on his muscular thighs. 'Isaac. I want you.' He raised his head and looked back at me, full of anguish. 'I don't understand why I feel this way. But you do something to me. And I don't really want to question it.'

He placed both of his hands on top of mine. 'I need to be honest, Rose. As much as I want you, I can't get the image of what happened to you out of my mind.' My heart sank. 'I'm torn between feeling so angry that I want to find him and fucking kill him for what he did and feeling so confused because I still want you. And frustrated because if I'd come looking for you when I first saw you, none of it would have happened to you in the first place and I wouldn't have to feel like a predator myself.'

'What?' I exclaimed, launching myself to my feet again.

'Come on, Rose. What type of monster watches a girl get raped and still wants to take her to bed?'

I'm not sure what made my anger boil over, but god, did it boil. 'I don't understand you. You're making out like this...reluctance, is for my benefit, to save me, the poor little rape victim. But I'm here, essentially offering myself to you on a plate, wanting to give you what we both want and you're still saying no? I don't want to make you seem like the bad guy, Isaac, but what about my choice? I had that taken away from me last week and now here you are, doing it again! In a different way, sure, but you're still doing it.'

'Rose,' he groaned.

I took a deep breath to calm myself, worrying when I was starting to get hysterical. 'Do you still want to fuck me?' I asked him again.

'Yes, more than you know. But I can't, Rose. It feels too soon.' He stood and took my face in his hands once more. 'I don't want to deny you. I really don't but I'm trying to be the good guy here.' I could feel my eyes filling with tears at his tender words. 'I want to do more than fuck you. I want to make love to you and when I do, I don't want you to be thinking about any other man but me.'

'I don't want to think of anyone else,' I told him, unable to stop the tears rolling down my cheeks. He kissed each one away, increasing my longing for him. 'I just want you to make me forget him.' I leaned into him, seeking his mouth again, revelling in the feel of his lips against mine.

'You'll be my undoing, Rose,' he whispered against my lips. 'Please, let me take you to dinner. Let me treat you differently to how I've treated every other woman.'

I sighed as I pulled away from him, my emotions all over the place. 'Okay,' I said. 'I'll just shower. Help yourself to wine or whatever you want to drink.' I headed to the bathroom, stopping at the door as he whispered my name.

'Don't be upset, please?' He looked devastating, standing there in my living room looking at me with a mixture of longing and reticence.

'How could I be,' I said with a sad smile, 'I get to spend the evening with you.'

In my bathroom, away from the sight of him, my sanity started to return. What was I thinking? Berating him for not wanting to jump me as soon as he got me alone? Jesus. I'd been sat worrying about this situation with Zara earlier in the week for the opposite reason. His motives were a blessing or should be, at least. But one kiss from him and I'm all ramped up. Maybe there *was* something wrong with me. I needed to apologise. The last thing I wanted was for him to start to view me as a hysterical mess and think I wasn't worth the trouble.

I slid the cubicle door open to start the water and undressed, dropping my clothes in a pile on the floor. While I waited for the water to get warm, I released my mass of hair down my shoulders and surveyed my reflection in the mirror. My pupils were wide and my cheeks were flushed. Is this what pure lust looked like? The only thing I knew for certain was how I'd never felt like this before. Not with anyone.

Steam billowed around me so I stepped in the shower and made a quick job of washing my hair, finger combing my conditioner through and scrubbing the splashes of paint from my skin. Once I'd rinsed my hair for the final time, I turned to leave, hand on the tap to stop the water. I froze as I turned, finding Isaac stood in the doorway of the bathroom, eyes locked to me. My breath hitched and my heart started pounding a frantic tattoo in my chest. He made no move towards me but allowed his eyes to move down my body, taking in every single inch of me. They moved lazily back up to meet my eyes and I saw they'd darkened and were full of desire. My own eyes fell to his mouth, where I watched his tongue slip out to wet his lower lip, which he then proceeded to bite between his teeth.

He took five steps to the closed shower door, standing there in front of me, his gaze sweeping up and down my body once more. I was so exposed but felt unashamed, with no inclination to hide my nakedness from him. Raising my hand to rest on the door, I wiped the condensation away so I could see his face clearly. 'I can't deny you, Rose,' he said. I had no words to give so I just slid open the shower door, exposing myself totally to him in silent invitation. 'Tell me,' he demanded.

'I want you,' I told him, realising he needed to hear it.

Isaac pulled his jacket off, tossing it to the floor with my clothes. He tugged his shirt from his trousers, unbuttoning it slowly, revealing his body button by button. First his chest with a smattering of dark hair, then his muscular stomach, cut with lean definition. I followed the progress with my eyes, flicking them back to his own every now and again. He never stopped looking at my face, searching for something. A moment of weakness? I must have given nothing away because he slid his shirt down his arms where it joined his jacket on the floor. His belt was next, followed by his top button and his zip, lowering slowly. Pure, liquid need pooled in my belly as I watched him undress. He was so seductive, I was practically panting.

Putting his hand in his pocket, he pulled out a shiny foil packet which he placed between his teeth before pushing his trousers past his hips, letting them fall to the floor. He stepped to the side, kicking them away before removing his socks. Then he stood to his full height, giving me one hell of a view. Isaac in a suit was sexy as hell but Isaac in nothing but a pair of fitted boxers was something else. I could see his arousal bursting to break free and so I met his eyes, hungry. He hooked his thumbs in the waistband of his boxers, then paused. He looked at me, waiting. He wasn't getting a response, I was incapable of speech. Sensing I was having trouble, Isaac smirked and pushed them down his thighs, letting his erection spring free. Good god. He lacked nothing. His cock stood out, thick and long. I licked my lips as I stared, brazenly drinking him in. I only looked back into his eyes when he gripped the base with his left hand and rolled the condom on with his right.

I stood back, giving him space to enter the shower. Isaac wasted no time, walking under the spray with me, taking me in his arms. He pulled me close to him, his erection folding up against my belly. He was so hard as he rolled his hips, pushing against me. I moaned aloud, which he swallowed as he claimed my mouth with his own. He kissed me with a ferocity that lifted my hunger to new levels. I thrust my hands in his hair, grasping hard but he reached up behind his head, taking my hands and lowered them to his back in an attempt to calm me and halt my eagerness. He moved from my mouth to my neck, trailing gentle kisses down to my collarbone while he raised a hand to cup one of my full breasts, rolling his thumb across my already hard nipple. I gasped, pressing myself further into his touch, stroking up his back, urging him closer to me. His other hand reached around to my bum, caressing gently.

I was pushed back to the wall of the shower, pressed against the tile as Isaac returned to my mouth, his tongue sweeping tenderly around. He was being so careful; I could sense him holding back. 'I'm not going to break,' I whispered to him, reluctant to break the kiss even for a second.

He pulled back to look at me, water running down his face. 'Let me take my time with you, Rose,' he implored, lifting my leg to his waist.

'Don't treat me like I'm delicate,' I warned, biting into his lower lip, pulling it between my teeth. He gasped at the sharp sting of pain. 'Let me be with you, all of you.' I met his stare, daring him to refuse me. I needed this. To be loved properly, intensely. As I would have been if he'd had his way with me last week.

Isaac dropped my leg, his gaze going even darker. He seemed to grow in size, intimidating and powerful. His shoulders moved up and down in time with his deep breaths. 'You sure?' he asked. I nodded, desperate to feel him inside me. 'Turn around,' he growled. The rasp in his deep voice caused my core to throb painfully. I wanted to clench my legs together to ease the pressure but I complied with his demand instantly. 'Touch the wall.' My hands shot out, slipping on the wet tile, trying to find a grip.

My feet were spread further apart and Isaac took hold of my hips, yanking my arse further back. He positioned himself at my entrance, already slick with my longing. He paused and tightened his hold on my hips. 'Rose?' he asked, the strain evident in his voice.

'Oh, god,' was the only response I could give him before he jolted forward, filling me with his hot, hard length. He held himself deep, holding his breath as he gave me a moment to adjust to his size. There was pain and there was pleasure, the two mingling together to create one sensation. He slid back out slowly on a groan. I moaned at the loss of him, a desperate mess.

'Isaac,' I breathed. He became unleashed, slamming forward on a yell, my hands sliding up the wall. I tried to strengthen my upper body as he rammed into me over and over again. I felt every stroke, every forceful thrust, the pounding of my heart drowning out the roar of the water beating down around us. He barked out a shout each time my arse hit his groin as he pulled me back onto his cock by my hips; I matched his yells with my own. A pressure was building within me, growing more intense with each thrust. My legs grew weak and my arms struggled to find purchase on the slippery tile. When I thought I could support my weight no longer, Isaac curled one arm under my stomach, holding me upright. He lowered his chest to my back, resting his other hand next to mine on the wall, grazing my shoulder with his teeth, leaving me whimpering at the new sensation.

When he moved his hand from the wall and onto my clit, my orgasm ripped through me, catching me completely off guard. I screamed my pleasure, feeling Isaac thicken inside me. He was close. He moved faster, pumping into me until he found his own release on a shout, slowing his thrusts to bring us both down from the high.

I could hardly form a thought, let alone words. We straightened together, my muscles liquid. I needed all of his help to turn me around to face him, his breathing coming as hard as mine. He lowered his face to mine, searching. I smiled up at him, wanting to be able to tell him how utterly mind-blowing he was. He returned my smile on a relieved sigh and leaned close, placing a soft kiss on my forehead, his tenderness as sweet as his lovemaking was powerful.

Unbidden, my breath hitched as a sob clawed its way up my throat. I was so overwhelmed by the pleasure he'd just given me, by his tender kiss and his look of concern, it erupted out of me without warning. My shoulders shook as my sobs turned to full cries, my hands coming up to my face so I could hide. I dropped to my knees, Isaac falling with me as I continued to cry, struggling for breath. 'For fucks sake, Rose,' he groaned, anguish in his tone, reaching up to turn the water off and gathering me in his arms. He arranged me on his lap and held me tightly. I buried my face in his chest as he held my head close to his body, stroking his other hand up and down my back, shushing and soothing me. He held me until my cries turned back to sobs, before I finally fell silent, making no effort to move me from the floor.

When I'd been quiet for a while, he stood with me in his arms, carrying me to my living room, grabbing a towel on the way. I wanted to say something to him, to tell him I was sorry, to make him understand the reason for my tears but I felt exhausted. I just allowed him to lay the towel down on my sofa, before laying me on top of it. More tears - silent this time - threatened to fall as I watched him turn and walk away, but he only went into my bedroom, returning with my duvet. Isaac lay it over me before crawling under, himself, snuggling close behind me. He tucked me in, my back pressed to his front. I relaxed as his arms circled me, holding me close. I could feel his breath on my cheek as my exhaustion threatened to overwhelm me. With my eyes growing heavy I muttered, 'you won't leave?'

I thought I might have heard him utter the word 'never' in my ear, but I couldn't be sure as I allowed sleep to take me under.

Chapter Nine

It was pitch black when I woke up, comfortable and warm. A brief moment passed when I was unsure where I was. I knew I wasn't in my bedroom. Everything felt different, but it didn't take too long to remember where I really was; curled up on my sofa, wrapped up in my duvet, Isaac's arms squeezing me tightly.

Memories of last night flooded my mind. The sound of his laugh, his playful smirk, that dark desire in his eyes. The feel of him moving within me, the force of my orgasm, like nothing I had ever experienced before. The tears and the way he comforted me. The way he was still comforting me. What time was it? I had no idea. My phone was on the other side of the room, dumped near the door. I wriggled a little, testing how much freedom I had. Zero, I realised as Isaac just pulled me closer to his chest.

I burrowed down into the sofa cushions in a bid to sink back into sleep but I was wide awake now. A pressing urge to pee made me wriggle a bit harder to get away. 'Stop moving,' Isaac muttered in my ear. I smiled and tried harder to escape but he tightened his arms around me. 'Stop it,' he mumbled again. 'I'm sleeping.'

'What time is it?'

'Time to sleep. Now shhh.'

He was grumpy. Not a morning person? I settled back in his arms, enjoying the sound of his steady breaths in my ear. Sleep was definitely out of the question now. I didn't feel tired in the slightest. My mind was racing all over the place and I couldn't help worrying about what Isaac might be thinking. What a first date, I was. No dinner, an argument, mind blowing sex, hysterical weeping. Good god, what a prospect I was. Not! I sighed, dropping my forehead to Isaac's forearm. 'Stop it,' he grumbled again.

'I'm not moving!'

'Stop thinking.' I whipped my head up, nearly head butting him on the nose. 'Fucking hell, Rose!' How did he know? 'Look at me,' he demanded, sounding more awake now. I held my breath as I shuffled around on the sofa, not graceful at all. I settled on my other side, meeting his fierce gaze. His face was filled with a steely determination and he took my face in both of his hands. 'I'm starting to read you like a book.' I dropped my eyes to his chin, suddenly feeling ashamed. 'Look at me,' he snapped. My eyes flew back to his. 'What are you worried about?'

'What do you think?' I was unable to hide my sullen tone.

Isaac narrowed his eyes and scrutinised me closely. 'Don't spare any thoughts in that beautiful head of yours for me,' he said, watching my face flush guiltily. 'I had an amazing time last night. I'm more concerned about you.'

'I'm okay,' I said, making Isaac tut and roll his eyes. 'I didn't want you to think...I wasn't crying...it wasn't...' I stuttered, the ability to speak a coherent sentence abandoning me. Isaac stilled my mouth by placing his lips to mine, moving softly. I moaned at the feeling, remembering instantly how he felt. My moan allowed his tongue space to slip inside, dancing gently with mine. I brought my hands up to fist in his messy hair, revelling in the pleasure our kiss created. My body moved against his without thought, rubbing against his erection that stirred between us. He groaned into my mouth as his hand moved from my face, down my neck to my breast, massaging softly, squeezing my nipple between his thumb and forefinger. His touch was featherlight but left a scorching trail across my body.

He worked my mouth with unparalleled skill while his fingers worked my body into a near frenzy but he kept the pace slow and steady. His fingers traced a path down my stomach, rubbing me at my core. I shivered at the touch. He broke our kiss to rest his mouth against my ear. 'You want me,' he whispered. It wasn't a question so I said nothing as he slid first one finger, then a second inside me. I cried out at the feeling. He took my earlobe between his teeth, dragging slowly before kissing and sucking my neck softly. 'Feel good?' he asked as his fingers kept up a maddeningly slow pace which was still building an intense pressure in my core. I squeezed my legs together around his hand in an attempt to alleviate the pressure, moving against his palm for more friction. My orgasm was approaching steadily.

Isaac brought his head up, watching me unravel under his touch. 'You're beautiful,' he said, focusing all of his attention on me, fingers still stroking in and out, an unrelenting sensation.

'Isaac!' I cried his name as he brought his thumb to my clit, my impending orgasm rocketing closer. I lowered my hand to his cock making him jolt forward as I stroked the length of him.

He lost no focus, still holding my gaze. Passion radiated from his eyes as he brought me closer to release. 'Are you close, Rose?' he asked, a firm circle of my clit with his thumb making me shake beneath his touch. I nodded, gripping him tighter, working him with a desperate intensity. He thrust himself against my hand, less controlled now as his release built, too. 'Let me see you,' he said when I lowered my head to his shoulder, my explosion imminent.

My eyes flew back to his at his command. He drove his fingers inside me and circled my clit once more, my body imploding on a wave of pure pleasure. I kept my eyes open and locked on his as my orgasm engulfed me, thrilling at the look of lust on his face. He shuddered in my grip once, twice and groaned his release as he emptied himself onto my stomach. He was stunningly beautiful, his wavy hair mussed with sleep, his eyes hooded with a look of pure rapture. He brought his hand back to my face, holding me still. 'My god,' he whispered, lips pressing to mine. I just sighed my agreement, snuggling close to his chest.

We lay like that for a while, just holding each other but it was clear neither of us was going to get any more sleep. 'I wonder what time it is,' I mumbled into his pecs.

'Too bloody early,' he said, squeezing me even closer.

I giggled. 'You're really not a morning person, are you?'

'Definitely not,' he replied, struggling to rise to a sitting position on my tiny sofa, which was much too small for his frame. 'Although I don't think I'd mind them as much if they all started that way.' He fixed me with a serious stare before breaking into a big grin, making me laugh out loud. I pulled myself up, keeping myself huddled in the duvet.

'Thank you,' I whispered.

He gave me a small smile, moving closer to me. 'The pleasure was all mine, really.'

I giggled again. 'I mean for staying, for understanding, for not running a mile.' Isaac pulled me into his embrace once more, kissing the top of my head. 'I don't know where that came from last night. I wasn't even thinking about anything but you, and us. It just came from nowhere.' I pulled back to look at him, finding him staring at me, listening intently. 'I really am sorry,' I told him, hurrying on when he started shaking his head. 'I just need you to know it wasn't you, it wasn't anything you did.' He tried to stop me speaking when he pressed his lips to mine. 'I don't want to make you run a mile,' I mumbled around his lips.

'You haven't. You won't.' Isaac rose from the sofa, leaving me wrapped up in the duvet. 'Jesus, it's cold in here,' he complained, looking around for my thermostat.

I raised my eyebrow at him. 'Oh yeah,' I said, looking at his still semi-erect length. 'You can tell.'

Isaac looked down at himself, laughing and unashamed. 'Sarcasm suits you,' he said, heading to the bathroom. It was only a second before I heard him exclaim, 'fuck me, it's only four.' He returned in a moment having thrown his clothes back on, finding me laughing silently into my hands. I couldn't believe how outraged he sounded to be up so early. 'It's alright you laughing, I'm normally still awake at this time on a Saturday morning.' Oh yeah, the life of a club owner. 'Coffee,' he said, mooching into the kitchen. I listened to him fill the kettle and set it to boil. 'Listen,' he said, coming back in to look at me, hands stuffed deep in his pockets. 'I'm just gonna say this now and I don't want to say it again.'

My heart dropped but I sat up straight, preparing myself. 'I don't ever want you to apologise to me if you get upset. I want you to talk to me, tell me what's wrong, but never tell me you're sorry.' He pursed his lips in thought. 'I can't begin to imagine how you feel, what's going on in your head.' Isaac walked forward and dropped to his knees in front of me. 'I'm taking my cues from you. What you say, goes. You have the control here, okay?'

'Why does that sound like something you never normally say?' I murmured.

'Because it isn't,' he said. 'I won't deny you again, Rose.'

I reached out my hand, cupping his chin. 'I don't want to be treated any differently to any of your other women,' I told him, moving my hand up to stroke his cheek.

He caught my hand in his, turning his head to kiss my palm. 'You are different,' he said.

Wow, that made me feel good to hear him say that. 'I just mean I don't want you to tread lightly around me. Don't treat me like I'm made of glass, please?' I slid off the sofa, straddling his lap. 'I don't want you to treat me like I'm fragile.'

Isaac stroked up and down my back before sliding his hands down to cup my bum. 'I won't,' he told me, kissing the end of my nose. 'I'll only stop when you tell me to.' He suddenly clasped my face in his hands. 'But you have to tell me to stop if you need me to.' He was serious. 'I mean it, Rose. Do not ever let me be with you if he's in your head.'

'I wouldn't,' I told him, meaning it with my whole being.

'It will only ever be about you and me.'

'I promise.' I kissed him hard, my heart thumping in my chest. Isaac rose effortlessly, holding me to him and started walking to my bedroom where he proceeded to throw me on the bed. He wanted round two? He could have it.

My disappointment was palpable when he leaned over to place a chaste kiss on my lips. 'No condom,' he said.

'Oh,' I said on a little pout. He chuckled. 'Me neither.' Why couldn't I be more prepared? Nana *and* Zara would be shaking their heads.

'Get dressed, I'll make some coffee.' Isaac turned and sauntered from the bedroom, my eyes glued to his arse the whole time.

After darting into my bathroom for a quick clean up, I pulled on some grey leggings and a black, oversized jumper. It was definitely cooler today. My hair was misbehaving massively, having being left to dry naturally again so I just scooped it back into a loose ponytail to get it out of my face. My bruises were faring very well, all things considered, which pleased me no end. I was reaching for my makeup bag when Isaac's soft voice made me jump.

'You shouldn't hide that face,' he said, handing me a cup of steaming coffee. 'You're beautiful enough without it.'

'I don't normally wear it,' I admitted, blowing on my mug to cool my drink.

'I didn't think so,' he said, taking a sip of his coffee, unable to hide his grimace. 'God, that's awful.'

I laughed, taking a sip of my own. I agreed, it was awful. 'No caramel macchiato, eh?'

'No, it certainly isn't.' He sat on the end of my bed, pulling a face at his mug. 'You don't have any sugar,' he grumbled. 'Or food, for that matter.' He looked up at me. 'Why don't you have any food?'

I shrugged. 'I'm not much of a cook.'

'Or an eater, by the look of that fridge.'

'Are you hungry?' I asked him.

'Starving. I missed dinner last night.' He smiled to let me know he was only teasing. I abandoned my makeup bag since he seemed to prefer me without it and took my coffee into the living room, Isaac following behind me.

We sat on my sofa drinking our awful coffee and talking until the sun came up. I'd have been content to sit there all day, getting to know him better but Isaac needed something to eat. 'Come on,' he said, jumping up from the sofa. 'Let me take you to breakfast since I missed taking you to dinner.' I let him pull me to my feet.

'I'll just finish getting ready,' I told him, heading to the bathroom to clean my teeth. I couldn't help my smile as I loaded up my toothbrush. I'd been so concerned after my hysterics last night that I was going to scare him away yet here he was, still wanting to spend time with me. I couldn't help being reassured by the things he said to me. He was going to take his cues from me, I had the control. Everything he said made me feel like he genuinely wanted to be with me, despite knowing I might have more moments like last night. I was so sure he would run a mile. I wouldn't have blamed him either, but he'd stayed, wrapping me in his arms all night. And he wanted to treat me differently to other women he'd been with. My stomach was full of butterflies and I felt full of hope. Nana would be pleased; she'd been looking forward to me meeting someone more than anything. She'd wanted to see me happy and in love.

I spat and rinsed, wiping my mouth. I jumped slightly when Isaac leaned across me, taking hold of my brush and toothpaste. 'You mind?' he asked, the corners of his mouth twitching in a cheeky smile.

I shrugged nonchalantly. 'Have at it,' I said, brushing past him, making sure my arm maintained contact for as long as possible. He caught my wrist as I moved towards the door, pulling me back to him. He lowered his head to mine, his tongue slipping past his lips, running up my chin before he kissed me hard on the lips.

'Missed a bit,' he winked, making me smile.

'Meant to,' I retorted on a wink of my own, walking back into my living room while he cleaned his teeth.

I made sure to grab my phone and shove it in my bag when my pile of post from yesterday caught my eye. I flicked through the few envelopes and leaflets, noting a new water bill and nothing much else of importance when I found the plain white envelope at the bottom. No name, no address, no stamp. I dropped everything else back on the corner table and slid my finger under the flap, opened it up and pulled a folded A4 sheet of paper out. Confused, I unfolded the paper to find two handwritten lines in the middle of the paper.

We are not finished
I will have you again

Chapter Ten

I stared at the paper, reading the nine words over and over again. I couldn't fathom what it meant. This wasn't addressed to me. The postman had not delivered this. Someone else had pushed this through my letterbox. By hand. Yesterday, while I was at work. *We are not finished. I will have you again.* My hands started to tremble, making the paper flutter in my grasp. There was only one person I could think of who would write something like that. This was my worst fear, manifested on a cheap piece of printer paper. He knew where I lived? He'd had his hand on my property. He could have been waiting for me any night this week, waiting for me to come home.

'You ready, Rose?' I could hardly hear Isaac moving behind me, I was so focused on the note. I couldn't speak. 'Rose?' I could hear the change in his tone, could sense his concern but I still couldn't speak. I just stared at the letter in my hand. Nine words only. Nine, but they said so much.

Isaac came right up behind me, looking over my shoulder. 'What's wrong?' Still, I stared at the paper. *We are not finished.* 'Rose, give that to me.' My knuckles were white. 'Let go.' He took hold of my wrist and squeezed gently. I didn't let go. The shakes in my hand spread into my arms and through my whole body.

'Rose!' Isaac's sharp tone shocked me from my reverie. I released my grip on the letter and watched Isaac carry it into my kitchen, holding it gingerly between his thumb and forefinger in the top corner. *I will have you again.* I wasn't safe. He knew where I lived. He *would* come back for me. 'Do you have a plastic wallet?' I could hear him but could only concentrate on my thoughts. I was spiralling. 'Fucking hell, Rose, snap out of it!' I flinched when Isaac stalked back into the living room, grabbing my shoulders and shaking me firmly. He lowered his head, getting right in my eye line. 'We're leaving, right now, okay?' I nodded, beginning to focus. 'Do you have anything to put that letter in?'

'A carrier bag,' I mouthed, my voice getting lost in my throat. I coughed to clear it. 'In the bottom drawer, in the kitchen.' Isaac flew back and grabbed a bag from the drawer, placing the letter inside. He came back over and pulled the envelope from my other hand, laying that inside as well. 'Isaac-,' I started.

'We're going. Get your stuff.' I picked up my bag, shoved my feet into my Converse and allowed him to steer me through the door and down the stairs. Outside, I attempted to lock the door but I couldn't still my shaking hand. Isaac took my keys from me and locked up, keeping me tucked close to his body. 'Come on,' he said, walking me down the street to his car.

Isaac opened the passenger door and helped me lower my shaking form into the seat. I grabbed the seatbelt but my vibrating hands couldn't click it in. On a small sigh, he took hold of the belt and secured me in. I flinched again when he slammed the door. I heard his frustration when he rounded the front of the car. 'Fuck's sake,' he muttered, snatching a parking fine from beneath the wipers.

'I forgot to give you the permit,' I muttered as he slid smoothly into the car, tossing the fine and the bag on the back seat.

Isaac revved the engine, peeling away from the curb on a lurch and performed a questionable three-point-turn to get out of the narrow street. 'Forget that,' he said, pulling onto the road. As it was only early on a Saturday morning, it was quiet out and Isaac was able to roar into the centre of the city without any delay. I usually loved seeing York in the early morning when it was just waking up, free of tourists but I saw none of it today. *We are not finished.* Where was he? Had he seen me leave my flat? I turned my head to look at Isaac. He was sitting silently, jaw clenched tightly, eyes hard and focused, his knuckles white on the steering wheel. He looked so angry, it was frightening.

'Are you okay?' I whispered. He flicked his eyes to me before returning them to the road. He placed his hand on my knee and gave it a comforting squeeze. He nodded his response, leaving his hand where it was.

We made our way through the one way streets and slowed as we approached Shiver. I expected Isaac to pull up at the front but he indicated left and swung down the side, turning again into an opening beneath the building. We started down a steep ramp before being stopped by a steel roller door. He dropped his window and keyed a code into a panel to raise the door. When there was just enough clearance for the car, Isaac pulled forward into an underground car park and straight into his reserved space. He swung himself out of the car and reached my side before I'd even managed to undo my seatbelt. My shaking had subsided now but I felt like I was moving through sludge. I just couldn't get my limbs to obey my brain.

After releasing me from my seat, Isaac took my outstretched hand and pulled me gently from the car, guiding me to the door which he unlocked with another eight-digit code. The door opened into a white-walled and grey-carpeted corridor. We were clearly in the bowels of the club. Isaac led me down the corridor, making a couple of turns I wasn't paying attention to before pulling up short outside a white wooden door. He had already removed his keys from his trouser pocket and he used them to let us into what I now realised was his office.

It was a clinical space; the same grey carpet and white walls. There was a cream leather sofa against one wall, facing a black and white painting of York Minster. A glass coffee table stood before the sofa, containing nothing but a silver bowl, which also stood empty. At the rear of the room, facing the door was a large glass desk, a leather swivel chair behind it. The desk contained nothing but a white phone and an Apple Mac. Arranged in front of the desk were two black leather tub chairs. It all felt very cold and very apt considering the name of the place.

Isaac moved me to the sofa with his hand on the small of my back and encouraged me to sit. He was still seething; I could almost taste it in the air around him. He moved straight to his desk and picked up the handset of the phone. After scrutinising the screen of his computer for a moment, he dialled a number, running his other hand through his hair. I noticed he'd placed the bag containing the letter and envelope next to me on the sofa; I hadn't even seen him pull it from the car. I rose from the sofa and gingerly placed myself in one of the tub chairs. I wanted to be as far away from the thing as possible.

'Constable Neil,' Isaac spoke firmly into the phone, following my movements across his office with his steely blue eyes. 'Isaac Yates. There's been a development you need to be aware of.' I looked into his eyes while he told the detective about the letter, marvelling at how quickly I could feel myself bonding with him. I'd only known him a week, had only spoken to him a handful of times before yesterday, yet I felt incredibly attached to this man. He made me feel things I had never felt before, both emotionally and sexually. He made me feel safe. I was scared to death but having seen the way he'd taken control immediately, I knew I would come to no harm when I was with Isaac. That thought calmed me and I felt some tension leave my shoulders, starting to feel more like myself. Relief passed visibly through Isaac's eyes as he released some of his tension on a sigh. I gave him a small smile as he finished up the telephone call. 'She's on her way here now,' he told me, rising from his chair and sitting beside me. 'You okay?' he asked.

I wanted to say yes but knew he'd see straight through me. Instead, I crawled into his lap, needing the security of his embrace. He didn't hesitate and swathed me in his strong arms, squeezing me tightly. I snuggled close. 'I'm keeping you from another meal,' I muttered into his shirt. I felt Isaac's chest move in a silent sigh as he stroked up and down my spine. I was feeling more relaxed the more he did it.

'I was going to order something for us to eat while we wait for the detective.'

'I'm really not feeling very hungry,' I told him.

'When was the last time you ate?' he asked me, absentmindedly running his fingers through my hair now.

I thought for a minute. 'Day before yesterday, tea time.'

Isaac tutted in my ear and tugged on the ends of my hair, forcing me to lift my head and meet his eyes. 'Do you have a problem with food?'

'No.'

'Then why do you not eat?' Isaac frowned down at me, his brow furrowing in concern.

'I do eat. I just wanted to be hungry for our dinner yesterday, so I didn't have anything for lunch. And then we fell asleep so early, so...'

'And now?'

'And now, what?' I asked on a shrug, circling one of his buttons with my finger.

Isaac grabbed hold of my hand, stilling my movements. 'Why won't you eat now? It's been so long, you must be hungry.'

'I feel quite sick if I'm honest,' I told him.

'How about I order you something light, then? There's a nice cafe down the street, they'll do anything you want.'

'But I really don't want anything,' I said.

'Rose, you need to eat.' He spoke firmly and his eyes had hardened. I could tell this wasn't a fight I was going to win, nor was it a fight I wanted at all.

'How about I have a breakfast smoothie now and eat something more substantial later?' I reasoned with him. Isaac glared down at me, narrowing his eyes, wondering, I'm sure, whether he would be able to persuade me otherwise. I just stared right back, not giving in to his silent challenge.

On a huff, Isaac adjusted me on his lap and pulled his iPhone from his pocket. 'Any particular preference?' he grumbled, begrudgingly conceding to my compromise, opening up the Deliveroo app.

'Would you like to choose for me?' I asked him sweetly. He just fixed me with a hard stare and tapped away on his phone.

'Fifteen minutes,' he said when he was finished. 'DC Neil should be about half an hour.' I nodded, snuggling back into his chest, content to stay like this until the food arrived, which is exactly what we did.

Isaac alternated between tracing patterns on my back and stroking my hair, seemingly happy to hold me in his arms and sit in comfortable silence. My thoughts shifted between my growing feelings for Isaac, how much I enjoyed his touch and how I was ever going to feel safe at home again. We only moved when a knock at the door startled us from our companionship. I made to jump straight up but Isaac held me tight. 'Yes?' he shouted towards the door.

The door opened and a lean Asian male walked into the room carrying a polystyrene container in one hand and a plastic cup full of the most deliciously pink smoothie I had ever seen. He had a lined face, appearing to be in his fifties. He lit up when he saw me sitting on Isaac's lap. He had the kindest eyes; I liked him instantly. 'Your food, Mr Yates.' The man placed the containers on the desk with a little nod to me in greeting.

'Hi,' I said shyly, a bit uncomfortable still clutched to Isaac's chest.

'Miss,' he said with another incline of his head.

Isaac rose from his chair and placed me on the floor, wrapping his arm around my shoulder and pulling me close. 'Thanks, Charlie. This is Rose. Rose, this is Charles Matsumoto, head of my security here.' Isaac made the introductions. Charles beamed at me and took my hand in his in a firm handshake.

'Pleasure to meet you, Miss Rose.' He turned his attention to Isaac. 'Jack came by last night. He was looking for you.'

I felt Isaac stiffen beside me. 'What state was he in?'

'He seemed alright. He just said he wanted to speak with you.'

'After money, no doubt.'

'He didn't say.'

Isaac pulled away from me with a shake of his head. 'Thanks, Charlie. I'll call him later.' He indicated for me to sit and start on my smoothie as he accompanied Charles to the door. They spoke for several minutes in hushed tones. Not wanting to eavesdrop, I took a sip of my smoothie. It was as delicious as it looked. Strawberry and banana and I'm sure there were oats and honey in there too. 'Good?' Isaac joined me back at the desk and took a seat in front of his food. I moaned around my straw as I took another sip. Isaac nodded his approval and started in on his breakfast; avocado toast and poached eggs. It did look lovely but my stomach was just about managing to cope with the smoothie. I'd definitely made the right choice.

I watched him eat for a few moments; he was very neat and ate with as much deliberation as he did everything else. He stopped with his fork halfway to his mouth when he noticed me watching, eyeing me warily. 'That looks very healthy,' I said.

'Hmm,' he replied around his mouthful, chewing slowly.

'You look like you like to take care of yourself.'

Isaac lowered his knife and fork and wiped his mouth with a napkin before answering me. 'I wouldn't say I *like* to take care of myself but, the older I get, the more I *need* to.'

'And how old are you?' I asked him.

He sat back in his chair and crossed one ankle over his knee. 'How old do you think I am? he countered, a small smirk dancing across his lips.

I gulped. I'd always hated this game. 'I asked you first.' Aware I sounded sulky, I still couldn't help crossing my arms across my chest.

Isaac laughed. 'I'm thirty-nine,' he told me. Oh? He was older than I'd thought. My surprise must have been evident on my face because Isaac studied me closely. 'Better or worse than you were expecting?'

I smiled. 'I thought you were younger. Whatever you're doing is working.'

'And the age gap?' He looked nervous all of a sudden.

'What's ten years?' I answered with a shrug.

On a grin, Isaac replied. 'What's ten years, indeed.'

Another knock at the door made us both turn our heads. Rather than shouting this time, Isaac stood, brushing down the front of his shirt and went to open the door. It was Detective Neil.

Isaac showed her in, gesturing to the seat he'd just vacated. He grabbed the bag from the sofa and sat in his chair behind the desk. 'Tell me,' she said to me, taking the bag from Isaac and peering in, being careful not to touch anything as she looked.

I took a breath and told her everything, which admittedly wasn't much. 'And you've both touched it?' I glanced across at Isaac who just nodded. 'You'll need to provide your fingerprints so we can isolate anyone else's on there.'

'Is it likely to help find out who he is?' I asked her.

DC Neil looked at me, a sad look crossing her features. 'His DNA isn't in the system so this is either his first offence or you're the first woman to come forward. I'll be honest, Miss Carter, I'm not holding out much hope that we'll be able to identify him through his fingerprints.'

I felt a deep exhaustion overtake me. This wasn't going to end quickly. 'What about the name on his booking? Nancy? Norma?' Isaac asked.

'Nicola.' DC Neil replied. 'We spoke to her. Unfortunately, her voucher was stolen from her bag and she can't tell us exactly when. It hasn't left us with very much to go on.' *Wonderful*, I thought to myself. 'I am deeply concerned about this,' DC Neil said. 'I will do all I can to find him, that I can promise you. But you do have a choice to make now, Miss Carter.'

'Oh?'

'Where do you want to go from here?' she asked. 'Is there anyone you can stay with? Or do you want to stay at home? I can arrange for a police patrol to keep an eye on your home periodically, to make sure you're safe there.' I thought about that. Where did I want to stay? I loved my home and hated the thought of being forced to leave, but I had already been thinking about how safe I was going to feel, or wasn't, as it were. I opened my mouth to speak, but Isaac beat me to it.

'You can stay with me.' He spoke quietly but firmly.

'Isaac, I'll be fine at home,' I said at the same time as DC Neil said, 'Mr Yates, I'm sure Miss Carter would be more comfortable with a family member.' I knew that wasn't true; I couldn't imagine anything more uncomfortable than going back to Mum and Dad's. Between Mum fussing around and Dad's coldness towards me now, I think I would go crazy.

'You can stay with me,' he said again before directing his attention to the detective. 'She won't be spending another night in that flat until that man is locked away and poses no threat.' He was fierce and DC Neil seemed to wilt under his gaze.

'Isaac,' I said quietly, dragging his attention back to me. 'I will be okay at home, honestly.'

He shook his head, pressing his lips into a thin line. 'Please don't argue with me about this, Rose. I need you safe.' I was about to open my mouth to do just that when I really heard what he said. I looked at him, trying to read his face. His eyes were pleading. I thought back to how worried he was when he knew I was walking home; his comments about needing a light on my front door. His fury when he saw the letter. 'Please, Rose,' he said.

I nodded my agreement. Yes, I would stay with Isaac. Because I knew I would be safe. And because I knew he would drive himself crazy if he couldn't be the one to keep me that way.

Chapter Eleven

Detective Constable Neil informed me she was sending a forensics team to my flat to check for further fingerprints and to see whether there were any signs of a break-in. I knew there hadn't been, that much was obvious. It did mean I wouldn't be able to get anything from home to take to Isaac's for a little while. I didn't need much, just a few changes of clothes. Some toiletries. Maybe a book or two. I wasn't sure what his work hours were like and I didn't want to feel at too much of a loose end while he was busy.

I tried hard not to think about what Mum and Dad would say when they found out. First and foremost, the thought of my attacker knowing where I live, that I was being targeted, that it didn't appear to be a spur of the moment assault. Secondly, what would they think about me staying with Isaac? They knew I didn't know him well and it was so unlike me. I know they had often worried about my lack of love life, just like Nana did. I'd heard their whispered conversations when I still lived with them. I'd never really committed to any relationship before. Sure, I'd been on dates, often more than one with the same person and of course I'd been to bed with a few of them but nothing serious had ever developed. I hadn't wanted it to. But here I was now, having known Isaac a week, been intimate with him twice and had just agreed to move into his house for an undetermined length of time. All the while trying to come to terms with the depth of my feelings for him, which had developed so fast I was frightened.

Was it a result of the rape? Would I be feeling like this with *any* man who had tended to me? Was it some sort of hero-worship? Or was it only Isaac? I thought back on his comments last night. If he had approached me in the club before I was attacked, would I feel any differently?

I jumped when Isaac laid his hand on my shoulder, crouching down to study my face. I looked at him, taking in his look of concern; brow furrowed and lips pursed. His piercing gaze with eyes so blue they took my breath away. *No*, I thought. I wouldn't feel differently. I would be just as captivated by him if I'd met him under regular circumstances. Realising DC Neil was stood, ready to leave, I leapt to my feet, catching Isaac off guard. 'I'm sorry,' I told the detective. 'I was miles away. You said we needed to provide fingerprints?'

'Yes.' She wrinkled her nose. Had this already been discussed while I was daydreaming? 'Isaac will bring you to the station later on today. The sooner, the better.' I nodded my understanding. 'Miss Carter, I have to ask.' Oh no. I could feel Isaac bristle beside me. 'Are you sure you wouldn't feel more comfortable staying with a family member for the time being?'

I could sense Isaac struggling to rein his frustration in. 'No," I told the detective. 'I really don't think so.'

'I just don't want you to feel pressured into going somewhere, or doing something you aren't comfortable with.' And there it was. The thing I was worried about. Being treated like I don't know my own mind. As though I was suddenly incapable of making my own decision. I could feel my anger beginning to bubble up in my stomach again.

It appeared, however, that Isaac's anger was already at boiling point. 'Just what are you insinuating?' he practically snarled.

His anger was so palpable, DC Neil visibly flinched. I placed my hand on his arm. 'I'm not being pressured into doing anything. I trust Isaac and want to stay with him. I can assure you that if I didn't want to, I wouldn't.' I looked across at Isaac, feeling upset for him. This was probably what others would think too, and it wasn't fair. 'Could we leave now?' I asked him.

Still tense, Isaac nodded, indicating towards the door. DC Neil took the hint and left after reiterating her determination to find my rapist. I could feel the tension radiating through the air. I placed my hand back on his arm; he was like a tightly coiled spring. His eyes remained on the door like he was trying to burn a hole through it. His mouth was pressed into a tight line. 'I'm sorry,' I whispered, leaning into him. He snaked his arm around my waist and pulled me close before completely enveloping me in both of his arms, squeezing tightly, his nose sinking into my hair. I could hear him inhale, breathing me in.

'What are you sorry for?' he finally asked, relinquishing his death grip but keeping me pulled against his chest. I circled my arms around his back to return his hug and lifted my head to look at him.

'I hate that you feel like people think you're acting out of some ulterior motive. That you're pressuring me into doing what you want.'

'Aren't I, though?' he asked, looking down at me. He wasn't smiling. I furrowed my brow in confusion. Isaac sighed and lowered his mouth to mine. His kiss was gentle and tender. 'I can take you to your mum's if you would rather,' he said.

'I don't want to go to Mum's,' I told him firmly, fisting my hands in his lapels and pulling him closer still. 'I know I've got the choice and I'm choosing to stay with you.' I stood on tiptoes and pressed my lips back to his. I stroked his lower lip with my tongue, slipping it inside when he parted his lips. Our tongues danced together and I moaned into his mouth as he lavished me. His hands moved to cradle the back of my head, not giving me an opportunity to pull away, not that I would have wanted to. I was feeling flushed and breathless when he finally broke the kiss.

Isaac took my face in his hands, running his thumbs gently across my cheeks. 'If you're sure,' he said. It wasn't a question.

I smiled up at him. 'I'm more than sure. It might sound crazy, all things considered, but I feel incredibly safe with you.' I took great pleasure in the fleeting look of relief that fluttered across his face. 'I don't quite understand where my feelings have come from and, to be honest, I'm not used to feeling this way but I'm also not wanting to question it. Not much, anyway.'

Isaac tugged me towards the sofa where we both sat, knees pressed together. 'Is this what you were thinking about before? When you drifted out of the conversation?' I nodded, unsure whether I should tell him how I was feeling. Surely it was going to scare him away. I hardly knew him and yet my heart was telling me I could be falling for this man. Falling hard and fast. It made no sense to me, but the only thing I *was* sure of was that, without a shadow of a doubt, I would have always felt this way about him. How could I not? His magnetism, his tenderness, his raw power. His instinct to protect me. A familiar doubt flooded my mind; would he have that same instinct if he hadn't seen what he'd seen? Did he only feel this way because of *what* he'd seen? My heart sank at the thought. What would that mean for us? 'Rose?' I jumped out of my reverie to find Isaac bent close to me. 'Where are you? What are you thinking?'

'I don't know.' I looked down at my hands resting on my knees.

'Look at me.' His demand was spoken softly but left no scope for defiance. My eyes shot up to his blues without a seconds hesitation. 'Whatever's going through that beautiful mind of yours, I'd like to know.'

I bit my lip, unable to tear my eyes away from his. 'What if it makes you run away from me?' I asked, throwing it out there.

Isaac took hold of my hands and gripped them tightly. 'Nothing you could say to me would make me run from you.'

I wasn't so sure about that. 'Not even knowing how scared I am?'

'I won't let anything happen to you, Rose.'

'I know that. I'm scared of what I feel about you.'

I expected him to pull away, to start distancing himself. I was surprised when his hands left mine and took hold of my cheeks once more. He rested his forehead against mine. 'Trust me when I tell you that my feelings are as frightening for me as they are for you.'

Stunned, I froze in his grip. My heart pounded in my chest. I opened my mouth to speak but only a breathy whisper escaped. Isaac consumed my mouth with a passionate kiss. 'I'm also struggling to come to terms with how I feel because it's nothing I've ever experienced before, either. I told you last night, I'm not usually like this with women.' I smiled up at him, remembering what he'd said. 'Feelings and emotions don't generally feature in my romantic life.'

'You don't really strike me as the romantic type.'

Isaac raised his eyebrow on a smirk. 'I'm not accustomed to wining and dining.'

'You haven't wined and dined me yet, either.' Isaac threw his head back on a laugh but sobered quickly. I felt bad. 'I'm sorry,' I told him. 'That's not your fault, I know that.'

'Before you stay with me, I need to tell you.' He nibbled on his lower lip. He looked vulnerable and, quite frankly, adorable. 'You are the most captivating woman I've ever met. You're beautiful and guileless and strong. There's a connection here, I'm sure you feel it too.' I could only nod my agreement. 'I have the strongest urge to keep you safe, that's true. But I do have an ulterior motive to having you come and stay with me. I want to keep you close. I want to explore this connection between us. While how I'm feeling is completely alien to me, I like how it feels and I don't want it to stop.' He paused, looking at me with wonder and a little bit of fear. 'I've never fallen in love before, Rose.'

I gasped. 'Is that what's happening?' I murmured.

'I don't know.' Isaac caught my gaze and held it without blinking. 'Is it?'

'I'm scared it might be,' I whispered back.

'Why are you scared?' he asked, taking both of my hands in his once more.

I wanted to tell him, to let him know how worried I was; that our feelings, our growing attraction, was a result of the trauma I'd experienced. The trauma he had witnessed. That we had become inextricably linked because of it. I don't think I could have stomached it if he agreed it was a possibility. 'Because I haven't felt this way either,' I told him instead.

Isaac brought my hands up to his lips and kissed them softly. 'So we'll just have to figure this out together, then,' he said. I nodded my agreement, feeling overwhelmed all of a sudden.

Rising to his feet, Isaac pulled me up to stand beside him. 'Come on,' he said, leading me towards the door. 'Let me show you your new home.'

I was surprised when Isaac led me back through the bowels of the club, to the car park but walked me straight past his car. He had a firm grip on my hand and faltered in his steps when he felt me slow down. He tugged gently. 'We don't need that,' he said, leaving me feeling more confused. He tugged again and led me through the car park, under the roller door and onto the street.

It was turning into a beautiful autumnal day, albeit a little cold. The sun was shining; light sparkled across the river like little diamonds. I detested winter; had always hated any cold, wet weather ever since I was a little girl, but crisp autumn days like these in York were some of my favourites. The city was stunning, with the leaves turning a golden brown and beginning to fall from the trees, lining the street and crunching underfoot. The sun, sitting lower in the sky, warmed the old stone buildings and cast a burnt orange glow across the landscape. Truly beautiful and today was fast turning into one of those days.

I felt a piercing moment of panic when Isaac led me onto the street in front of the club and passed the steps I'd been thrown down previously. I couldn't help tensing as I peered down there; Isaac squeezed my hand and yanked me forward without a word. I glanced up at him as he power walked me towards the bridge which spanned the river. His jaw was clenched, a muscle twitching. His eyes were narrow and hard. He only relaxed when we had crossed the river and were stood on the other side.

To the left of us, directly opposite the club across the water stood the Waterfront. One of the most expensive sought after properties in the city. It had the best views of the river and was comprised of six luxury apartments. I'd seen a vacant one for sale when I was looking for my own little flat and remembered laughing my head off at the price. Never in my wildest dreams would I be able to afford a place like this. Not even with Nana's inheritance.

I was only mildly surprised when Isaac pulled me toward the entrance. Considering how he earned his living, it was no wonder he was able to live somewhere like this. We walked into the lobby which was all white marble and gold. Every surface gleamed and the air smelled like lilies and lilacs. There was a stunning blond manning the reception desk who stood up straighter and flicked her hair over her shoulder when she clocked Isaac walking toward her.

'Good morning, Mr Yates,' she practically purred. I felt an instant, irrational pang of jealousy.

'I need a second key cutting, Veronica,' he told her, as abrupt and to the point as ever. He pulled me to his side. 'I also need Rose Carter adding to the list of approved guests.'

'Certainly, Mr Yates. I'll have the key brought up within the next hour if that will suffice?'

'Fine. Thank you.' I was led towards a lift with golden doors which opened as soon as Isaac touched the button. I was ushered inside without a word.

I could hear Veronica's stilettos clicking on the tile floor as she rounded the reception desk. 'Is there anything else I can assist with, Mr Yates?'

I felt Isaac tense. He pulled his keys from his pocket and placed one in a small lock above the panel of floor buttons. 'Just the key, Veronica,' he told her, looking anywhere but at her as the doors slid closed.

'Always so abrupt, Mr Yates,' I said, nudging him playfully with my hip.

Isaac smiled down at me. 'Do you think I'm rude?'

'No, but she might.'

He sighed. 'I wish.' I thought about questioning him but was surprised to find the lift doors opening onto a small foyer facing only one white wooden door.

'I thought there were six apartments here?' I asked as Isaac urged me forward.

He opened up, leading me inside. 'There are,' he replied. 'To purchase. I had the penthouse built for me.'

'You built this place?' I couldn't hide the shock and awe in my voice.

Isaac laughed, placing his finger under my chin to close my gaping mouth. 'Not with my own hands, but yes, I had it built.' He turned me around and ushered me into the most beautiful open plan living area I'd ever seen. It was all antique wood, everywhere. Hardwood floors covered with soft coloured Aubusson rugs. Directly in front of me was a sitting area with two large cream sofas facing each other, a sturdy coffee table between them. Behind that was a floor to ceiling window which ran across the full length of the penthouse, showcasing that amazing view of the city. To the right was a kitchen that looked as though it belonged to a modern country home, complete with pale grey arger oven and other built-in appliances, cream units and a four-seater wooden table and chairs in the centre of the area.

The left side of the space was kitted out as an office area with, to my delight, floor to ceiling bookcases, each shelf filled with more books than I could count. An enormous desk stood before the shelves, the chair positioned to face the window; how he managed to concentrate on work with that vista was beyond me. A little reading nook took up the far corner of that side of the room with two squishy cream armchairs, side tables and lamps.

I noted the walls - *magnolia* - and turned to face Isaac. 'Not a fan of colour, I gather,' I told him wryly, remembering also the stark lack of colour in the club.

'You would not be surprised to hear vanilla is my favourite ice cream flavour,' he replied, looking on as I moved slowly through the space, taking in the splendour and beauty of it all. 'There are two bedrooms, one on either side of the space.' Isaac indicated white doors, one beyond the kitchen and the other beyond the reading nook. 'Both ensuite.'

I turned to look at him. 'All this space and only two bedrooms?'

Isaac shrugged. 'I don't have many visitors.'

'Not even family?' I asked, regretting it instantly as I caught the small flicker of pain passing across his handsome features. Before I could apologise, however, Isaac walked over and pulled me into a tender embrace.

'That's perhaps a story for later,' he said, kissing my hair. 'I'm really sorry, but I do have to dart back across to the club and take care of some business.'

'That's okay,' I told him, greedily eying up the wall of books. I couldn't wait to peruse his collection.

'I'll be back in a couple of hours if that's alright?' I nodded, taking half a step across to the library. I could hear him chuckle under his breath. 'Master bed is on the left. Guest is on the right.' I flicked my eyes back to him, eyebrow raised in a silent question. I enjoyed the sight of his lip raising in a smirk a little too much. 'You can choose your favourite but I would much prefer to see you in my bed.' Now my eyebrow raised suggestively as I straightened up in front of him, causing him to laugh out loud. 'Later, as much as it pains me to say.'

I pouted my displeasure playfully and stood on tiptoes to give him a chaste kiss on the lips. 'Thank you for letting me stay here,' I told him. 'It's a beautiful place.'

'I'm glad you like it,' he said, returning my kiss. 'Now, I'm going before you distract me. I'll see you soon, okay.'

I gave him my goodbye, unashamedly staring at his magnificent backside as he left. I was already counting the minutes until his return.

Chapter Twelve

I could have spent an eternity browsing the shelves before me. There had to be well over one hundred books, many of which looked very well-read. I noted that Isaac had a very eclectic taste; many classic novels with some in vintage binding, thrillers, crime, sci-fi and fantasy. Some non-fiction and autobiographies too. I felt like a kid in a sweet shop. There were so many authors I hadn't heard of. Genres I hadn't tried, and I generally prided myself on being a prolific reader; clearly not a very broad one. There wasn't a television in the sitting area of the penthouse and judging by the creased spines on many of these books, I could only assume Isaac spent the majority of his time lost in his literature.

Knowing I was going to be alone for a while, I wanted to get stuck into something that would keep my mind occupied. My thoughts tended to drift away when I wasn't focused on something or someone and I didn't like where my mind ended up in those moments so I was constantly in search of things to keep my brain busy. My gaze fell upon a battered copy of Andrzej Sapkowski's *The Last Wish*. I'd been considering reading this ever since I watched *The Witcher* on Netflix the previous year and became intrigued by the lore and fantasy of it all. I pulled it down and placed it on one of the armchairs before heading across to the kitchen and set about making a cup of tea.

It took far longer than it should have to figure out the Quooker tap to get my hot water and took even longer to find the teabags. There was nothing out on the units, not even a toaster. I chuckled when I finally came across the cupboard with his crockery in - *grey*. All so very monochrome. He must have had a heart attack when he saw my mismatched collection of colourful mugs.

With my tea in hand, I sank into the chair and started reading. I became lost in the story and devoured more than a quarter of the book before I realised how hungry I was. As I was looking around for something I could use as a bookmark - there was no way I was going to fold the corners of the pages over, despite Isaac doing just that - when I was startled by a knock at the door. I jumped and froze, staring in that direction. My heart clattered in my chest. Isaac wouldn't knock, he'd just come straight in. No one knew I was here yet, except the police but they were waiting for me to visit them at the station.

I swallowed and used my trembling legs to carry me across the penthouse. I was gingerly stretching towards the peephole when another knock made me jump again, my teeth cracking together. Good god, I was sweating. My heart was pounding in my chest, I could hear my blood whooshing in my ears. I felt sick to my stomach and my breaths were coming in short, shallow gasps.

I took a step back when I heard muted voices behind the door, another when I heard a key scraping in the lock. I was lost in my memory; no longer indoors but outside again, hearing the birds and smelling the river. Tears pooled in my eyes, tracing a scorching path down my cheeks. I backed up more and more until I was pressed against the window, unable to move any more. My vision grew blurry and white, whether through my tears or my lightheadedness, I couldn't tell.

A hazy shape approached me, growing closer and closer. I held my arms out in front of me in a weak attempt to protect myself, to keep them away from me. I couldn't suck a single breath into my lungs. I tried to beg but my voice came out in nothing more than a whimper. I squeezed my eyes closed so I wouldn't see the punch coming. The figure was talking to me but I couldn't hear a thing. They took hold of my wrists and pulled me to them, wrapping their arms around me, one rubbing my back and the other cradling my head.

I tried to pull away, still desperately trying to get some air through my lips but their arms only held me tighter. I felt lips close to my ear and they stayed there until the roaring in my ears began to subside and I started to hear a gentle shushing. 'It's Isaac, Rose. It's Isaac,' he repeated, over and over again. 'It's okay. You're safe, you're okay.'

Realisation dawned and I clamped my arms around his waist, holding onto him for dear life. Isaac slid his hands down my back and took a gentle hold of the backs of my thighs. He pulled me up to his chest with little effort and carried me over to one of the sofas where he sat down, leaving me straddling his lap, body pressed up against him, face buried into his shoulder. My senses eventually returned to me as I matched my breaths to the steady rise and fall of his chest. My limbs stopped trembling and I no longer felt like I wanted to throw up. After an age of feeling Isaac stroke up and down my back in a steady rhythm, I lifted my head to look at him, sniffing loudly. 'Bet you're sick to death of seeing me look a puffy mess,' I told him, lowering my gaze to his collar, focusing on his tie knotted at his throat.

'Shut up,' he said. I leaned back on his legs to look at him, feeling so embarrassed that he'd seen me like that again, especially when I kept telling myself I was going to pull it together. He nudged me and took my hands in both of his. 'Do you know what brought that on?' he asked.

I nodded, watching him rub his thumbs over my knuckles. It felt nice. It helped ground me back to reality. 'Someone was knocking at the door. I don't know where it came from. I was just thinking about who it could have been and then I started shaking.' I shook my head. 'It happened so fast. One second I was alright, the next I was a mess.'

'It was Veronica,' he told me. 'Bringing your key.'

I shook my head. 'God, I'm ridiculous.'

Isaac jerked his hips, jolting me in his lap. 'Shut up,' he said again. 'I should have thought about something like this happening before I left you alone here. Strange place and all that. I shouldn't have left.'

I shook my head again. 'You have to work. You shouldn't have to change your routine just because there's a maniac after me.'

'I'm glad to change my routine. You're worth it.'

I smiled, feeling happier than I'd any right to, considering. 'I really don't know what happened there,' I said again, snuggling closer to his chest, glad I was feeling more like my normal self again.

'I'd have said a panic attack but, honestly, you didn't look like you were here.' He tapped the side of my head lightly.

'I didn't feel like I was here,' I admitted, realising I needed to come to terms with the fact that I couldn't just brush this whole experience under the carpet. I had been hurt, badly, and as much as I wasn't going to let that define me or rule my life, I still had to process it. Not ignore it. I was going to have to start talking. 'I could see you but I didn't know it *was* you if that makes sense. I wasn't reliving anything but I did feel like I was outside, back by the river.' I enjoyed the feeling of Isaac's arms circling my body, cuddling me close. I could feel him winding my hair through his fingers. 'Am I crazy?' I asked in a whisper.

Isaac buried his face in my hair, inhaling deeply. 'Not at all,' he eventually replied. 'Is there anything I can do? Can I help at all?'

I smiled into his neck before pulling myself upright on his lap again. I pressed a very gentle kiss to his lips. 'You already are,' I told him, watching my fingers slide across his chest. I started to slowly loosen his tie, frowning when he stilled my hands with his. 'You're always saying no to me,' I pouted playfully.

Isaac narrowed his eyes and took a firm hold of my hips, swivelling his groin into mine. I gasped as I felt his hard length beneath me. 'Does that feel like a no?' he asked, exasperated. 'Your timing is shit.' I raised my eyebrows in question. 'We're expected at the police station.'

'Now?'

'Yes, now.'

'And later?' I bit my lip.

Isaac held my chin, keeping me in place so he could kiss me deeply before sucking my lower lip into his mouth. 'You'll see,' he practically growled.

It was an arduous visit to the police station. DC Neil was otherwise engaged but Constable Mcloughlin greeted us in the waiting area. She was very young, hardly looked old enough to have left school, let alone enforce the law. Her brown hair was today pinned up in what once must have been a neat bun but was now falling loosely around her face. She looked as though she had worked long enough to pass tired and was now just bone-weary but she still greeted me with a kind smile.

She led us into a room and took both of our fingerprints. I'd been expecting inky fingers so was surprised how technological the process actually was. She made idle chit chat with me but couldn't seem to find any words for Isaac. She just kept flicking her eyes up to his face and back down to his hand, her cheeks becoming more enflamed the more she looked at him. I could sympathise. He often rendered me speechless and turned my mind to mush when I looked at him. I was becoming no more immune despite spending more time with him.

Isaac was seemingly oblivious to the effect he was having on the constable. He spent the time it took him to be fingerprinted looking only at me, frowning when my stomach rumbled audibly. I groaned inwardly, knowing it was going to be even longer before he took me back to his now. After refusing a proper breakfast, he wasn't going to let this go. I shifted in my seat, catching his smirk as he watched me. Bastard. He knew exactly what I was thinking. My timing really was shit.

Once we were finished, PC Mcloughlin walked us through to the exit and told us the forensic team was almost finished at my flat, so we would be able to stop in anytime and pick up some things I'd need. DC Neil must have filled her in on the fact that I would be spending some time at Isaac's. I thanked her for her time and allowed Isaac to escort me back to the car.

He opened the door for me, still smirking as his fingers brushed against my hips when he guided me into my seat. I just smiled up at him sweetly, buckling myself in. He was calculating. He knew very well the effect he had on me and was going to use it to torture me. I just knew it. I also knew it would be pointless to argue with him. He wasn't happy that I'd shunned breakfast and I *was* hungry. Plus, I figured I could help increase his own anticipation too. Two could play at his game. I fully intended to make sure he was as affected as me.

My phone buzzed in my bag while Isaac slid into his seat. It was Mum. I silenced the call, letting it ring out to voicemail. I knew I needed to have a chat with her, tell her where I was going to be staying for the next few days but I wasn't ready to have that discussion yet. It meant telling her about the note. I was still trying to come to terms with it myself and judging by my panic attack this morning, I wasn't coping very well. Mum finding out would only increase her panic and I wouldn't be able to handle her fussing. If I could just avoid speaking to her for a little while longer, I knew I'd be able to explain the developments better and leave myself better able to deal with her hysteria. I just wanted to be able to spend this time with Isaac and explore my developing feelings for him without worrying about anyone else. Selfish it may be but I wasn't sorry about that.

I switched my phone off and shoved it back into the bottom of my bag, deciding I wasn't going to allow anything further to spoil my day with Isaac. It had started amazingly and I was going to make sure it finished the same way, despite the blip in the middle. I looked across at Isaac as he started the car and pulled out of the police station onto the main road. He kept flicking his attention between the road and my bag in the footwell. His brows were turned down in a deep frown. 'You okay?' I asked.

'Someone bothering you?'

I laughed, surprising both myself and him. 'Yeah, my mum.' I took a long look back at Isaac, really seeing the worry and concern on his handsome features. For the first time, I began to realise the sense of responsibility he was shouldering in his attempt to keep me safe. I was shocked all over again at how quickly our feelings seemed to have sprung up out of nowhere. The now-familiar fear of the cause of those feelings started to bubble up in my mind once again, but I squashed them back down. There would be time to consider and contemplate all that another time. 'She'll only carry on trying to get in touch with me if I leave it switched on. I'll have twenty-odd missed calls before she packs it in.'

'And finding you've switched it off altogether won't wind her up more than you ignoring her?'

'I'm renowned for not leaving my phone charged. If she rings and it's off, she'll just assume I've let the battery drain again.' I chuckled to myself and shook my head. 'That way, she can remain blissfully ignorant to the fact that I am, in fact, ignoring her.'

As Isaac drove toward my flat, I let my hand drift across the centre console and rest lightly on his knee. He stiffened under my touch. I couldn't help my private smile when I ran the tips of my fingers up and down his strong thigh, my touch featherlight, and I could hear his steady breathing falter. I would swear I could hear his heart rate increasing. He wasn't unaffected by me. I maintained my gentle stroking absentmindedly, enjoying the feel of him beneath my fingers. I turned my head towards the window to watch the world go by and hummed along to the radio. After a couple of miles, I felt Isaac relax in his seat and lay his big hand on top of my small one, linking his fingers with mine. I turned my head to offer him a smile and found him looking down at our hands resting on his thigh with a confused expression. It was fleeting and passed with a bemused shake of his head.

I squeezed my fingers around his, making him flick his head in my direction. His piercing gaze heated my blood in an instant. My breathing grew shallow and my heart was thumping wildly in my chest. I couldn't take my eyes off him, even when he turned back to watch the road. I marvelled again at how handsome he was. Everything about him was effortless. He was obviously aware of how attractive women found him, how could he not be? He was a gentleman about it though. He didn't use his good looks as a weapon, at least not with me. But he had admitted to just taking what he wanted in the past, when he wanted it and there was no doubt in my mind he would have had plenty of choices. I'm sure women just threw themselves at him. Veronica's behaviour was proof of that. If he could fluster a level headed policewoman with just his very presence, what would he be like when he turned that dial up? I'd already seen his charm at work and was nearly a pooling mass of desperate want, yet I knew he was holding back with me. He was treating me differently and I didn't really know why and, being completely honest with myself, I liked it. It made me feel special.

Isaac pulled up outside my front door just as his car speaker started ringing. The name 'Jack' was flashing on the centre console screen. Isaac's mouth pressed into a thin line, his brows turning into one hell of a frown. He made to cancel the call but I unbuckled my belt and hopped out of the car, wanting to give him his privacy. It must be the same Jack who had been at the club looking for him earlier. 'I'll be five minutes,' I said before I shut the door on his stunned face and headed down the alley to my flat.

'Hello?' I called up the stairs, in case any CSI were still up there. There was no reason for anyone to be up there; it wasn't like my attacker had broken in, but I found I couldn't take a single step towards my flat until I knew for certain it was empty. I called out one more time before feeling fully comfortable and darted up the stairs.

There was an eerie atmosphere in my living room. I couldn't quite describe it but it didn't feel like my living room anymore. Like it now belonged to someone else. I know I'd told Isaac I would be happy to come back home but, now I was standing there, I wasn't so sure about that. I felt even more grateful that he'd offered me a place to stay.

I could feel my heart beginning to pound and my fingers were starting to get tingly so I quickly rushed into my bedroom and pulled an overnight bag from the bottom of my wardrobe. I made short work of throwing enough clothes and underwear in to last me a few days. I wasn't going to be presumptuous; I knew this couldn't be a long term thing. The last thing I needed was to become afraid of my own home. Or stay afraid, at least. I couldn't avoid being here forever, even though I *did* need this time away.

Heading into the bathroom, I grabbed my toothbrush and some other toiletries and shoved them in my bag. My heart was drumming wildly in my chest now and my blood was roaring in my ears. I grabbed hold of the edge of the sink, lowered my head and took a shaky breath in through my nose before releasing it in a rush from my mouth. I gripped the sink until my knuckles went white, counting my breaths in and out in an attempt to slow my racing heart.

I jumped about a foot in the air when I felt hands circle my waist. I heard a gentle shush in my ear. Staring straight ahead at my reflection in the mirror, I found Isaac stood close, arms wrapped tightly around my stomach, his head nestled close to my face, chin resting on my shoulder. His cerulean stare was watching our reflections in the mirror. I looked pale, panicked. He looked concerned and shockingly handsome. I watched as his eyes met mine in the mirror for a moment before he placed a tender kiss in the crook of my neck. I closed my eyes, feeling the tension begin to leach out of my body. I took a deep breath, taking in the scent of his aftershave. Everything about him was so comforting, so calming. I opened my eyes again to find him still studying my reflection. I offered him a small smile, which he returned. 'Are you ready to leave?' he asked me softly. I nodded. I was so ready to leave.

Chapter Thirteen

Despite wanting nothing more than Isaac to take me back to his, I really was feeling quite hungry, so I was happy to indulge his desire to take me out to lunch. After dumping my bag in the boot of his car, he drove back to the club and walked me through the city streets to a small bistro cafe called Spring Espresso. It was quaint and quiet and the food was delicious. I enjoyed a mozzarella and pesto ciabatta while Isaac polished off a croque monsieur. His appetite was astounding and, considering there wasn't a millimetre of fat on his body, he must work hard to keep himself in shape. I lowered my knife and fork, silently appraising him while he wiped his mouth with a napkin. He paused, raising his eyebrow on a smirk. I'm sure he could read my mind.

'You like what you see?' he asked softly, placing his napkin on his plate and leaning back in his chair.

I gulped as I took in the full length of his lean torso, sweeping my eyes up and down what I could see, a blush blossoming on my cheeks. 'A bit,' I shrugged with a nonchalance I didn't feel, rearranging my knife and fork on my plate. Isaac barked out a laugh so I shot my eyes back to his face, not wanting to miss a second of my favourite smile.

'You want dessert?' he asked, proffering the menu. 'They do really good pancakes.'

'I don't want pancakes,' I said, eyes down on my plate, feeling a wave of shyness roll through me.

'What do you want, Rose?' He spoke quietly, suggestively. I lifted my eyes to meet his gaze. His eyes gleamed, burning a hole right through me. Good god, he only had to look at me and I was burning up.

I let my tongue sweep across my lower lip, catching Isaac's sharp intake of breath. 'I think you know,' I whispered.

I jolted in my seat when Isaac rose from his chair, pulling his wallet from his back pocket. I stood too, reaching into my bag for my purse. Isaac rounded the table, taking hold of my elbow and gently removed my hand from my bag. 'My treat,' he said.

‘Next one’s on me, then,’ I replied, ignoring his quiet *hmm.* He strode over to the cafe counter and settled up so I headed out into the street, tilting my head up towards the sun. I basked like a cat for a few minutes until I felt a tug on the end of my ponytail. I opened my eyes to find his face just above mine. I started to smile but was stopped when he took my mouth in a hard kiss, one hand caressing the back of my head, the other pressing into the small of my back. The force of his kiss bent me backwards and I grabbed onto his arms to steady myself. Not that I had any need to worry; his arm was wrapped around me so tightly, I don’t think I was ever in any danger of hitting the deck.

I responded to his kiss with as much passion as he was giving me. I ran my hands up his arms and across his shoulders, before fisting them tightly in his hair. I was lost in him; the movement of his lips against mine, the feel of his tongue stroking against my own. I lost all notion of where I was, so consumed by his power over my senses, until a cocky school boy’s jeering brought me back.

I laughed into his mouth as I broke our kiss, feeling a little embarrassed to have given myself over to such a public display. Isaac was unbothered as he took my hand and started walking me back through the city to the Waterfront. His long legs swallowed up the streets and I was practically having to jog to keep up with him. I couldn’t help giggling as I struggled to match his pace, tugging on his arm to try to slow him down. He turned to face me with a look of such exasperation on his face that I lost it. I was belly laughing in the street, bent at the waist, tears streaming from my eyes while Isaac stood, gazing impassively down at me. ‘I’m sorry,’ I said on a snort, feeling like I was losing control. I hadn’t laughed like this for ages and the more I tried to get a grip of myself, the harder I found myself laughing.

Isaac took hold of the front of my jumper and hauled me close, pressing his lower body into mine. I gasped, sobering in an instant. He was as hard as iron. ‘I’m not above carrying you, if it gets you naked and beneath me faster,’ he growled in my ear. I’d have thought he was joking but the steely look in his eye and his erection pressing into my abdomen made me think twice. I just placed my hand in his and started walking, matching his pace easily now, fuelled by a heat burning deep within me.

It didn't take long to navigate the streets, even though they were rapidly filling up with tourists. Isaac seemed to know all the little shortcuts to avoid the busiest thoroughfares that I'd neglected to learn since moving to the centre of the city. I kept wanting to break the silence. Not because it was uncomfortable, far from it. I just wanted to keep learning more about him. I offered no conversation, though. Isaac was radiating too much tension and I was as eager to get back to his as he was.

Once we made it into the lobby of his building, Isaac practically dragged me toward the lift. Veronica came around the reception desk as soon as she saw us, clicking her heels and shaking her arse. I couldn't make out what she was saying and Isaac gave her no time to finish as he bundled me through the open door of the lift. 'Later, Veronica,' he said on a growl. I tried to ignore the incredulous look on her face as the doors slid closed in front of her.

The wall met my back before the lift had even started moving. Isaac was all over me; it felt like he had hands everywhere. My own hands found their favourite spot in his hair and pulled him to me, melting once more into his kiss. He parted my legs with his thigh, catching my sweet spot with delicious friction, making me moan into his mouth. My breath was coming in frantic gasps as Isaac dragged his lips across my cheek. He grazed my lobe with his teeth; shivers rippled up and down my spine before he dropped his head into my neck, nibbling and sucking gently. 'I don't know what you do to me, Rose,' he said into my neck. I shuddered in his grasp as he cupped my breast, finding my nipple through the material and squeezing tightly, the pleasure almost bordering on pain.

The lift pinged as it came to a stop and I only half cared if someone else was getting on. There was nothing that would have made me stop this, not even an audience. Isaac lowered both hands to my bum and lifted me from the ground. I circled his waist with my legs, my fingers still tangled up in his hair. Our lips were fused as Isaac walked me from the lift, running his hands up and down my back. He held me against him with one hand as though I weighed nothing at all while he fumbled in his pocket for his keys. I knew I wasn't helping by staying in his arms but I didn't want to break contact. It was impossible to let him go.

Eventually, Isaac opened the door and walked through it, kicking it closed behind him with a bang. He wasted no time moving through his apartment, straight to his bedroom, pulling my hair tie as he went. My hair cascaded down my back, then flew all around me as Isaac launched me from his arms onto the bed. He was breathing heavily, watching as I writhed on the bed before him, taking in his dishevelled state. My fingers had pulled his hair in all different directions, mussing up his glorious waves even further. I'd yanked his tie and his shirt was half untucked.

He spent a few moments getting his breath back, holding me in place with only his stare. He swept his gaze up and down my body, his eyes burning with pure lust. I was a wanton mess, desperate to put my hands on him again so I rose to my knees and crawled down the bed towards him. Spreading my hands across his chest, I ran them down his shirt, feeling the tight muscle beneath before running back up his chest, making his nipples harden beneath the fabric as I gently teased them.

Slowly, I pulled his tie free from its knot and slid it from around his neck with a smooth yank, looking up at him from beneath my eyelashes and sinking my teeth into my lower lip before starting to undo his shirt buttons, one by one until his body was revealed to me in all its glory. I dropped my gaze to admire him, running my hands all over him, circling his nipples with my fingertips. I moved my hands around his back and urged him to step closer to me so I could place gentle kisses on his chest before applying a little pressure on his nipple with my teeth.

Isaac sighed and took my face in both of his hands, stroking his thumbs tenderly against my cheeks. 'Do you know how beautiful you are?' he asked me.

'I know how beautiful you make me feel,' I replied, lifting my head to receive a soft kiss on the tip of my nose.

In a swift motion, Isaac reached down and whipped my jumper over my head, before pushing me back down to the bed. He made short work of undoing his belt and slipped out of his trousers, losing his shoes and socks at the same time. His boxers quickly followed suit and then he was with me on the bed, smothering me with his body.

'You are the most beautiful woman I've ever seen, Rose,' he said, kissing each of my eyebrows, my nose, my lips. 'You are so beguiling.' He moved down to my neck, trailing kisses across my collarbone before he reached my breasts. 'You are sexy.' He ran his fingers beneath the cup of my bra, teasing me with his touch. 'You're even sexier because you have no idea how sexy you are.' Isaac reached around my back to unclasp my bra, sliding the straps down my arms and releasing my breasts. My nipples puckered as he took each one in his mouth one at a time, swirling his tongue around the tips. 'You enthral me like no one else ever has.'

Isaac moved lower, raining kisses across my stomach, making me twitch when he dipped his tongue briefly in my belly button. He rose to his knees, leaving me feeling cold, desperate to have him back on top of me. 'You confuse me,' he said, hooking his fingers into the top of my leggings and drawing them down my legs, taking my knickers with them. 'You make me question the man I've been.' He tugged my Converse off and tossed them over his shoulder to allow him to remove the rest of my clothes, which joined the growing pile on the floor. I moaned my pleasure when he dragged his teeth across my skin, nibbling his way up my calf and inner thigh before running his tongue firmly between the junction of my thighs. I cried out sharply, the shocking stab of pleasure so unexpected I could hardly contain it.

'You scare me,' Isaac muttered into my flesh before licking and sucking my sensitive folds towards a release so powerful, my whole body was shaking on the bed. I screamed his name as I fisted my fingers in his hair, yanking hard in my ecstasy. Isaac brought me down from my orgasm slowly, letting me ride out the waves of pleasure before he rose over me and reached into the drawer beside his bed. My head fell back against the pillow in a daze as I listened to the foil packet of a condom ripping. Tension had leached from my body, leaving me more relaxed than I can ever remember being.

I lifted my head again when I felt Isaac part my legs with his muscular body, crawling up the length of me and settling himself on top, bearing his weight on his forearms, which were caged around me. I was cocooned in his warmth and was so protected in his embrace. I smiled up at him, bending my knees and spreading my legs to give him more room. He returned my smile, his eyes softening as he brushed some stray hair off my forehead. 'It's like you're holding a mirror up in front of me, Rose, and I don't know what to do.'

I circled my arms around his back, holding him tight to me. 'You make me want to be a better person,' he said, lowering his head and taking my mouth in a gentle yet passionate kiss. I returned his kiss with fervour, unable to understand how he could see himself in any other way than how I saw him now. He seemed so full of doubt and I wanted to show him that he had no reason for it. I didn't know what he was like with others or how he'd been with other women, but I couldn't comprehend him being anything less than the kind, funny, protective person he was with me.

The realisation that I was falling for him rushed up quickly. It made my heart feel like it was swelling to twice its normal size. I was glad to be his mirror. 'I don't want you to be scared of me,' I told him, breaking our kiss and seeking out his eyes once more.

He shook his head. 'I'm just in complete awe of you,' he said, looking down at me. 'You're everything I didn't know I was looking for and I'm a little overwhelmed.' He was overwhelmed? He was taking me over, body and soul, yet I found I was relieved beyond measure that I wasn't the only one feeling this way.

Isaac inched forward, his broad erection teasing my entrance. Unbidden, my body froze, my muscles locking into place. Panic threatened to swamp me once more. My eyes clamped shut and Isaac halted immediately. 'Who are you with, Rose?' he whispered in my ear, raising his lower body ever so slightly so I couldn't feel him anymore. I shook my head, fighting to stay here in bed with him instead of disappearing into my memories. I didn't want this moment ruined. 'Look at me,' he demanded softly. Still, I kept my eyes closed. 'Rose,' he breathed. 'Please, look at me.' I couldn't do it. I was drifting away. It was only noticing Isaac tense his arms in preparation to pull away from me that brought me back. I squeezed his shoulders in a bid to keep him close. 'Open your eyes,' he demanded again. This time I did. I opened my eyes and saw him, inches above my face. His eyes were like crystal clear lakes, full of anguish and lust and a tenderness I had never seen before. I exhaled on a shaky breath, letting him take over my senses. I focused on the comforting weight of his body on top of me and the familiar fragrance of his aftershave combined with his uniquely masculine scent. He was grounding me back to reality. 'Who are you with, Rose?' he asked me again.

'I'm with you,' I told him, the memories beginning to fade.

'Are you sure?' he asked, lowering his hips again.

'Only with you,' I assured him, tilting my pelvis to meet his descent.

On a long exhale, Isaac slid inside me, my body offering no resistance. He stretched me as he sheathed himself to the hilt, burying himself deep inside. He held himself there for a moment or two, his own eyes squeezing closed as he absorbed the pleasure. I stroked my hands up and down his back while I felt him twitch and throb inside me. 'You feel incredible,' he said, beginning to rock his body, moving in and out at a deliciously slow pace. I felt a tugging sensation deep in my belly as I savoured each drive of his pelvis.

Needing to be closer to him, I wrapped my legs around his lower back, urging him deeper still with each thrust. I moaned his name, my head thrashing on the pillow. On every advance into my body, he rotated his hips a little, circling deep within me. That was the beginning of my undoing. Isaac pushed me higher and higher with every thrust and each rotation. I started circling my hips, catching onto his rhythm and matching it, stroke for stroke. The now-familiar tension started in my belly, my core heating up as my orgasm powered forward. Isaac was starting to lose control, his hips jerking forward a little faster and a little harder, hitting me in just the right spot. I cried out as he hit it again and again, my legs stiffening as my orgasm ripped through me.

Isaac followed moments after, dropping his head into my shoulder on a shout. He continued to move lazily in and out, spilling all he had, working us both down. We were both covered in a sheen of sweat, our breathing taking a while to slow as we recovered. Pulling out, Isaac rolled onto his side, pulling me with him so we were facing each other. He moved more hair from out of my eyes, running his fingers through the tangles. 'I can't stop looking at you,' he said, tucking himself close to my body, wrapping his arms around me and holding me close.

'And why's that?' I asked him, although I knew exactly how he felt; I had trouble tearing my own eyes away from him.

‘I don’t want to miss a single second of you.’

Chapter Fourteen

The afternoon passed us by while we lay together on the bed, wrapped up in each other's arms, talking about anything and everything. He told me some more about the club and his plans to expand with more exclusive venues throughout the country. He had the six apartments in his property portfolio and was considering looking into procuring more land to enable him to build more luxury properties. Even though they didn't give him a regular rental income, the profit he made on the sales left him with plenty to reinvest elsewhere for future ventures, plus enough to allow him to live a more than comfortable life.

He didn't live extravagantly, though. Although it was a *very* comfortable life as he wanted for nothing, he spent it in relative quiet. He enjoyed to travel when work allowed him to, he ran - a lot - regularly managing a half marathon at least once a fortnight, sometimes even once a week. With as many as five trips to the gym a week, no wonder his physique was as perfect as it was. I felt exhausted just listening to him, not to mention feeling lazy and unfit. I wasn't carrying much additional weight but that was mostly due to skipping a meal or two. Not because I was particularly concerned about my size but because I tended to wait until I was truly hungry to eat, which I didn't always feel. I did no exercise to speak of, though, apart from walking to work and I knew I was a little soft in the middle. Luckily Isaac didn't seem to mind my fitness levels not being up to snuff.

I decided not to quiz him on girlfriends, knowing already how unaccustomed he was with "wining and dining". I had already gathered he had plenty more experience than me and didn't want to hear about it or dwell on it. What I really wanted to know about was the sheer amount of books in the other room. 'Have you even read them all?' I asked him.

'Not even close. I'll definitely die before I get through them. I've got a bad habit of buying more and adding to the collection.' Isaac frowned when he saw me suppress a shiver. He got on his knees and tugged the duvet from beneath me before laying it over my body. He crawled beneath it too and snuggled back up, propping his head on his arm. 'I just love reading. I'm so busy at the club and it's always so loud. Either the music or people clamouring around wanting to speak to me. Just coming home and sitting in the quiet, getting lost in someone else's story for a while? It's just bliss.' I knew what he meant. Reading had always been my escape too.

I stretched my arms over my head and rolled over onto my back, burrowing deep under the thick duvet. The bed was so comfortable and the weight of the duvet felt so comforting, reminding me of my Nana's old eiderdown duvets. When I was a kid, staying over with her during the school holidays, I remembered feeling like I couldn't move under the weight of them. 'I could spend hours picking through those books, sitting reading in one of those chairs. But do you never just fancy vegging on the sofa, watching tv or a film?'

Isaac placed his hand on my stomach, rubbing gentle circles across my flesh. He smiled at my question. 'Of course I do.'

'But you don't have a tv.' I thought back to my little snoop around his living room.

I jumped when Isaac started laughing, curling his body closer and hooking his leg over mine. 'No, I don't,' he said. 'I do have a projector that drops from the ceiling, though.'

I tutted and rolled my eyes. 'Flashy bastard,' I muttered playfully.

'It's hardly flashy when you can't see it,' he said, making me giggle. 'I don't like clutter, alright?' Now he sounded defensive. I was about to turn to face him, to tell him I was only teasing, when his hand started digging in my ribs, tickling me like crazy.

'Alright, alright!' I gasped, trying my best to wriggle away from him. I detested being tickled. Always had. 'Isaac, fucking hell, stop it!'

My wriggling had turned me around to face away from Isaac and he stopped his tickling fingers immediately, yanking me to him. I could feel his chest shaking with laughter while I huffed and chuffed. 'You're lucky I didn't try to kick you in the balls,' I spat out, not even remotely joking. Isaac just laughed more.

'I'm sorry,' he said in my ear, shuffling even closer, spooning tight against me. 'Forgive me?' I just wriggled my bum against his groin, trying to get comfortable again, smiling when I felt him harden behind me.

'You're forgiven,' I said, stopping moving and settling into the cuddle.

'Tell me what made you want to start your own business.'

My heart simultaneously sank and soared. I was so proud of what I was doing but I hated what it had taken to give me the opportunity. 'It was my Nana,' I told him. 'She always wanted to see me doing something I loved. We had a mutual love of cats and she always hated leaving her own in what she would call "sub-par" accommodation when she jetted off on her holidays. We would spend ages talking about all the things she wished she could give her babies when she was away. Everything in my place is a collaboration, really, of all those things that she would have wanted.'

'Is she no longer with us?' he asked softly.

I shook my head, feeling the familiar crushing sensation in my chest. 'No, she passed just over ten months ago now.'

'I'm sorry,' he said with sincerity, kissing the top of my head and stroking my arm.

'I miss her every day,' I continued. 'She left me a generous inheritance and I decided to blow it on one of the few things she really wanted me to do with my life.'

'She wanted you to start your own business?'

'Not really. She just wanted me to be happy. She could see me settling in my job at the accountants and knew I would be missing out on chasing my dreams. She didn't want that. I didn't necessarily need to start my own business but I knew that working with animals would make me happy and I figured I could honour her with what I'm doing with the place, you know?'

'Having seen what you've done with it, I think she would be incredibly proud of you.'

'I think she would, too,' I said. Almost absentmindedly, I added, 'she'd have got a kick out of you.'

Isaac propped himself up on his elbow so he could look down at me. I felt my face flame instantly. 'Oh yeah?' he asked.

'Oh yeah. You're exactly what she wanted for me, above and beyond anything else.'

He snorted. 'And what's that, exactly?'

A sex god, I thought to myself. 'Something unexpected,' I told him. Isaac said nothing, just continued staring down at me, waiting for me to elaborate when a pounding at the door startled us both.

We whipped our heads toward the open bedroom door. 'Hang on,' he said, hopping out of bed. 'I'll just see who that is.' He pulled a pair of grey skinny sweatpants on and shrugged his way into a loose white t-shirt. 'Wait here. I won't be long.' He padded out of the bedroom and pulled the door closed.

I snuggled down further under the duvet while I waited for him to return. For the first time since being carried into the room, I took a proper look around. It was beautiful. Cream walls - obviously - and a soft grey carpet. But the bedding was a deep blue, the furniture a pale, natural wood and the walls were adorned with blown up, framed photographs of the sea. They were all taken from a little way up the beach, the shore giving way to various shades of water. They were wonderful to look at. Some of the beaches were white sands, others were golden while others still were shaley. One was even black; a volcanic beach. The blues of the water varied from bright to deep, the sun sometimes sparkling off the rippling waves. There were no people or objects in any photograph, just an endless horizon. I could have looked at them for hours. They were stunning in their simplicity, evoking a feeling of serenity and calm.

After a while, I began to wonder what might be keeping Isaac. I climbed out of bed and dressed quickly, moving towards the closed door. I pressed my ear to the wood, listening for sounds in the room beyond but couldn't hear anything so I opened the door a crack and popped my head out. There was no one there.

Confused, I walked into the open space. I looked around for a moment before spotting the front door, ajar. I headed over, curiosity getting the better of me. As I got closer to the door, I could hear muted voices. Isaac sounded as abrupt as ever, pissed off, even. His companion was male and spoke in a whisper. I couldn't hear him very well. I wanted more than anything to go out into the hallway but judging by Isaac's tone of voice, I don't think I would have been welcome. I was, however, feeling a bit like a spare part. I headed closer to the door and cleared my throat. 'Isaac?' I called through the gap, wanting to make my presence known.

Both voices stopped at once. 'And who are you hiding in there, big brother?' I heard through the door. *Brother?* I took a step back as the door started to swing towards me. I expected Isaac to walk through but it was his companion instead. There was just barely a family resemblance. He was tall, like Isaac, but he was reed-thin. His face was sallow, his eyes - a blue-grey colour - were sunken into his skull. He was sporting a scruffy, stubbly beard and his hair was the same shade of brown as Isaac's but was longer and more unkempt. He looked like he had been a handsome man once, but was ruined now, somehow.

He'd called Isaac big brother but looked older than him; despite Isaac looking younger than his years, I would have put this man in his late thirties. He didn't so much as walk into the room, instead, he sort of swaggered. No. He slithered in. There was something predatory about him. My heart thrummed a rapid patina in my chest, making me take another step back, away from him. A lump formed in my throat. 'Hey, girlie,' he said as he approached me.

'Jack.' Isaac's tone was cold, a clear warning when he followed him into the room.

I moved back another step. There was a sour smell to him. I really didn't want to be near him. I looked from him, to Isaac and back again. I didn't like the look on Isaac's face. It was the look someone had when they were approaching a snarling dog. Wary.

'Look at you,' Jack said. He stopped a ways in front of me and shoved his hands in his jeans pockets. They were worn and frayed with holes in the knees. He was wearing a thin, baggy khaki coloured jumper. Tattoos covered what I could see of his hands. 'You're not his usual type.'

'Jack.' Isaac spoke again while I took another step back.

'Take it easy, Zac,' he said, not looking over at his brother. 'Are you going to introduce me, or not?'

I gulped. I think I was only a few minutes away from losing my shit and the tension radiating from Isaac was making me feel worse. I needed to do something. 'I'm Rose,' I said on an unsteady breath, holding a shaky hand out to him.

Jack took my hand in his clammy one. I expected him to give it a quick shake and then release me but instead, he yanked me forward until I was practically pressed up against him. He took a chunk of my hair and wound it around his fingers before bringing his hand up to his nose to inhale. 'Hmm,' he breathed, under his breath.

The next second, before I could even react, I found myself tumbling to my knees, a tearing pain shooting across my scalp as some of my hair was ripped out. I landed on the floor with a thud and looked across the room to find Isaac with his hand around Jack's throat, walking him backwards until he was pressed against the wall. Isaac's face was pushed right up to his brother's and I could see his lips moving as he growled something at him but I couldn't hear anything he was saying over the sound of Jack's laughter. He sounded utterly crazy.

'You don't want to share this one, then?' he asked. *What?* Isaac didn't give Jack any time to elaborate and he offered no answer to the question except to launch his fist into his brother's face. It made a sickening noise, knuckles meeting skin, bone crunching under the impact. I winced from my prone position on the floor.

Jack made to crumble to the floor but Isaac's grip tightened around his throat and kept him on his feet. Blood was gushing from his nose, covering his face and Isaac's fingers, dripping to the floor. 'If you come back here again,' he snarled in his ear, 'I'll-'

'What, big brother? What the fuck will you do?' Jack wheezed. I staggered to my feet, seriously concerned that Isaac was going to choke the life out of his brother in front of me. I needn't have been too worried. Before I could move a step towards them - not that I would have been able to pry them apart - Isaac propelled Jack through the open door, leaving him sprawled on the floor of the hallway.

'You need to fuck off, Jack. Get a fucking grip and get the fuck out of my life.' He slammed the door and pounded his knuckles into the wood. Once, twice. I hesitantly moved over to him and placed my hand on his shoulder. When he offered no resistance to my touch, I stepped closer and wrapped my arms around his stomach and rested my head against his back. We stayed like that, me wrapped around him and him breathing heavily, his angry shaking subsiding until we heard movement in the corridor. We listened until we heard the bing of the lift and the whoosh of the doors as they closed. 'You really can't choose your family,' he said, his forehead pressed against the wood. It sounded so much like he wished he could.

I guided Isaac away from the door and led him across to the sofa. He sat down in a rush, his head in his hands. 'I'm so sorry,' he said.

'What for?'

'For him. For letting him touch you. For his very existence.' He lifted his head. 'Are you hurt?'

I shook my head. My knees were throbbing and my scalp was stinging but I was more worried about Isaac. Any panic I'd been feeling was forgotten in the face of his turmoil. I did have a few questions but I didn't know where to start. It turned out I didn't need to. 'We're not very close, I'm sure you can tell.' I didn't say anything, just waited for him to continue. He didn't look like he knew where to begin but I didn't want to interrupt his train of thought by asking questions. I just put my hand on his knee and squeezed my encouragement.

On a sigh, Isaac covered my hand with his and flopped back onto the sofa. He pulled me down with him so I ended up curled into his side, my head on his chest. He kept one hand gripping mine and the other cradled my head, his fingers massaging my scalp. It felt nice on the tender patch. 'Jack is eleven years younger than me.' *Good god,* I thought to myself. He was not looking good. He was only twenty-eight? 'He was babied. Our parents struggled to conceive me and were told that having a second child was practically impossible. He was a very welcome surprise, even if they were a little long in the tooth to be caring for a newborn.'

'How old were they?'

'When Jack came along? My dad was fifty-three. Mum was fifty-one.' He sighed again, running his fingers through my hair. 'Neither of us wanted for anything growing up. My dad was in stocks and shares and Mum was in television production. They made a good living and left a big legacy for us.'

My heart sank. 'They've passed?' I felt him nod.

'Car crash. Lorry driver fell asleep behind the wheel on the motorway. Their car got in the way. They were killed instantly.'

I squeezed him tight. 'I'm so sorry,' I told him, so heartbroken. I couldn't imagine losing even one parent, let alone both of them, and so tragically too.

'Jack was eighteen. Legally an adult, supposed to stand on his own, live his life. He had all the means at his disposal to make a really good one.'

'But he didn't?' I don't know why I bothered asking. I could see he hadn't.

'Of course he didn't. He partied hard for a few years. I can understand that. Young man, immature, wealthy, grieving. Not a good combination, not at that age. He fell in with a crowd of people who just wanted him for his money. I know the type, they gravitate to me too, only I've always kept them at arm's length. He was too impressionable, though. They ruined him.'

'Drugs?'

'Yep. Started off quite light. Dabbling here and there. It wasn't long before he got on to the hard stuff, heroin being his particular favourite. He injected the rest of his inheritance and has been a pain in my arse for the last several years. In and out of rehab. On and off the wagon. He can't hold down a job and keeps coming back for money. He swears he's clean, that he's going to use the money to start over, but before long, it's been shoved back in his veins and the cycle starts over again.'

I didn't know what to say. Pain laced Isaac's words. It was clear he wanted to help his brother but it was also clear that Jack needed to help himself. I wasn't sure Isaac would appreciate that observation. I was just opening my mouth to offer what would only be another redundant sorry, when he said, 'what a way to spoil a lovely afternoon, eh?'

I smiled and propped myself up. 'Don't be silly,' I told him. 'I'm glad you told me.' I hated to see the light in his eyes fading out. I wanted to lift the mood, despite having a million more questions. 'I don't know about you, but I could really go for a drink right about now.'

'Oh yeah?'

'Yeah. I know you'll have to work tonight, so I thought it might be nice if I took you up on your offer before you do.'

'And what offer was that?'

I jumped up off the sofa and held out my hand for him to take. 'You said you'd have me back in your club anytime. I quite fancy a cocktail, so long as the owner promises to mix it for me.'

Chapter Fifteen

While I showered, Isaac darted over the river to grab my overnight bag from the car. I told him it didn't matter, that I would grab it on the way back from the club but he wasn't having any of it. I used the master en-suite to get ready, getting a little thrill from using Isaac's shower gel. The fragrance filled the room, stirring my senses. I towel dried my hair in the bathroom, not bothering to do anything more than braid it over my shoulder. It was too long to faff with and, being completely honest with myself, I was falling out of love with it. My hair was one of my most striking features, reaching right down to my lower back and being a bright, natural blonde. It was what people noticed about me first. That, and my larger chest, narrow waist and plentiful hips. Jack had taken a lock of my hair, literally ripping it from my head, however inadvertently. I had no doubt my attacker had been attracted to it, too.

I hung up my damp towels on the heated rail and clocked a pair of nail scissors on one of the glass shelves opposite me. I started to wonder whether there might be a bigger pair in the kitchen. I could take care of my hair then. Lop it all off and make sure no one looked twice at it again.

A quiet knock pulled me from my reverie. Isaac popped his head in, his hair damp from the shower, too. He must have used the other en-suite. 'You okay?' he asked.

'I'm great,' I told him, putting all thoughts of a DIY haircut from my mind. 'Sorry, have I been ages?'

Rounding the door, Isaac dragged a slow stare up and down my body. I wanted to cover myself, suddenly shy. But I kept my arms by my sides, letting him drink me in. He had changed into a pair of dark blue jeans, slim-fitting. He was wearing a grey v-neck jumper with an open-collar white shirt beneath. He looked lovely, all casual and relaxed. Still sexy as hell. I sighed as I stared right back at him. Isaac chuckled under his breath. I smiled, shrugging my shoulders in apology. 'It's your fault,' I told him. 'You're a distraction.'

'Right back at you, gorgeous,' he said, indicating my nakedness with an appreciative nod of his head. 'You still want that drink or am I taking you straight back to bed?' Desire pooled low in my belly, making me press my thighs together. Isaac just laughed. 'Get dressed, woman,' he said on a shake of his head, heading back into the bedroom. 'You're just too tempting.'

I definitely had a spring in my step as I followed him into the bedroom. Isaac had placed my bag on the end of the bed so I headed straight over and pulled out some underwear, slipping it on quickly. A quick peek over my shoulder told me Isaac was reclined in a wicker chair, one ankle resting on the opposite knee, his hands linked over his taught stomach. I fluttered my eyelashes coquettishly, bending at the waist to pull my black skinny jeans from my bag. 'I like your tattoo.' he said.

I straightened and looked back over my shoulder at him. 'Thank you,' I told him simply before stepping into my jeans and pulling them up my legs. I only had the one and, never having caught the bug, had zero desire to have another. I adored it though and regretted every day not having it somewhere I could see it. When do you ever get the opportunity to look between your shoulder blades?

It was a black and grey piece and was a pretty young woman, hair bundled untidily on top of her head. The inside of her head was full of books, each one a title from my favourite authors. It was the most accurate representation of the inside of my own head I had ever seen and knew I needed it on my body from the very first time I'd seen the design. I had it done on my twenty-first birthday. It was a gift from Nana and she had sat with me for the full five hours it had taken to get it done. The biggest surprise was her getting a small rose on her ankle at the same time. 'To remind me of you,' she'd told me.

I jumped slightly when I felt Isaac stroke down my spine, caressing the ink. 'C.S Lewis. Emily Brontë. Linwood Barclay. Karin Slaughter.' He read across the shelf on my skin. 'JEM?'

'My Nana's favourite,' I told him, grabbing a lightweight white jumper from my bag. 'She had a filthy mind and was a sucker for a romantic alpha male.' I stood and enjoyed the feel of him tracing the spines of all my favourite books before placing a gentle kiss on the centre of my back, his arms wrapped around me, hands splayed across my stomach.

'I meant to compliment this last night,' he told me, resting his chin on the top of my head. 'I couldn't take my eyes off it while I had you in the shower. I've never been so turned on by a tattooed woman before.'

'Well,' I said lightheartedly, turning in his arms to look up at him. 'I've heard I'm not your usual type.'

Eyes turning cold at the memory of his brother's words, Isaac kissed the tip of my nose. 'No, you're certainly not.' No matter how much pride I felt at that statement, I still didn't want to find out what his usual type was.

I yanked my jumper over my head. 'Come on, then,' I said, bouncing on the balls of my feet. 'I'm parched.'

We headed out to the lift and down to the lobby. I expected to go straight out to the street but Isaac headed instead to the reception desk. For once, Veronica made no move to round the desk. 'Do you know the security protocols for this building, Veronica?'

I swear I could see Veronica's throat moving in a gulp. She knew she'd fucked up. 'Mr Yates?' Her voice was mouse quiet.

'The security protocols. Do you know them?' Isaac spoke softly, was standing a respectful distance from the desk but still radiated authority. I was glad I wasn't on the receiving end of his questions.

'Yes, I know them, Mr Yates.'

'And they are?'

'What, Sir?'

"What are the security protocols?' Good god, she was wilting. She looked over Isaac's shoulder at me; I could only grimace in sympathy. 'Specifically the visitor protocol.'

'Um, anyone not on the approved guest list is to wait in the lobby until the resident has confirmed entry.'

'Is the gentleman you allowed up to my penthouse earlier on my approved guest list?'

'He said he was your brother, Mr Yates. I thought...' She broke off as Isaac took a step closer to the desk.

'Is he on my approved guest list?'

'No, he isn't.' Veronica dropped her gaze to the desk in a bid to escape Isaac's scrutiny.

'Veronica, I take these security protocols very seriously. I also operate a three strikes policy with my employees. You can consider this your first, do you understand?'

I could see Veronica's cheeks flaming all the way across the lobby. 'Yes, Mr Yates,' she whispered, still looking at the desk.

'Good.' Without offering anything further, Isaac turned and walked back to me, pulling me to his side and escorting me from the building. I let out a puff of air, not sure what to say. 'What?' he asked, looking down at me.

I shrugged. 'Did she deserve that?' I asked, perhaps a little more harshly than I intended.

'Yes,' he replied, as curt as ever. 'If the man who attacked you finds out you're staying with me, you want to hope she doesn't let the fucker up.' *Well, when you put it like that,* I thought.

I repressed a shudder at the thought of him finding out where I was staying again and put my arm around Isaac's waist, leaning into his embrace. The walk to the club was pleasant, the sun just beginning to drop lower in the sky. It was cool, but not cold. It wasn't as busy, either. We crossed the bridge in comfortable silence. As we passed the stone stairs to the riverbank, I turned my head further into Isaac's chest, trying to ignore the lump in my throat. I felt relieved to walk inside. There was already a doorman in position, although no one had started queuing for entry yet. 'What time do you open?' I asked.

Isaac glanced at his watch as he greeted some of the staff, walking me through the club to the bar. 'In an hour and a half,' he said, before placing me on a stool in front of the bar. 'Plenty of time for me to ply you with alcohol. Unless you want to stay tonight?'

I laughed. 'Dressed like this?' I indicated my casual attire. Isaac smiled and headed through the hatch, behind the bar. 'Shaun, I'd like you to meet Rose.' He placed one hand on the shoulder of his barman and held the other out to me. I waved hello, recognising him to be the barman who served me on my leaving do.

'Can I get you both something to drink?' he asked, wiping his hands on the front of his apron.

Isaac nudged him aside with his hip, coming to a stop in front of me. 'I'll handle this. You get on with the prep.'

'Yes, boss.' Shaun saluted and headed back over to the tower of lemons and limes he'd been slicing when we arrived.

'So, what'll it be?' Isaac asked, leaning down to get eye level with me. 'Let me guess...' He stroked his chin with his fingers, thoughtful. 'Something fruity? A little sweet?' I nodded, a small smile teasing the corners of my mouth. I had the feeling he might already know what my cocktails of choice were. I'd have bet money on Shaun having filled him in. 'Hmm, something refreshing? A porn star martini?' I wobbled my palm in the air in front of him. Occasionally, but not my favourite. 'No, I know. Something I can blend with fresh fruit. How about a strawberry daiquiri?' I started to nod my agreement in excitement when another memory of that night shot into my brain, stopping me short. I could taste the fresh strawberry, the tang of the rum sliding down my throat. Could feel the crunch of the seeds between my teeth. I could also feel his hands sliding up and down my bare arm while he tried to get me to dance with him. 'Or maybe something different?' Isaac quietly asked.

'Yes, please,' I said, grateful for his intuition. 'Surprise me. What do you think I'll like?'

There was a long moment where he just stared at me, lips lifting in a slight smile. I could almost hear what he was thinking. He knew exactly what I liked and it wasn't a beverage. Eventually, he stood and grabbed a glass tumbler and a martini glass. He tossed a handful of ice in both. He turned and took a bottle of Grey Goose vodka and Chambord from the shelf behind him. With one hand, he poured a long pour of the vodka and a couple of seconds later used the other to add a shorter pour of the Chambord. I raised my eyebrow. 'No measuring?' I asked him, in a playful mood.

Isaac scoffed. 'Not in this joint, baby,' he said, making me smile wide. He reached under the bar and removed a bottle of pineapple juice, adding a measure to the tumbler. He then slammed a silver beaker into the glass and started shaking the hell out of it. He made it look effortless, especially when he shook with one hand and dumped the ice from the martini glass with the other.

Grabbing a strainer, Isaac removed the glass tumbler from the shaker and poured the delicious-looking purple liquid into the chilled glass. The moment Isaac placed the shaker back on the bar, Shaun tossed a lemon peel over his shoulder - which Isaac then caught without looking - in a move that looked so natural it had to have been practised many, many times. I barked out a laugh, revelling in the cheeky, boyish wink Isaac sent my way. God, he was adorable. He twisted the peel over the glass, releasing a drop of oil onto the surface of the drink before he slid it in front of me. 'French martini for the lady,' he said.

I picked up the glass and took a small sip, sighing in pleasure before enjoying a healthier swig. 'Mmmm, beautiful,' I said, my approval evident.

'Indeed,' Isaac retorted, his eyes not moving from mine.

The next hour and fifteen minutes passed far too quickly, as did the cocktails. I had another French martini and a cosmo before they were ready to open the doors to the public, while Isaac enjoyed a couple of godfathers, which were rather delicious themselves. He asked me, again, if I wanted to stay but I really didn't. I felt comfortable there with Isaac, and Shaun was a perfect little charmer but the thought of being in there with the crowds...in all honesty, I felt ill thinking about it.

So, fifteen minutes before Shiver was due to open, Isaac walked me back across the river and up in the lift, greeting the new receptionist in the same curt manner as Veronica. 'So you're not just rude to your female staff, then?' I joked, after noticing the night receptionist was a big bald man named Tony.

'I'm not rude, I'm an efficient conversationalist,' he replied. I rolled my eyes and followed Isaac into the lift. I was feeling a nice little buzz from the alcohol so I was leaning against Isaac's chest, my arms wrapped around his back, his wrapped around my shoulders. It felt so lovely, to just be held. I sighed when I felt Isaac drop a kiss on the crown of my head, enjoying the feel of his hands tracing my spine through my jumper. 'Are you going to be alright tonight?' he asked me as he walked me through his front door.

I followed him into the bedroom, not wanting to miss a chance to see him undress and suit up. Nothing wore him like a suit, that was for sure. 'I will. I'm going to curl up and read and probably get an early night. I'm shattered,' I told him, stifling a yawn.

'Do you want me to order some food in for you before I leave?' I studied the planes of his chest for a moment, watching his deft fingers button up a crisp white shirt, from bottom to top. I think I may have been drooling as he tucked it into his pale grey trousers. 'Rose, don't look at me like that. I'll never get to work,' he said on a laugh.

'I can't help it. You're just too lovely.' I shook my head, inwardly groaning with pleasure when he shrugged into a light grey waistcoat. 'And no, thank you. I'll make something here. I don't want another meltdown when a delivery person knocks on the door.' He completed his look with a pale pink tie, which he tucked beneath his waistcoat before pulling on the matching jacket. 'No wonder you sell so many tickets to the place,' I muttered dryly, definitely drooling now.

'I use god-given gifts, that's true.' He smiled at me on a slight shake of his head and headed into the sitting room. '*Will* you make yourself something, though?' he asked, fixing me with a hard stare. 'Or will I come home and hear your stomach rumbling in your sleep?'

'I'll make something. I honestly don't have a problem with food,' I added, seeing his eyes awash with concern. 'Okay?' I asked.

He nodded. 'Alright. I have to go. I'll try to escape before closing but I'll be quiet when I come in in case you're asleep.'

I kissed him deeply goodbye, having to fight the urge to tell him something crazy like, "I love you". I was done for. Forget falling for this man; I had long since surpassed a full free fall. I'd already fallen.

Chapter Sixteen

My evening was quite lovely. I found that I didn't mind being alone. Despite almost losing my mind earlier, there was something incredibly comforting about being in this penthouse. I couldn't tell whether it was because it was so damn luxurious, the calming - if a little dull - colour scheme or whether it was because the place just made me think of Isaac. I took such a level of comfort from him, I was growing concerned it was unhealthy. This concern grew when I headed into the bedroom after seeing him out the door and, instead of pulling on the comfy pj's I'd packed for myself, I grabbed the white t-shirt he'd been wearing earlier and slipped it over my head. It fell to my mid thighs and the penthouse was so warm, I felt comfortable enough to pad around in only that and a pair of socks. I inhaled deeply, taking in the fresh masculine scent that had permeated the fabric.

I headed straight back across to the chairs in the office area after grabbing a big glass of water from the kitchen and dived straight back into *The Last Wish*. Dusk had fallen by the time I looked up and I thought I'd better make good on my promise to eat something. I pottered around the kitchen and, after taking a good look through his fridge and cupboards, I settled for a pizza from the freezer. Utterly shameful but I really was that terrible a cook. At least it was real food. I'd been contemplating a bowl of soup but something told me Isaac wouldn't have considered that proper food.

After eating and clearing away, I was feeling too sleepy to concentrate on my book. I had a look around for the hidden projector but had no joy, so I grabbed my iPad and, after connecting it to my phone's hotspot, settled down on the sofa with Netflix.

At some point, I must have fallen asleep because I woke up in the dark, disturbed when Isaac picked me up and carried me to bed. He laid me down under the covers, crawling in with me after he undressed before tucking me into his front. It didn't take me long to fall back asleep with his arms wrapped around me and his warm breath in my ear.

The sun was shining through the crack in the curtains when I woke up properly the next morning. I felt more rested than I had in a while. Isaac was still wrapped tightly around me; I wondered how long it had been since he'd arrived home. Careful not to disturb him, I untangled myself from his grip and headed to the bathroom to freshen up.

Back in the bedroom, I dressed quietly, enjoying watching him sleep. He was so relaxed and cute in his slumber. I wanted to crawl right back into bed with him but I did need to get back to the cattery. I had the last of the prep to sort out because I had my first paying client coming in less than a week and I wanted the place to be finished before then. I didn't want Mrs Pepper to be bringing her precious Noodle to a sub-par establishment. So, with a last longing look at him, I moved through to the living room to leave him a note. Not a scrap of paper to be found. I was a little hesitant to rummage through his desk for a notepad but I couldn't leave without letting him know where I was going.

A quick rifle through the top drawer revealed a week-to-view diary and more pens than I'd ever seen in my life. He was like a serial hoarder. I smiled, enjoying finding out about his little foibles and opened the diary to today's date to scribble him a note, telling him where to find me. I grabbed my bag and made my way down the lift, stepping out into the autumn sunshine after giving Veronica a little wave of greeting. She returned it hesitantly. She looked as though she was waiting for Isaac to follow me out of the lift. Poor woman. He really was a force of nature.

My walk to work was a steady meander. On a Sunday morning, York was more like a sleepy village than a bustling city. I window shopped my way through the streets, stopping to grab a frappuccino from Starbucks on my way past. Slurping on my white chocolate mocha, I approached my hairdressers, almost on autopilot. Still thinking about the lost love for my hair, I pushed the door open and made a spontaneous appointment for the following Saturday. If I bottled it, there was plenty of time to cancel.

It wasn't long before I had to decide whether to stick to the main road or whether I was going to take the river walk. My gut instinct was to stay by the main road but I knew if I did, I would forever be avoiding the river. It would become a phobia and I couldn't allow that to happen. So, I took a deep breath, then another, and a few more, and then I crossed the path and joined the river walk.

My heart was pounding the whole time and I had to resist the urge to break into a run, but I did it. I walked as far as I could before I had no choice but to veer back onto the main road. The sense of relief I felt was immense, but I had made it. Nothing bad had happened to me. I was safe. But it did feel great to be back where there were more people. My heart rate slowed down, as did my footfalls and I had pretty much stopped gasping for breath by the time I unlocked my cattery door. I locked up behind me and dumped my stuff in the office. I rooted through my bag, looking for my phone. 'Shit,' I muttered to myself, upending the contents of my bag over my desk. It wasn't there. Of course it wasn't. I'd used it the night before to connect my iPad to the internet. It was probably still on the sofa or slipped between the sofa cushions. 'Fuck.' I chewed on my lower lip, worrying. Isaac would be pissed off, I just knew it. He was going to wake up, see I wasn't there and was going to call me. Probably before he even saw my note. His protective instinct would kick in and he was going to freak out when he couldn't reach me.

Should I go home? I could be back in plenty of time before he woke up. But I was so close to getting the cattery finished. I was taking my last delivery of stuff in the week and Sunday was one of the best days to crack on and get the decorating finished. No, I decided. I was going to stay and work. I didn't even know how long Isaac would sleep for. I might even be done and back before he woke up and then he'd be none the wiser. Decided, at last, bemoaning the fact that I would have to work without music, I grabbed my roller and tray and got to work.

I was sweaty and splattered in paint by the time I'd chucked my roller away but it was finally finished. Apart from the delivery of various foods and the soft furnishings I needed, I was done. By the time Noodle arrived, I would have a fully functioning, luxury cattery. I just needed Mrs Pepper to leave me a good review and tell all her cat-owning friends about what a wonderful place I ran. My fingers were crossed.

Now ready to leave and head back to Isaac's for a shower, hopefully *with* Isaac and not by myself, I was startled by my office phone ringing. Excited at the prospect of a potential new customer, I darted back to the office and grabbed the phone. 'Hello, Carter's Cattery?'

Dead silence on the other end. 'Carter's Cattery, Rose speaking. How can I help you?' More silence.

I was about to hang up but then whoever was on the other end started to speak. 'That's a pretty name, Rose.' I dropped to the floor like a stone the instant I heard his voice, the receiver clutched to my ear in a death grip, the plastic creaking. 'Rose. Rosie. Rosslyn.' His voice was deep, gentle, at complete odds with his brutality. I wanted to hang up but couldn't bring my arm down. I couldn't even attempt to stand up. I could hardly breathe. 'Are you there, Rose?' I couldn't say anything. 'I've been thinking about you a lot, Rosie. When I'm at work, when I'm at home. When I've got nothing else to do. I think about how you looked, lying beneath me. How you felt when I fucked you.'

Bile rose in my throat. I swallowed it back down before I asked, 'what do you want?' My voice came out in little more than a croaky whisper.

'What do I want?' he repeated, sounding deep in thought. 'What do you think I want?' I said nothing, only capable of squeezing my eyes closed in a bid to escape. 'Rose. What. Do. You. Think. I. Want?' he enunciated slowly. His voice whispered in my ear, becoming guttural, filled with lust. I knew what he wanted. 'You liked it,' he said. 'You might have played hard to get in the club but when it really came down to it, you liked it. You bitches always do.'

'You fucking raped me,' I snarled down the line.

'It's what you're for,' he countered, matter of fact. I groaned, my stomach spasming when he started laughing down the line. 'I'll admit, Rosie, I'm not usually as taken with bitches like you. I can't quite put my finger on what it is about you in particular but you intrigue me. You caught my attention, with that tight dress, your big tits and long hair. I imagined fucking you right there, in the club. Just taking you to a dark corner, lifting that dress up, having you there and then. But what a shame that would have been, not being able to look into those eyes. Seeing the blood spill from your nose. Feel your breath on my face. The taste of your tears.'

'Please, stop,' I whispered, tears falling freely down my face.

'Oh, the feel of you, Rose,' he continued, as though he hadn't even heard me. 'That moment, when I put my cock in you. I've never felt anything quite like you. And then he came and ruined it.' He went quiet for a while. Why couldn't I just hang up the phone? Just hang up and get out? 'Has he fucked you yet, Rose? I know all about him. I know how he likes it. I know what he does with the sluts in his club. Do you know that if it wasn't me that night, it would have been him? He'd set his sights on you and he doesn't like to let go either. We're alike, like that.'

'He is nothing like you,' I barked into the receiver, fire blooming in my belly.

'Hmm, there's a spark in you,' he said. 'I'd like to see what that's like. Have you thought about me at all, Rosie?' I was gripping the receiver so hard, it was in danger of shattering in my grip. I was going to crush it. 'I think you must have thought about me. You were moving so quickly down the river path earlier, I could hardly keep up with you. I must have been in your thoughts.'

'You followed me?'

'Yes,' he answered. 'I've been everywhere with you. I can't stop looking at you. I meant what I said in my letter, Rose. I will have you again. And again. There's nowhere I can't find you. You're mine now.'

'You won't get near me again, you sick fucking bastard,' I spat each word down the phone at him, disgust roiling in my gut.

'Are you sure about that, sweet girl?'

'More than anything.' I was shaking now, anger boiling my blood and giving me strength. I lurched to my feet.

'Turn around, Rosie. Let me see that fire in your eyes.'

I pivoted round in an instant, spinning towards the window facing the rear of my property. There he was. He was staring at me through the window, his mobile phone held to his ear. I got my first real good look at him. Sloping nose, fuller face. His hair was a close buzz cut and his lips were thin and cruel. His eyes were dark green and unblinking. He lifted his free hand and rested it on the window. I could hear him breathing in my ear. 'You make me hard, Rosslyn,' he said, just as a loud banging started up at my front door. I watched his shoulders rise in a sigh. 'And here he is. The hero. Getting in my way.' The banging grew louder and louder. 'This isn't goodbye, Rose.'

He disconnected the call and started walking backwards, away from the window. I was still stood facing the glass, the phone still pressed to my ear when the front door was kicked in with an ear-splitting crash. 'ROSE?!' I could hear Isaac's bellow but could do nothing more than watch his retreat. I didn't even react when Isaac grabbed hold of my shoulders and shook me. 'I've been so fucking worried. I woke up and you weren't there! I didn't know where you were and you didn't even take your fucking phone! Are you stupid?!'

'No!' I shouted, shoving him in his chest and throwing the phone in his direction. 'No, I'm not stupid. I came to work, like a normal person. I didn't mean to leave my phone, it was an accident. And I left you a bloody note so you wouldn't worry!' I realised I was nearly screaming but I couldn't seem to stop. 'I bet you just woke up and started tearing through the house like a mad man and didn't even spend a single second thinking about where I might have gone. Right?'

Isaac was pacing up and down in front of me, running one of his hands through his hair and using the other to massage his chest. 'What the hell was I supposed to think? I've been going out of my mind.'

'I'm so fucking sorry,' I yelled. 'For wanting to live my life, to do my job. To carry on like normal.'

Isaac stopped his pacing. 'Things aren't normal for you, though, are they? You've got a fucking stalker. It's not safe for you.'

No, it's not!' I screamed in his face, flying across the room to him, raining punches on his chest. He grappled with me, trying to get me under control. It was like someone had lit a fire within me; I was rabid. I was shouting unintelligible words, hitting him harder and harder until, eventually, Isaac swept my legs out from under me. He caught my weight to stop me from hitting the deck and lowered me to the floor, straddling my waist in a bid to keep me still. I just writhed underneath him, trying to buck him off. I kicked my legs and flailed my arms in his grasp.

'Rose, STOP IT!' He pushed my arms up and over my head, laying his whole body on top of me, rendering me completely immobile, his face right up close to mine. I stopped struggling at once, gasping for breath. 'Has something happened?' he asked, his face afraid.

I nodded, totally spent after my outburst. 'He was here,' I muttered.

'Has he hurt you again?' he asked through gritted teeth.

I just shook my head. 'He was there, through the window. He followed me here. He phoned me.'

In an instant, Isaac jumped to his feet and raced from the room. I could hear him clambering over the remains of my door. I just lay on the floor until a soft cough startled me to a sitting position. Stood just inside the doorway to my office was a young Asian man, tall and thin. 'Can I help you up, Miss?' he asked me. I nodded, trusting the kindness in his chocolate-brown eyes and his polite voice.

The young man practically glided across the floor, he was so light on his feet. He held his hand out to me and I placed mine in his, allowing him to pull me to my feet. 'Are you hurt?' he asked, looking me up and down.

I followed his gaze. 'No,' I told him. 'I'm okay.' I didn't mean it, not at all.

He smiled at me, casting his gaze to the window. I turned to look as well, making out Isaac in the field, hands on his hips while he swept his head back and forth. 'My name's Hiro Matsumoto,' he told me. 'I work with Isaac.'

'Charles's son?'

Hiro nodded once, his gaze still on Isaac who had now started walking back to the building. 'Yes, Miss,' he replied, his tone gentle.

I left the office with Hiro close behind me. 'Fucking great,' I muttered under my breath when I saw my front door, completely detached from the frame, splinters everywhere.

'I'll fix that,' Isaac said as he clambered back over it, coming towards me. I didn't miss the slight shake of his head as he glanced at Hiro.

'You'd better,' I shot back at him. I didn't know whether I was pissed off or scared to death. Probably both in equal measure.

Chapter Seventeen

Once again, my life was a mess of activity. I was left to sit, shaking, in my office while Isaac called the police - again. He also arranged to have my front door fixed and CCTV installed around the building. That morning I would have called it overkill. Now I wasn't so sure. Was this ever going to end? I couldn't see it. He'd made his desires quite clear. Not only had he told me but he'd also demonstrated his desire all over the wall behind my office, either while he was talking to me or while he was watching me. I felt sick, thinking about him pleasuring himself back there. Hiro grabbed a bucket of water after he'd shown the police and given them chance to take their samples. I knew the moment he told Isaac what had been found because I heard his phone bounce off the wall.

It was a policeman who took my statement this time. He avoided my eyes pretty much the whole time he was talking to me. I wanted to punch him in the face. That or scream at him to look at me. I did neither. Just sat there and answered all his questions until he left. He didn't even try to reassure me that they were doing everything they could, or that they were going to find him. I was glad because I had next to no faith in them. Even with samples of his DNA, they couldn't find out who he was. The part that concerned me most was the fact that he knew my name. My full name.

Initially, I thought he'd learned my name when he called, and I told him when I answered the phone but, the more I thought about it, that couldn't have been the case. He knew my full name. Rosslyn. It isn't a common name and not even my mum and dad call me that. There was no way he could have known that without doing some digging. He obviously knew where I was staying, too, if he'd followed me all the way here. God, I was stupid. I'd put myself in so much danger, walking by the river. He could have grabbed me any time. He could have done anything to me and no one would have known. I wouldn't have even been able to call for help, it was so deserted that morning.

I was lost in thought, feeling sick and scared and guilty. 'Rose?' Isaac moved in front of me and dropped to his knees. 'Do you want to go home?'

'Mine?' I asked in a panic.

He gave me a sad smile. 'Mine.'

I nodded my agreement, leaning forward and resting my forehead on his. He rubbed his hands gently up and down my thighs. 'I'm sorry for hitting you,' I muttered.

'Don't be.'

Shaking my head, I told him, 'there was no excuse for that. I'm disgusted with myself.'

Isaac gripped my cheeks and lifted my head so he could look at me. 'I want you to give me your pain, Rose. Give me as much as you can. If we share it, it'll make the burden easier.' A lone tear dribbled down my cheek. He caught it with his thumb and wiped it away. 'However that pain comes, I want it. I promise I will never judge you.' I closed my eyes, unable to bear witness to the love and compassion shining through his own.

'Isaac, he knows me,' I spoke in a rush.

'I know he does. I don't know how, but I know.' Leaning in, he placed a gentle kiss on my forehead. 'That's why I've asked Hiro to spend time with you when you're out and about.' I looked up at Hiro, who stood unobtrusively in the doorway. 'Would that be alright with you?'

'You're asking?' I looked back at Isaac, noting his wince at my words.

'I am. I realise I've taken a degree of control away from you. That was never my intention.'

'I know,' I reassured him. 'I get it. I'm grateful. Honestly.' I wrapped my arms around him and pulled myself onto his lap. I breathed in his scent, feeling my whole body relax. 'Thank you,' I said into his shoulder.

He wrapped his arms around me, squeezing me tight. 'I love you, Rose,' he breathed into my hair. 'I'm tired of fighting this, of questioning every feeling. I love you so fucking much. I can't bear the thought of anything else happening to you. I'd do anything to keep you safe.'

Rearing back from our embrace, I kissed him hard on the lips. 'I love you, too,' I told him, surer of this than I'd ever been about anything before. 'I trust you and I'm so glad I have you. I can't imagine getting through any of this without you.'

Isaac rose to his feet with me still clinging to him. He held me to his front with one hand while he smoothed my hair from my face with the other. 'Can I take you home?' he asked between peppering my face with kisses.

'Yes, please,' I replied.

The days that followed were much the same. If I wasn't with Isaac at his house or the club, I was with Hiro at the cattery. He had an incredibly calming presence and I very much enjoyed spending time with him. Initially, he was reserved and sort of blended into the background but, after a couple of days, I was able to coax him out of his shell. I was glad because it was making me feel a little uncomfortable, having him lurking in the corner while I worked, no matter how calming and unobtrusive he was.

He told me all about his father's upbringing in Okinawa, and how he fell in love with an English teacher who was working abroad. When it was time for her to return home, Charles followed her, leaving his family behind to follow his heart. Hiro had one sister, named Amma, after his grandmother on his mother's side. Hiro came several years later and was named after his paternal grandfather. He had joined his father's security team the moment he'd completed his IT degree and had never looked back. He took great pleasure in telling me how much they both enjoyed working for Isaac. It wasn't long before I felt like I could rely on Hiro and count him as a friend. He certainly did make me feel safe when I was out and about. He might have been thin and wiry but he carried himself with a surety and confidence that left me in no doubt he could handle himself. I knew that must have been true because Isaac would never have trusted my safety with someone he didn't trust himself.

During the next week, I took my final deliveries to get the cattery up and running at full steam. My front door was replaced and I took a massive amount of comfort in seeing the CCTV cameras circling the building. I could see the footage on both my phone - which I was making a point to have fully charged and with me at all times - and on my office computer. Isaac was also able to access the feeds at home and the club, along with Charles, Hiro and the rest of the security team.

Things had definitely started to look up because I'd even taken bookings from two other people, one of which was for a fortnight. I was relieved that my website and social media campaign was paying off.

On Thursday night, I went for dinner at Mum and Dad's. Isaac wanted to come with me and introduce himself to them properly but, at the risk of upsetting him, I told him I thought it was too soon. I needed to be able to explain where I was staying and with whom, without him being there. If he was, I was worried they would jump to the wrong conclusion, and I couldn't have that. I didn't want anyone else casting aspersions on his character. As it was, Mum didn't take the news well.

'But who is he, sweetheart, really? You hardly know him.'

I had to bite my tongue as I swallowed my mouthful of lemon meringue pie, another one of Mum's speciality desserts. 'Mum, I need you not to freak out about this.' I lowered my spoon and started faffing with my wine glass. Why the hell couldn't I be more assertive. 'He's been amazing about everything and he's done nothing but try to look after me.'

'To what end, though?' I turned to Dad, shocked that he was weighing in on the discussion. He had been uncharacteristically quiet throughout the meal *again*. 'What does he want for his efforts?'

I was ready to fly off the handle and let them have both barrels but then I heard his tone. 'He just wants me, Dad. He wants me safe and he wants to look after me. He wants all of me.'

Mum looked back and forth between us. I just stared at my dad, waiting to hear his response. 'Does he treat you well, Rose?' he asked, focusing down on his untouched pudding.

I let my wine glass go and reached across to take hold of his clenched fist. 'Better than I ever imagined I could be treated, Dad.'

'That's all we want, Cassie. Just leave it there, okay? Don't badger the girl.' Mum opened her mouth to say something. I wanted nothing more than to receive one of Dad's hugs or even one of his smiles. Instead, he stood and left the table, disappearing upstairs.

Mum and I just stared after him for a few moments, stunned into silence. 'Why is he being so strange around me, Mum?' I asked her, feeling utterly heartbroken. My closest parental relationship seemed like it was hanging on by a thread.

'Baby girl, I don't even know where to start.' That was a surprise. I thought she would brush me off, tell me I was imagining things.

Resolute now I knew for certain something was amiss, I pushed my chair back and stood up. 'Well, then,' I said, throwing my napkin onto my plate. 'I'll just have to go and ask him, won't I?' If Mum tried to stop me, I couldn't hear her.

I stomped my way through the house and up the stairs, making zero effort to hide my approach. There had been something off about Dad since the assault and I was sick of it. We'd always been so close and what happened to me was starting to ruin it. We were having this out and sorting it. Whatever elephant was in the room, we weren't ignoring it anymore. It stopped now.

Having worked myself up into a near frenzy, I pushed my way through into their bedroom. I stopped short when I saw Dad sat on the end of his bed, head in his hands. He looked up, startled when the door slammed into the wall. There were tears in his eyes, which shocked and unsettled me. Dad was stoic and I could count on one hand the number of times I'd seen him cry in my twenty-nine years. I padded into the room and dropped to my backside next to him on the bed. 'Dad, please tell me what's wrong,' I pleaded with him.

'Oh, Rose. I hate this.'

I couldn't bear to hear the desolation and despair in his tone. 'Talk to me, Dad. Whatever it is, just talk to me.' He stayed silent and lowered his head back into his hands. I decided to ask him what had been on my mind for the last few weeks. 'Do you think less of me, because of what happened?'

His head shot up so fast, I'm surprised he didn't give himself whiplash. 'Jesus. No, never! How could you even think that?'

'Because you've been distant with me ever since it happened.' I shrugged and started chewing on my bottom lip in a bid to stop it from wobbling.

'Honestly?' he asked me. I nodded. 'I don't know how to behave around you. I don't know whether you want me near you, whether you want me to hug you. I'm second guessing myself all the time. If I cuddle you, will it make you remember him and what happened? Is it better if I stay away?'

His questions were rhetorical but I gave him an answer anyway. I launched myself into his arms, squeezing him tightly. I was relieved to feel his arms tighten around my back. 'I need you, Dad. I need you to be strong for me and help me feel normal again. I want to forget what happened as much as possible.' I ignored the pang of guilt I felt at not telling him and Mum the whole truth about what was happening now. They knew about the note, that being the reason I was staying with Isaac but I hadn't found the courage to tell them about his visit the other day. 'I've had my sense of safety taken away and I do feel scared still. Not all the time, but sometimes. And yeah, there are times I remember the attack vividly. But it's knowing that the people I care about, the people who care for me, are going to be there to see me through it.' I pulled away from our embrace. 'You've always made me feel safe, Dad, and I don't want something like this to put a distance between us.'

Dad took hold of my hand in both of his. 'I don't want that either, Rose. I've just felt so uncertain. Which has made me feel selfish, because what right do I have to be getting absorbed in my feelings? When you've been dealing with so much?'

'You're not selfish, Dad. Yes, it happened to me but you've had to deal with the fallout, too. I've realised that the after-effects of something like this reach further than just who it happens to. Does that make sense?'

My dad brought my hand up to his lips, kissing my knuckles and rubbing up and down my forearm. 'It does, sweetheart, it does,' he said.

We sat in silence for a while but, thankfully, it was a more comfortable one than we had enjoyed in a while. I kept hearing Dad take a breath, as though he wanted to say something, but remained silent. 'Is there anything else, Dad?' I asked him.

He smiled at me, sadly. 'You remind me so much of your Nana.'

'How so?'

'Your fight. And your strength.' He sighed. 'She never told you what happened when she was about your age, did she?' I shook my head, confused. 'Your grandad had gone on business. I was ten and woke up in the middle of the night. I don't know exactly what woke me but I got up because I was thirsty. I went down to the kitchen and there was a boy. He couldn't have been any older than seventeen. He had your Nana pinned down on the kitchen table, and was, well...' He drifted off, looking down to the floor.

I lifted my hand to my mouth. I couldn't believe it. 'Oh my god,' I breathed. 'Nana?'

'When I walked into the kitchen, I disturbed him and he ran off. Your Nana was more concerned about me and how I was. But afterwards, I could see how withdrawn she'd become. Even with your grandad, for a little while. When I was a bit older, I found her crying in the bathroom, all alone. She told me some of what happened. Said she'd woken up when she heard a window breaking in the kitchen. She went downstairs to see what was going on and saw the boy rooting through the drawers, looking for things to steal. She shouted at him and tried to shove him out of the house but he managed to overpower her. That was when he started to, uh... god, why can't I say it?'

'You don't need to say it,' I told him, knowing the struggle he was having. I found it difficult to vocalise, too, sometimes. 'Was he ever caught?

Dad shook his head. 'She never reported it. She didn't even tell your grandad for a while. Just left him wondering why she was struggling so much until he threatened to leave her unless she told him what was going on. She just soldiered on. Business as usual, for the most part.'

'I can't believe it,' I said. 'You would never have known, she never said anything.'

He shrugged. 'She didn't like upsetting anyone. Told everyone she was okay, just the same way you do. Carried on as normal, just like you. Except you're braver, I think.' I started to disagree but he quickly shushed me. 'I only mean because you're talking about it, you've been to the police.'

'I don't know whether that equates to bravery though. If Isaac hadn't called them, I don't know whether I would have had the strength to do it.' Would I? Or would I have kept it to myself like Nana?

'Well,' he said. 'I'm glad he did. I want them to find him and I want him to suffer for what he's done to you.'

Chapter Eighteen

Hearing about what Nana had been through made me wish more than ever that she was still here. I knew I would have been able to talk about how I was feeling and would have been able to take her advice on how to manage my conflicting emotions. I know Dad said I was strong and a fighter, and I felt like one, most of the time. But in my most vulnerable moments, when I woke up in the middle of the night, a scream dying in the back of my throat, sweat pouring out of my skin? Isaac did a great job calming me down, holding me until the echo of the nightmare faded away, but I know Nana would have understood. She would have been able to empathise in a way Isaac could not. And Dad was right. I bottled up a lot of my thoughts for fear of upsetting people. I kept the worst of the thoughts from even Isaac and Zara.

But I endured; soldiered on, just like Nana. I was better when I kept busy. Whether that was busy with work or busy with Isaac, it was all the same. It was when he left me alone so he could work that I struggled the most. Late Saturday morning saw him needing to go to work and deal with some paperwork he'd been postponing. I knew he was neglecting various aspects of his business to spend time with me but I was only feeling a little bit guilty. I enjoyed the time I got to spend with him. But when he told me he really needed to head into the office for a while, I told him to go, not to worry about me. Because I had another appointment. Not that I told him that.

When he left the apartment, I picked up my phone and dialled Hiro's number. He answered on the second ring. 'Yes, Miss?'

'Hiro, how many times do I have to tell you to just call me Rose?'

'At least once more, Miss.' I sighed. He was unfailingly polite, just like his father.

'I have a hair appointment in half an hour. I was wondering whether you would mind coming with me?'

I could hear movement on his end of the line. 'Of course, Miss. I'll be in the lobby waiting for you when you come down.' Bless him. He was so lovely. It must have been torture for him this past week, and a few hours hanging around at the hairdressers was no doubt going to be worse. But he did everything without complaint, and I thought he did enjoy spending the time with me; I was hopeful it wasn't *just* because he was well compensated.

I threw on an old pair of leggings and a worn t-shirt and stuffed my feet into my tatty Converse before bounding down the stairs to the lobby, making a point to ignore the lift. I'd been feeling increasingly bloated lately, making me realise I wasn't active enough. Taking the stairs up and down would be a start at least. True to his word, Hiro was in the lobby, waiting with his hands behind his back. He was more casual today, wearing black jeans and a plain white tee. He usually rocked a shirt and trousers. But then, it was the weekend.

Shooting a quick wave at Veronica as I passed the reception desk, I practically skipped towards Hiro. I was feeling buoyant today. 'Hiya,' I sang, linking my arm with his and walking out into the bright sunshine. Indian summer was now in full swing after the previous cooler spell, and it was unseasonably warm. I wished I'd brought some sunglasses with me.

Hiro turned to me and smiled. 'You seem brighter today,' he observed.

'I feel brighter. More positive. Like I'm finally starting to turn a corner.' I returned his smile with a truly genuine one.

'It suits you,' he said.

'Thank you. I'm not normally as maudlin as you've found me.' I laughed a little. 'I'm a very happy person, generally.' We walked arm in arm through the city, stopping only so I could buy a very large coffee for Hiro to keep him going while I was in the hairdressers. I also picked up another white mocha frappuccino for myself. I was developing an unhealthy obsession with them, buying one every couple of days. I offered to buy him a book to keep him occupied but he told me he'd got some things to take care of. It was then I noticed his satchel. He did tend to carry his tablet everywhere with him.

The salon was bustling but Sophie was ready to see me straight away. With an apologetic smile at Hiro, which he waved away with courtesy, I was led across to one of the chairs. When I was seated, facing myself in the mirror, I told Sophie exactly what I wanted. I swear I saw her pale as she ran her hands through my hair. 'Are you sure?' she asked me, at least fifteen times before she reached for the scissors.

Three hours later, my waist-length, straight, natural blond hair now tumbled around my shoulders in a mass of layered waves and was the most gorgeous chestnut brown with subtle caramel coloured highlights. I hardly recognised myself, which was the whole point. My locks were shiny and luscious and my complexion looked much healthier. I couldn't stop touching it. Sophie slapped my hand away again. 'Stop it,' she hissed playfully at me. 'You'll make all the waves drop out.'

'I can't help it.' I laughed, shaking my hair around my shoulders. 'It's beautiful, Soph. Thank you so much.'

'You're so welcome. Will you let me put the before and after on my socials?' How could I refuse her after she'd done such an amazing job?

My bank card practically screamed when I handed it over. Or maybe it was me. It was so worth it though. I was in love. Once I'd paid and thanked Sophie a dozen more times, I walked back into the waiting area, towards Hiro. He looked up from his tablet, then looked back down again. Then his head shot up, his eyes went wide and his mouth dropped a little. On a small shake of his head, he stood, shoving his tablet back in his satchel. 'I almost didn't recognise you,' he said, unable to hide his smile. 'That colour looks really good on you.' I fluffed my hair at the roots, laughing at Sophie's 'leave it alone!' from across the salon.

'Thanks, Hiro,' I told him. I glanced at my watch. 'Do you think Isaac will be interruptible by now?'

On a roll of his eyes, he said 'Mr Yates is always open to interruptions from you. In fact, I have strict instructions to take you to him whenever you want.'

Before Hiro escorted me across to Shiver, I wanted to go back to mine to pick up a few things. He told me he could go and fetch his car but that was going to take far too long. So we hopped on the red line bus and rode to the stop opposite my flat. As the familiar thrumming of my anxious heart kicked in, I forced my mind to think only of what I was coming home for. I wasn't going to be here for long, and nothing was going to happen to me. Hiro wouldn't let it.

Once inside, I left him in my living room while I went to the bedroom and pulled out my makeup bag. I knew Isaac didn't particularly like me to wear makeup; he said he preferred my face to show its natural beauty. I wasn't overly fond of a heavily made up face either but, for what I was planning, I needed something a bit more dramatic. I wasn't going to cover up. Instead, I was going to enhance.

I applied a very light powdered foundation and rouged my cheeks. Then I went heavy with the grey and black eyeshadow to create a smoky look, finishing off with some eyeliner and mascara. I went deep red on my lips. Surveying the look in the mirror, I realised I'd never have been able to pull off such a dark and dramatic eye with my blonde hair. I liked it. It made me look sultry. Once I was happy that my face was perfect, I went over to my wardrobe and pulled out my first date dress. I held it up against me for a moment, admiring it in the mirror. It really was the most stunning dress I'd ever owned. I pulled it over my head, loving the way it hugged my body, emphasising my curves without drawing attention to the parts of my body I liked the least. The flared skirt swung around me as I twirled in front of the mirror. I fell in love with it all over again.

Then, the *pièce de résistance.* From the bottom of my wardrobe, I removed the coveted gold box and lifted the lid. Nana's 'fuck me' shoes. They were stunning in their perfection. I placed them on the floor and stepped into them. They fit me like a glove. I had to use the wall to steady myself, as I was so unaccustomed to wearing stilettos. I walked around my bedroom, getting used to the feel of them on my feet, making sure I could walk gracefully in them. The last thing I wanted to do was fall flat on my face. Before I headed back out to Hiro, I took a last look at myself in the mirror. The nearly impossible height of the heels gave my calves a delicate, sexy shape and the red soles complimented the red roses on my dress perfectly. I felt utterly gorgeous and full of a confidence I didn't usually feel.

My confidence was further emboldened when I sashayed into my living room and saw Hiro's mouth drop. He rose from where he was sitting on my sofa, blowing his breath out on a huff. I gave him a little twirl before asking, 'how do I look?'

Hiro shook his head. 'You look truly beautiful, Miss Rose,' he said. 'An absolute knockout.' I flushed, his praise meaning so much to me.

'Well, thank you, Hiro. That really is a fine compliment,' I said, meaning it sincerely.

'As it should be,' he said, tapping away on his phone. 'I've booked an Uber. There's no way you can navigate the bus in those shoes.' I wholeheartedly agreed.

It was twenty minutes before our car picked us up and, by the time it pulled up outside Shiver, there was already the familiar line forming around the side of the building. I felt like a VIP as Hiro escorted me through the front door, nodding to the doorman as he passed. Shaun was already in position behind the bar, making eyes at one of the waitresses. He glanced my way and whistled through his teeth. 'Jesus, lady,' he said. 'I'd love to be a fly on the wall when he catches sight of you looking like that.' I smiled my thanks, blushing again. I really did struggle to take a compliment. 'Hair looks gorgeous. He's in his office.'

'Is he busy?'

'For you, right now, looking like that? Hell no, little lady. I think he'd fire me if I *didn't* send you straight in there.' Excellent, that was just what I'd wanted to hear. 'Can you find the way?'

I nodded. 'Yes, I think so.' I set off, my heart starting to beat harder in my chest. I hadn't done any of this for Isaac, I had only done it for me, to make myself feel better, but I very much wanted him to like it. If his reaction was as positive as Hiro's and Shaun's, I think I was going to be okay.

I got a little turned around in the labyrinth of corridors beneath the club but I eventually found myself in front of Isaac's office door. I raised my hand to knock but paused when I heard his voice behind the wood. He sounded angry. 'They've been absolutely fucking useless. I'm going to have to take care of it myself.' He paused as if listening to someone replying. He must be on the phone. I knocked quietly before I lost my nerve. 'Yes?' He was his usual abrupt self.

Almost hesitant, I pushed the door open and stepped into his office, finding him with the phone pressed to his ear. His eyes widened as he took me in, his mouth falling open. 'I'll call you back,' he said into the receiver before hanging up, not giving whoever was on the other end chance to reply.

I indicated the phone with a nod of my head. 'Problems?'

'Liquor supplier.' He stood and rounded the desk, sweeping his gaze up and down my entire frame. I closed the door behind me with a soft click. 'I don't know what to say,' he said, stalking towards me at a leisurely pace. Heat bloomed between my legs in an instant. His eyes. My god. They were all over me, burning a path up and down my body. I stood tall, letting him take me in. By the time he'd walked over, I was eye to eye with him, my heels were so high. 'You take my breath away.' He placed his hands on my narrow waist, squeezing me as he pulled his lower lip between his teeth. 'You look like a different person.'

'That was the point,' I told him, feeling his hands run up and down my sides, his thumbs rubbing over my breasts, my nipples hardening beneath the fabric. My breaths came faster and shallower as he heated me up from the inside. I shifted my legs in a bid to ease the pressure, which allowed Isaac to lean closer to me, his leg between mine, his hips pressing into me.

His fingers found my hair, running through it. 'You look beautiful,' he whispered as he watched the light catch in the strands.

'Thank you,' I whispered back. I could feel his erection straining through the fabric of his trousers. I had never felt more desirable in my life. I raised my arms and grabbed his tie, yanking him as close to me as I could get him. Before I could get him close enough to kiss him, he slammed his hands on either side of my head, making me jump. He dropped his head into my neck, his lips kissing and sucking gently. I arched my back, my chest pressing into his. One of his hands fell to the small of my back and the other fisted around my hair, pulling my head back, exposing my throat further.

He lifted from out of my neck and stared down at me. I was breathing hard now and had to grab hold of his shoulders to help support the angle he was holding me. 'You know, I never did like blondes that much, anyway,' he said, his voice husky with desire before he smashed his mouth to mine, the force of his kiss and the power of his strong body forcing me back upright, pressed against the door.

Our tongues began a passionate dance, each vying for dominance over the other. I could taste the sweet coffee he drank and the masculine taste that was just him, the taste I was becoming so familiar with. I moaned into his mouth, suddenly desperate to have him inside me, even though we were somewhere so public. I tried to reach my hand between us, eager to touch him, to please him, but he was pressing his body so close to mine, it was impossible. 'I want to touch you,' I breathed into his mouth when he eventually let me come up for air.

I felt him reach behind me, locking the door and giving us our privacy, before taking a small step back, his chest rising and falling, slow and deep. I took advantage of the room and cupped him over his trousers. He was solid. I needed to feel him properly and wasted no time unbuckling his belt and popping his button. I slid my hand inside, taking his warm hard length in my grasp, applying the gentlest of pressures. Isaac jolted in my grip and leaned forward to take my mouth once more.

With gentle nudging I walked him backwards, not breaking our kiss until his knees hit the cream sofa. He sank down, hands reaching to my waist to pull me down onto his lap but I released my grip and sank to my knees before him. I ran my hands down his thighs and pushed his legs apart, giving me room to crawl my way between them. I looked up through my eyelashes at him, pulling his erection free from his trousers. I licked my lips slowly, making my intention crystal clear. I loved the look in his hooded, lustful eyes as he watched me. I kept my gaze on him as I lowered my head, gently kissing the tip of his penis before I used the whole of my tongue to lick the underside, from base to tip.

Taking a deep, steadying breath in through my nose, I took his cock in my mouth and sank low. Isaac exhaled in a rush and I felt his body relax in an instant. I lifted my head and swirled my tongue around the tip, tasting the salty bead on the end before I took him again, feeling him at the back of my throat. I hollowed my cheeks and fell into a steady rhythm; up and down, alternating licks and sucks. I felt Isaac grip the back of my head and start thrusting his hips, matching my rhythm, stroke for stroke.

He was so thick in my mouth and the groans he was making as he pumped in and out were shooting straight to my groin, making me throb incessantly.

Looking up at him, I found him with his head thrown back against the sofa, his throat working as he absorbed the pleasure, his eyes screwed shut, tight. He was sexy as hell. It all spurred me on to take him faster and harder. I could feel his thighs tensing as he neared his release. I was so ready to take him all the way but he fisted his hands in my hair. 'Rose, stop,' he gasped, lifting me from him. I looked up at him in confusion. He urged me up until I had no choice but to straddle his hips. 'I want to come with you,' he told me, sinking his tongue deep into my mouth as his hands got busy moving my skirts out of the way.

My desire was becoming almost impossible to bear. Without thought, I was grinding myself into his erection and his probing fingers, which had now slipped beneath my panties and were stroking up and down my cleft, spreading my desire. My head fell back as I revelled in his touch, letting out a deep moan when he pushed a finger inside me.

'Isaac,' I moaned his name, forcing my head up before letting it fall forward, resting on his forehead. My hands caught the sides of his face. 'I need you,' I told him, circling my hips, increasing the pressure from his hand.

When he pulled his hand free to roll on a condom, I felt bereft at the loss of his touch. He smiled as he placed his hands back on my hips, lifting and positioning me above his cock. 'So impatient,' he said, moving my panties to the side, lowering me slowly. My lips spread as he stretched me. I moved my hands from his face and grabbed onto his wavy locks, pulling hard in my frustration at his gentleness. Isaac hissed at the sudden painful sensation. He jolted his hips up at the same time as he yanked me sharply down, impaling me completely. I cried out at the feeling of fullness, his hard length buried so deep within me.

My thighs tensed as I prepared to rise back up but he kept an iron grip on my waist keeping me still. He was breathing slowly, eyes seeking mine. 'I just need a second,' he said through gritted teeth.

I sat astride him, his cock spearing me. I could feel every twitch and throb as he fought for control. 'I love you,' I told him, capturing his gaze with my own.

Isaac smiled at me, the most beautiful beam spreading across his face. My eyes watered at the sight of him. He radiated such tenderness and love it brought a lump to my throat. 'There are no words to describe what you mean to me,' he told me with reverence. 'You've captured my heart and soul. I wasn't looking for you, but I'm so glad I found you.'

A single tear rolled down my cheek, which he swept away with a gentle kiss. His grip tightened further on my waist before he lifted me, slipping almost completely free before bringing me back down in an agonisingly slow motion. I was overcome. Incoherent words and moans tumbled from my mouth as he lifted and lowered me, over and over.

It wasn't long before I felt the familiar stirrings of an impending orgasm deep in my belly. I was overtaken by a desperate need to climax, so I moved my hands from his hair and grabbed onto his shoulders. I let him lift me again, slow and steady, but I tightened my grip and slammed back down, shouting my pleasure. Isaac echoed mine on a bark. I rose up myself this time and ground my pelvis back down, circling my hips once before rising back up.

As I fell back, Isaac once more yanked me down, hitting me deep with a ferocious force. A pleasure bordering on pain, I became lost in the sensation, giving myself over completely, trusting him to take me to rapture.

As my orgasm tore through me on a scream, I dropped my head, letting Isaac reach his release with a few fast, deep pumps into my core. We were both sweaty and breathing hard. Isaac wrapped his arms around me and held me close as we rode the waves of that delicious sensation together, lazily pumping his hips as I took everything he had to give me.

Isaac took my mouth in a tender and adoring kiss. 'You are so surprising,' he told me, staring at me with awe. 'You make me feel things I've never felt before.'

I smiled before I lowered my head into the crook of his neck. I knew precisely what he meant. 'I didn't exactly see you coming, either,' I said, suckling on his collarbone, tasting his damp, salty skin.

'You don't regret me?' He cradled my head in his hands, massaging my scalp with his fingers. His voice sounded so unsure, so totally unlike himself. I lifted my head to find his eyes searching, clouded with concern.

'Isaac,' I looked at him, making sure I had his eyes, needing him to see me and understand what I was about to tell him. 'Knowing what I know now, feeling how I feel about you, I wouldn't change a thing about how I met you.' I watched his beautiful blue eyes start to shine with tears.

'You can't mean that.'

'I do mean it. I could never regret you, Isaac. If everything had to happen that night the way it happened to have led you to me, then I'm glad of it. What was the worst thing that could have happened to me gave me the *best* thing. You.'

It was my turn to brush away one of his falling tears. 'I can't believe how strong you are.'

I smiled. 'I'm only strong because I have you,' I told him.

'Thank you, Rose.'

'What for?'

'For filling my empty life. I've kept myself busy with the business, travel and meaningless encounters with women. But for the first time, I'm really feeling. And that's all down to you.'

'Looks like we were made for each other, then, doesn't it?'

Isaac beamed at me once more. 'It most certainly does.'

We sat entwined in each other's arms for the longest time, Isaac still buried deep. The phone ringing on the desk interrupted our laziness. I rose onto my knees, feeling him slip from me. He removed the condom and tucked himself back into his trousers before he answered the phone. I rearranged my underwear and fluffed out my skirts while I waited for him to finish. Looking down at my Louboutins, I couldn't help but smile; 'fuck me' shoes was right.

'Something funny?' Isaac asked, hanging up the phone. I just shook my head in amusement. His answering smile was full of affection. 'Are you staying here tonight?'

I gestured down my body. 'I am. I'm not wasting the opportunity to wear this dress.' I gave him a twirl, delighting in his laugh.

'I'll give Zara's name to the doorman if you want to get her to come down. And I'll join you when I can.'

'Sounds perfect.' I gave him a chaste kiss and headed out the door towards the thumping bass of the club. It sounded like the night was already in full swing.

Zara didn't waste any time getting ready and arriving at the club. Anyone would have thought she'd been sat by the phone. Until she arrived, I was kept company at the bar by Hiro and Shaun. I handed over a ten-pound-note to pay for my first French martini, but Shaun waved it away. 'You don't pay here,' he told me, moving on to load a waitresses tray with cocktails and prosecco.

I knew when Zara arrived because I heard her screaming the moment she recognised me. I stood to hug her and let her take a good look at me, faffing with my shorter hair. 'I can't believe how different you look,' she all but shrieked in my ear. We enjoyed a couple of cocktails each while Zara and Shaun flirted outrageously between his mixing drinks. I suspected phone numbers might be getting exchanged before the night was through. Then, a pleasant buzz kicking in, we headed out to the dance floor, throwing some questionable moves. Hiro was never far away and I was sure I'd also seen Charles roaming the edges of the dance floor. There wasn't a moment that I felt unsafe.

After several songs, I was getting ready for a bottle of water and another French martini when I heard the piercing opening notes of The Killers *All These Things That I've Done*. I saw the crowd part as Isaac moved onto the floor, his jacket gone, tie loose and shirt sleeves rolled up. He'd left his waistcoat on. My mouth was watering. He stalked towards me, his lips mouthing for me to *hold on* in time with the song. My mouth spread into the biggest grin as he took me in his arms and spun me around. As the beat picked up, so did Isaac's pace and, before long, we were dancing with abandon, arms in the air, hips swaying, chests touching. His hands were everywhere, caressing my hair, touching me all over. I could sense every woman in the club looking at him, wishing they were the ones he was dancing with. But instead, it was me and my heart was full to bursting. I was in the midst of a dark and troubling time in my life, but Isaac was filling me with a light and hope for much better things to come. I never wanted this moment to end.

Chapter Nineteen

It was another week and a half before I realised my period was late. I'd welcomed Noodle into my cattery and seen him back into the arms of his owner without a hitch. On the back of her glowing review on my website and social media, I had taken further bookings from three of her friends, one of which was for *three* fur babies. This filled me with confidence. I was happy enough that people were trusting me with one cat, but to have them trusting me with three? I must have been doing something right.

Things were going so well with Isaac. The previous Sunday, I had taken him to Mum and Dad's for one of their dinners. I knew Mum was still concerned that things were moving too quickly between us, but he was the perfect charmer. He answered every single one of her probing questions at the table, even though they were often blunt and inappropriate. Between mouthfuls of his roast chicken, he lowered his knife and fork to his plate and placed his hand on my back, my shoulder or my knee. Every glance I snuck at him showed him either focusing on Mum while she spoke or looking at me with a loving smile. By the end of the meal, he'd pretty much charmed her knickers off, but what really endeared him to her was when he stood from the table and started clearing the dishes with her. I don't think this was a calculated move on his part; it was just something he was used to from all his years living alone. Needless to say, Mum was flattered and flustered and shooed him into the living room with a crack of her towel.

Originally, I'd have thought Dad was going to be the one Isaac would have to win round, but after our heart-to-heart, I'd got nothing to worry about. The moment he opened the front door to let us in, Dad shook him warmly by the hand, clapping him on the shoulder. That was as good as a hug in Dad's book. After dinner, before Mum served us victoria sponge and ice cream - that's how I knew she'd been flapping; she only pulled out the shop-bought pudding when she didn't want to risk cocking up the dinner - Isaac and Dad sat in an armchair each, eyes on the tv, chatting about the football. I sat curled up on the sofa, watching their exchange, warmth and love for those two men making my heart swell. I had no idea Isaac was such a chameleon; he could talk to anyone about anything. But he was definitely safe with sport as far as Dad was concerned. He was obsessed with all kinds of it.

By the time we left their house, it was almost full dark. Isaac had spent the evening telling us about the places he'd travelled to. I hadn't travelled much out of the UK and hoped very much I would be able to go somewhere exotic with him one day. I told him as much when we crawled into bed together, his hands roaming all over my naked body. 'Pick a place and a date and we'll go,' he told me before taking my nipple into his mouth. I had a feeling he would agree to anything if I was lying naked beneath him.

Wednesday rolled around and I'd just taken my morning trip up to the cattery to feed and play with my current resident, a very sturdy tuxedo cat named Binx. Hiro and I were walking back through the city centre, passing the chemist when I had a sudden jolt. How long had it been since my last period? I thought back, counting on my fingers. Was it one week before my leaving do?

'Miss Rose, are you alright?' Hiro asked from beside me. I ignored him as I rooted through my bag. Pulling my phone free, I unlocked the screen and loaded the health app. I'd got into the habit of tracking my cycle the older I got, becoming more and more anal retentive with the technology. I was wrong. My last period was *two* weeks before my leaving do. Which meant I was now a week and a half late.

I could feel the colour draining from my face. It was impossible. Isaac and I had used protection every time we made love. I'd taken the morning-after-pill after my assault and I hadn't been with another man for some time before that. It had to be the stress of the past few weeks, messing with my cycle. I counted through the days on the calendar again. I was definitely late and that was unusual for me. I'd always been as regular as clockwork. 'Miss Rose?' Hiro spoke again, placing a gentle hand on my elbow.

The contact made me jump. 'Can you wait here a moment?' I asked him, lurching through the door of the chemist without waiting for his response.

In a daze, I wandered up and down the aisles, looking but not seeing. Eventually, I was approached by a young staff member. 'You alright there?' he asked.

I looked over at him, feeling a lump form in my throat. I tried to swallow past it. 'Where are your pregnancy tests, please?' I spoke in a whisper, unable to prevent the wobble in my voice. The ding of the doorbell startled me, making me swing my head in that direction. It wasn't Hiro, though. Whoever it was had headed straight towards the rear of the shop.

The clerk pointed to the wall behind me. 'Over there,' he said, a blush spreading across his young cheeks. I moved over there, my limbs seizing up like a robot's. I grabbed hold of the first box I could lay my hands on and practically threw it at the cashier who had now moved behind the till, his eyes looking anywhere but directly at me. 'Thank you,' I told him, after tapping my card on the terminal and shoving it and the test in my bag.

Hiro was waiting outside, tapping away on his phone. He had the good grace to look guilty when he saw me exit the building, which meant he'd been sending a status report back to Isaac. I didn't even care, I just needed to get home and pee on the stick, if only to alleviate my worries. It had to be stress-related. There was no way I could be pregnant. I'd taken every precaution known to man.

'Everything okay?" Hiro asked me, putting his phone back in his pocket.

Painting a smile on my face, I linked my arm through his and started walking at what I hoped was a normal pace towards the Waterfront. 'Absolutely fine,' I replied. 'Just a headache coming on.' I looked down at my feet, pretending to watch my footing on the uneven cobbles. 'I just needed to pick up some paracetamol.'

We walked in near silence back to Isaac's. I could tell Hiro was deep in thought. Worrying. No doubt thinking about what he was going to tell Isaac. I needed to get this test done, and fast, before Isaac came barrelling through the front door, protective mode engaged. Once in the lobby, I gave Hiro a quick hug which probably increased his suspicions. 'I'll not be heading back to the cattery until later on this evening,' I told him. 'Isaac may even take me if he's finished at work.'

Hiro nodded once, eyes scanning my face. 'Of course. But you'll ring me if you need me.'

I told him I would, even though he wasn't asking. I bid him farewell and made myself saunter across to the lift, despite wanting to run as fast as my legs would carry me. I even called out a cheery hello to Veronica, who was warming towards me a little more now she'd seen me come and go for the past couple of weeks. Calling the lift down to the lobby from wherever it was in the building, I had to resist the urge to press the button repeatedly.

I could feel Hiro's eyes burning a hole in my back while I waited for the lift. When the doors slid open, I inserted the key for the penthouse without turning around. I didn't trust myself to be able to keep my worry from him.

It took an hour to reach the penthouse, or so it felt like. I fumbled with the key in the lock, nearly scratching the paint off the door in my haste to get inside. Stumbling my way in, I went straight to the bathroom, pulling the box from my bag. I struggled with the button on my jeans before I could push them down my legs, sitting on the toilet with a thud. Then I couldn't get the plastic wrapping off the box, or tear open the packet to pull out the test. But eventually, I was able to release my bladder and shove the stick between my legs with shaking hands.

I put the stick on the counter and started counting. One, two, three. Forty-four, forty-five. One-twenty-two, one-twenty-three. One-seventy-nine, one-eighty. Then I looked at the stick. At the box. Back at the stick. Two little pink lines. Impossible.

It couldn't be. I was still thinking the same thing half an hour later when I was still on hold to speak to my doctor's surgery. It had to be a false positive. Definitely. I was wearing a rut in the rug with all my pacing and hardly gave the receptionist time to speak by the time they finally answered the phone. 'I need to see someone, as soon as possible. My period is late and I've just taken a positive pregnancy test.' My words came out in a rush. 'I can't be pregnant. There must have been something wrong with the test.' I wished I'd picked up a box of two, but I'd been in such a rush.

The receptionist took my name and date of birth and spent far too long to tell me there were no available appointments today. 'You don't understand,' I pleaded. 'It shouldn't be possible for me to be pregnant.' My voice broke as my tears started falling. 'Please, I need to speak to someone.'

There was silence on the line while I sobbed into the phone. I don't know how much time passed but, eventually, a new voice spoke down the phone. 'Miss Carter, are you there?'

'Yes,' I sniffled, wiping my eyes and nose with the back of my hand.

'My name's Lucille. I'm one of the nurses here. My colleague has told me a little about why you're calling. You've had a positive pregnancy test?'

'Yes, but there's no way…it's impossible.'

'Are you sexually active at the moment, Rose? Can I call you Rose?'

'Yes,' I said, sniffing loudly. 'And yes, I'm sexually active.'

'And what protection are you using?'

'We use condoms.'

'Every time you have sex?'

I nodded. 'Yeah, every time.'

Lucille paused. 'Well, condoms aren't one hundred per cent effective. You haven't noticed any breakage?'

'No, never.'

'And you haven't had any other form of unprotected sex at all in the last several weeks?'

I opened my mouth to say no but stopped short. I felt sick to my stomach. 'I was raped,' I whispered into the receiver. 'A month ago. He didn't use a condom. But I was given the morning-after-pill in the hospital.'

'Any sort of stomach upset in the immediate hours after taking the pill?'

Oh fuck. I gasped and clapped my hand to my mouth. 'I threw up when I got home.' I started sobbing again, dropping to the edge of the sofa, my whole body shaking with the force of my weeping. Lucille was muttering soothing words to me, but I couldn't hear what she was saying over the racket I was making. 'Is that what's happened? Am I pregnant because of that?' I asked once I'd calmed down.

I could hear Lucille breathe a sad sigh. 'It's possible. Any vomiting or diarrhoea can lessen the effectiveness of the pill. Listen, Rose. There's only one way to know for certain, and that's for us to take a urine and blood sample to confirm the pregnancy. I shouldn't be doing this, but I'm just getting off shift now.

If you come straight to the surgery, I can run those tests. I can also do an internal ultrasound if you're comfortable. That will help us date the pregnancy.'

'So you think my test wasn't a false positive?'

'It's unlikely, Rose. I'm sorry,' she said softly, before instructing the receptionist to book me in.

I wasted no time leaving the penthouse and making my way to the doctor's surgery. I didn't call Hiro and I definitely didn't call Isaac. I noticed he'd tried calling while I was on the phone to the nurse and sent a couple of texts, inquiring as to how I was. It proved Hiro was reporting back. I knew I was going to be worrying him, but I couldn't reply. Not until I knew for certain, one way or the other.

My doctor's surgery wasn't far from the river, like most places in York, so it didn't take me long to get there. The receptionist took one look at me and pointed to the waiting area. Was I that obvious? After waiting only a couple of minutes, a young-looking nurse in pale grey scrubs called me through. She had a friendly, round face, big brown eyes and lovely plump lips. I felt at ease and comfortable in her presence.

Lucille gave me a specimen bottle and instructed me to go back to the toilet through the waiting room and fill it, which I did. She took a vial of my blood before putting a test strip in the jar of my urine. Seeing her lips press tightly together was all the answer I needed. 'The blood results will take a couple of days to come back,' she told me.

'And how likely are they to give me a different result?' I asked her. My voice sounded flat, even to my ears.

'Not very likely, I'm afraid.'

'Fucking great.' I looked up at her from my chair. 'I'm sorry,' I apologised for my language. She just shook her head, brushing me off.

'Okay.' She indicated a portable ultrasound machine. 'I mentioned an internal ultrasound on the phone. I do have a sonographer here today who can do this now if you're comfortable. I'd need you to lie back on the bed there and he'll insert a thin probe into your vagina. That will allow us to see into your uterus.'

'He?' My mouth went dry and I started wringing my hands together.

'Yes, sweetheart. It's a male doctor.' Lucille pulled her chair to face me properly and gently placed her hands around mine. 'This isn't essential. The blood results will give us a very good indication of how far along you are.'

I just stared at our hands resting lightly on my knees. 'But that will take a few days, won't it?' Lucille nodded. 'Will the ultrasound tell me now? How long ago? Who the father might be?'

'It would give you a more definitive answer right away,' she told me, squeezing my balled fists.

More tears formed in my eyes as I imagined another man anywhere near me. 'Will you stay in here with me, while he does it?' I asked her.

'Of course I will. If it helps, you can bring your partner here as well. Or instead of me, if that makes you more comfortable.'

I shook my head. 'No. I don't want him to see me like this.'

'Alright then. If you're ready, I'll go and bring Dr Tennyson in.' I nodded my consent and moved over to the examination table.

The whole ordeal only lasted around ten minutes. I found it very difficult to look at the doctor, even though he was professional and courteous with me. Once I'd removed my jeans and underwear, I turned my head to the wall and kept my eyes clenched shut. When I felt him insert the probe, my breathing came fast and I had to keep swallowing to try to get rid of the lump in my throat. Dr Tennyson talked me through the entire process and Lucille held my hand the whole time.

When he was finished, he told me that he couldn't see very much as the pregnancy was very early, but he could see a gestational sac forming. Which meant I was around three weeks pregnant. His best guess confirmed the father of my baby was my rapist. The morning-after-pill had failed. I had no tears left by this point. I was numb. Dr Tennyson left to leave me to get dressed, which I did, wordlessly. Lucille offered some words of comfort and gave me some leaflets, detailing all of my choices. She told me to go home, speak to my partner, spend some time thinking about what I might want to do. She told me not to worry, it was very early days which gave me plenty of time to make a decision. I thanked her profusely for her time and left the surgery in a daze. I didn't notice the rough hand around my wrist until it was far too late.

Chapter Twenty

The force at which I was pulled down the cobbled side street almost yanked my arm from its socket. I turned over on my ankle, pain shooting up my calf before I found myself pressed up against the side of a stone building. My stomach turned and my lungs seized when I felt his hot breath in my ear. 'Is it mine, sweet girl?' he whispered, taking my earlobe between his teeth and biting hard.

My body froze. I looked over his shoulder, counting the pits in the old stonework opposite. This was not happening, not again. I shut down, ignoring him. He couldn't hurt me if I didn't acknowledge him. He didn't like that. He took my chin in his hand and squeezed, bringing a tear to my eye. 'Do not ignore me,' he demanded, forcing me to look at him. 'Is. It. Mine?'

'I don't know what you're talking about.' My voice was toneless. Dead, like how I was inside.

He pushed his lower body into mine, pinning me to the wall. I tried to pretend I couldn't feel his arousal. 'I think you do know what I'm talking about. I saw you buy that pregnancy test in the chemist earlier.'

My heart sank. He was still following me? 'Please let me go,' I begged. His smile was sickening.

He trailed his hand down my chin, over my breasts and onto my stomach. His big hand spanned my belly, pressing firmly. 'I am growing inside you, aren't I?' He looked at me, moistening his lips with his tongue, rubbing small circles on my belly. It could have been a tender motion if he didn't look so psychotic.

I thrust out my jaw in defiance. 'I'm not keeping it.'

His other hand wrapped around my neck before I could blink. 'Shut your fucking bitch mouth,' he snarled, eyes narrowed into evil slits. 'You will. You'll keep it because I'll kill you if you don't. And I won't do it quickly.' It may have been an empty threat, but I believed him. At this moment, his hand squeezing my throat, he certainly seemed capable. 'I will watch this baby grow inside you. I will watch you grow bigger and bigger while I fill you.' He looked down at my stomach. 'You'll never be free of me now.'

My lungs were burning, trying desperately to suck in air. He loosened his hold just enough to allow me to take in some oxygen. My eyes watered with relief. 'Every day, you will feel me moving inside you. That is mine, which makes *you* mine.' He smirked. 'Daddies have rights.'

'Fuck you,' I snapped. He tightened his grip on my throat again, while he popped the button on my jeans with his other hand.

'Listen to me, sweet girl. You will carry this child and you will take very good care of it.' He slid his hand down my jeans and underneath my knickers. I tried to close my legs but he spread them apart with his own. He grunted, displeased. 'You will get wet for me, Rose,' he said, hurting me as he speared me with his finger. 'You will do whatever I want you to do, do you understand?'

I rolled my head from side to side, full-body shakes making me vibrate where I stood. His quiet laugh repulsed me. 'I told you before, I *will* have you again. And you will learn to like it.' His hand still rubbing beneath my underwear, he leaned his head towards me, breathing harder now. I swallowed and inclined my head towards his. I took his head between my hands. And I bit him. I bit him on his lip so hard, I tasted blood.

The pain he felt made him take a step back; he pulled his hand free of my clothes, the other released the pressure on my neck. I took advantage and shoved him hard, with all the strength I had. He stumbled backwards, hitting his head on the wall behind him. Then I ran. I didn't look back to see where he was. I just ran, hair flying behind me, lungs bursting with the exertion. People were staring at me as I fled through the streets but I didn't pay them any attention. I didn't stop running even as I burst through the doors into the Waterfront lobby. Tears were blinding me as I crossed the space, not wanting to stand and wait for the lift. Veronica may have shouted to me as I shoved through the door leading to the stairs, but I didn't stop. I just forced my legs to keep on moving, pounding up the stairs. I didn't feel the burn until I flew through Isaac's front door, slamming and locking it behind me.

Convinced he was behind me, I grabbed a knife from the drawer and backed through the penthouse with it in front of me, until I'd passed through the master bedroom and into the bathroom. Once there, I locked that door too and sank to the floor, my back sliding down the wall. It was only then that I allowed the true horror of what had transpired out. I screamed and screamed into my knees until I blacked out.

There was no way of knowing how much time had passed when I came round. It could have been minutes, but could just as easily have been hours. My unconsciousness had done little to ease the panic in my mind or the building sickness in my stomach. *My stomach.* I sat upright against the wall, my legs straight out in front of me, looking down at my abdomen. To look at it, there was no sign at all that I was growing a life inside me. But it was there. Cells dividing. Getting a teeny tiny bit bigger with every second that I did nothing. My thoughts were scattered; I felt out of control.

I had always imagined I would have a child at some point in my life. There were no set timescales that I wanted my life to follow, but I'd never been anti-children. Any man I'd been with, I'd always taken the proper precautions because it was never serious enough; because it wasn't the right time or the right man. The few times I'd been in a long term relationship, I'd made sure I'd been on the pill, even though I wasn't always my natural self on it, which was why I never hesitated to stop taking it again when a relationship ended. I could count on one hand the number of one night stands I'd had and had never been intimate without making them wear a condom. But a part of me had always acknowledged, however unconsciously, if it was meant to be...if whatever form of contraception I was using failed, for whatever reason...if I fell pregnant? I would accept the hand I'd been dealt and would love that child and raise it right.

But like this? How could this be the hand I was dealt? Raped, brutalised, stalked. Knocked up? What the hell had I done in this life, or even a past life, to deserve this? Never before had I considered that an abortion might be a viable option for me but if I could, I would. I didn't want to feel his baby growing inside me. I didn't want any part of him anywhere near me. But when he told me he would kill me if I killed his baby, I believed him. I could see how much he meant it. It was in his eyes and the force in which he squeezed my throat. He would hurt me and make me suffer. That much, I was certain of.

My eyes fell to the side, seeing the kitchen knife I'd grabbed on my way through the penthouse. I'd taken it for my protection, in case he'd followed me through the city. Could it be my salvation? I couldn't abort his baby because he would kill me. Painfully. But I could take control. For the first time in this shit show he had caused, I could take back the control and I could choose what to do with my body. With my life. One deep cut now and I could drift away. It might hurt, but it would only be for a short while. It would be a better way to go. Certainly more peaceful than what he would have planned for me.

Taking hold of the knife, I held it up in front of my face. My heart ached. Isaac would be devastated. Despite only knowing him for such a short time, I knew how deeply he cared about me. But because we had only known each other for so short a time, I knew he would be okay. He would recover and carry on with his life. In the long run, he would be better off. Because how on earth could I expect him to cope with me, my trauma *and* my illegitimate baby. Because I couldn't kill it. Even if I really wanted to, I couldn't do it. Every fibre of my being told me I couldn't terminate the pregnancy. Not if I intended to continue living, myself. Eventually, Isaac would be alright. I was sure he would grieve, but I would just be a drop in the ocean of his grief, compared to all he had already lost.

My blood whooshed in my ears, pounding a deep banging noise in my head. My mind made up, I raised the knife and placed it against my wrist. My hand did not shake as I pressed the sharp edge into my skin. Blood welled to the surface and rolled off my wrist, dripping onto my jeans. I could tell it wasn't deep enough, that I'd been too hesitant. The drumming noise in my head continued to increase in volume and tempo as I raised the knife again, ready to deepen my wound.

All of a sudden, the pounding rush of my blood stopped. I looked up, confused in the silence. Isaac was stood where the locked door had been, pale and shaking. I'd thought I had no more tears left, but the sight of him there brought on another deluge. I lowered my head to my clenched fists and just wept.

Whether it was the sight of me sat, utterly broken, on the floor or the knife in my hand or the blood dripping from my wrist, it brought Isaac to me in an instant. He knelt in front of me, straddling my legs to get as close to me as he could. Through my tears and heartbreak, I could feel his fury. It radiated from him; it was palpable and visceral, but he sounded so scared as he kept telling me to let go of the knife. My fists were clenched so tightly around the handle; it took him screaming at me to let go and physically pulling my fingers from the grip before I would relinquish my hold. He threw it behind him; I could hear it skitter across the tiled floor.

His hands were trembling as he grabbed a towel from the rail and pressed it to my wrist, trying to staunch the blood flow.

'What the hell have you done?' I heard him ask through gritted teeth. I just dropped my head back against the wall, unable to stop my tears from falling. 'Why, baby? Why have you done this?'

I said nothing, just stared across the bathroom over his shoulder. I could hardly breathe. Is this what a catatonic state was?

While I lay there, seeing nothing, Isaac continued to talk to me, asking me questions. He brushed my hair from my face, stroked my cheeks, kissed my forehead. He bandaged my wrist tightly, talking all the time, trying to get me to respond. I knew the moment he found the pregnancy test on the counter, where I'd left it in my hurry to get to the doctor's. His questions stopped.

Pressing my eyes shut, I willed myself to be anywhere but there. I felt, rather than saw, him drop back to his knees in front of me. 'Rose, you have to talk to me.'

I shook my head, over and over again. I only stopped when he took my face in his hands, stilling me. 'Rose.' His tone offered me no way out.

I peeled my eyes open. His face was right in front of me, as close as he could get. 'It's his baby,' I croaked, my voice hoarse from all the screaming. I watched his slow blink. Saw the pity fill his gaze. 'I'm carrying his baby and I can't get rid of it.'

Isaac sighed and pulled me to him. I flopped against him like a rag doll and I let him cradle me to his body. 'He was outside the doctor's. He knew. He'd seen me buy the test. He knows it's his.'

'Did he hurt you?'

'He tried,' I told him.

'Where was Hiro?'

I felt a flash of guilt light me up from within. 'I didn't take him with me,' I admitted. 'It wasn't his fault.'

Isaac pulled me away from his body, holding me at arm's length. I flinched at his anger. 'Why would you do something so stupid to yourself? Do you see no other way through this?'

I dropped my eyes in shame. 'No,' I muttered. 'He told me he would kill me if I got rid of it.'

'So you thought killing yourself was a better option?'

I shrugged, looking anywhere but at him. 'I could have done a quicker job.'

Isaac dug his fingers into my shoulder, so deep it hurt. It helped bring me back to myself a little. 'There are other options. You don't have to do this.'

Finding his gaze for the first time, I could see his anguish. 'I can't have an abortion. And I don't want to die.'

'Then what the fuck are you doing?'

'I DON'T KNOW!' I shouted, throwing my face back into my hands. 'I don't know what I'm thinking. I don't know what I'm doing. I'm so sorry!'

Once more, the floodgates opened. Isaac clutched me back to his chest, shushing me over and over until I calmed down as he rocked me gently. 'I would never let him hurt you, baby. Not again,' he said into my hair. 'If you made that choice, I would keep you safe.'

'I can't do it. I can't have an abortion,' I said again.

'Please don't leave me,' he begged, holding me tight. 'Please don't do anything to hurt yourself, I couldn't bear it.'

I lifted my head, looking up at him, feeling more in control of myself now. 'I won't.' I found I meant it. 'I don't know what I was thinking. I was panicking and felt so hopeless and scared. I really don't want to hurt myself. Please believe me,' I begged. What *had* I been thinking? If he hadn't come in when he did, it might have been too late.

He smiled and kissed my forehead. 'I've never been so scared in all my life,' he told me, 'seeing you like that, the knife at your wrist.'

'Try being in my head. I'm pregnant with a rapist's baby.' It made it seem more real, saying it out loud.

'It isn't just his baby, Rose,' he whispered, his gaze sweeping across my face. 'It's your baby, too. Good, like you. It would be perfect, like you.' He sounded strange. Wistful.

I just scoffed. 'If that was even the case, everyone knows what happened to me. Imagine the shame, of seeing my friends and family looking at me, at my belly, at my newborn baby, thinking all the time...rape did that. I don't know how I could handle that,' I said.

Isaac was silent for a minute, chewing on the inside of his mouth. 'What if people thought it was mine?'

Chapter Twenty One

Never before had I fully understood the phrase *deafening silence,* until that very moment. I could hear my breath rushing in and out of my mouth. I could even hear my eyelashes rustling when I blinked. The loudest sound I could hear was the bass beat of Isaac's heart. It was thumping steadily away, solid as a rock. I could only stare at him. Surely I'd misheard. 'What did you say?' I asked him, thinking it couldn't have possibly been what I thought.

Isaac brought his hands up and cradled my head, his hands fisting in my hair. He swept his gaze down to my belly before finding my eyes again. 'Rose, if you want to keep this baby and don't want people to know it's his, we can tell them it's mine.'

What was he even saying? 'You can't mean that.'

The tenderness in his eyes almost broke my heart. 'I've never meant anything more,' he said, dropping one hand to my tummy and holding it there. 'I've stopped questioning how I feel, baby. I'm so in love with you and I know I don't want to be without you. And this child, if you make this choice? I will love it, too, like it was my own. So why not just tell people I'm the father?'

'Why would you take on such a burden?' I couldn't believe what I was hearing.

'What burden?' I gestured at myself, my stomach, just shrugging my shoulders. Isaac's eyes hardened. 'Your opinion of yourself is appalling. I need you to hear me. You are not, could not, will not ever be a burden to me. You are my whole life. You and this baby, if you want me, too.'

I wasn't sure whether it was his sincerity or something else, but I was suddenly struck with panic so intense, I couldn't sit still. 'Isaac, let me up,' I said, pushing him away. He fell back, shocked. I jumped to my feet and dashed into the bedroom. Yanking my bag from the bottom of the wardrobe, I paced around the room, shoving what belongings I could lay my hands on into its depths.

'Please don't go, Rose.' His voice was quiet as he followed me from the bathroom, watching my every move. 'Don't run away from me.'

'This is too fast, Isaac. I can't even process this myself, and you're there, all noble, ready to play happy families.' I was shaking my head, darting back into the bathroom to grab a few toiletries. 'I need some space, some time. I've got to get my head together.'

Isaac stood in the doorway, blocking my path. His arms were crossed and his feet were planted. 'You don't have to leave for that. I won't rush you, or force a decision from you.'

'But I can't think straight when I'm around you. I need the space from *you*.' I was blunter than I intended. Guilt twisted my insides when I saw his face drop. 'I'm sorry,' I told him. 'I just need to get away for a while.' I could hardly bear to look at him.

'Where will you go?'

'Zara's.' I couldn't go home and I definitely didn't want to go to Mum and Dad's. 'I'll stay there for a few days, just to clear my head.'

I forced myself to lift my head and look at him. It nearly broke me. I wanted nothing more than to run into his arms, but I knew he needed this time as well. He didn't know what he was saying. 'I do love you, Isaac,' I told him. 'And I want to believe what you're saying, but I can't. I want this perfect life you're promising, but I'm so fucked up. It's not fair to you.'

'Why does it sound like you're saying a real goodbye?' Was I? Was I leaving him? 'Don't let me go, Rose. Hold. On.' He spoke the words slowly, reminding me of our first dance together, the way he'd mouthed those same words to me across the dance floor.

'Why do you make it sound so easy?'

'Because it can be,' he said. He made it sound so simple. He sighed and ran his hands through his hair. 'I'm not going to stop you from leaving. I'll give you your space so you can get your head together. But I'm telling you now, baby, I'm never going to stop fighting for you.'

My heart hitched in my chest. 'I don't want you to,' I told him in a whisper, even though I had no right.

He made as if to reach for me but held back. 'I'll be right here.' My lower lip wobbled, but I needed to hold it together. It was me who was choosing to leave, whether permanently or not. I was the one who needed to be strong. 'I just need you to promise me one thing.'

I didn't trust my voice. I couldn't respond. I just looked at him, counting my breaths in and out in a bid to keep myself calm. 'Use Hiro. Do not go anywhere without him. He is at your disposal, no matter where you go.' Isaac caught my gaze and held it. 'Where ever you go, do you understand?' I could hear the double meaning in his tone. He really was going to leave me to make this decision alone.

'I understand,' I told him, my voice tight. I was ready to lose it again. I needed to get away before I became totally swallowed up by him. 'Will he take me to Zara's?'

Isaac's lips pressed tightly together. 'Yes. He's downstairs now.' I nodded, praying as I walked past him that he wouldn't touch me. He didn't. It left me free to walk away, through the penthouse towards the front door. 'Maybe one more thing,' he called behind me. I didn't want to hear it, I knew it. I stopped where I was, eyes on the door, dreading his words. 'Never forget how much I love you,' he said. I swear I could hear his voice breaking.

I clenched my eyes shut in a desperate bid to stop more tears from flowing. I managed to whisper the word 'never' before I forced my legs to carry me from the penthouse. I didn't look behind me and it wasn't until I made it into the stairwell that I let my heartbreak loose, shouting my sadness into the empty space.

By the time I'd made it down the stairs and into the lobby, I'd managed to gather myself enough that I appeared almost human. The look on Hiro's face told me he was already up to speed. I shook my head on the way past him, not wanting to elaborate, moving instead into the street. His Audi A1 - gunmetal grey - was parked illegally. The door unlocked as I approached, leaving me free to sink into the seat and stare out of the window, in utter desolation. Hiro joined me in a matter of moments, after taking a quick call. He looked across at me but I turned my head away and rested it on the glass. I knew Isaac had told him where I was going; I didn't need to make the effort to open my mouth.

Zara lived a little way out of the city in a neat and tidy new build. Two bed. Plenty of room for her but if she ever met someone, she would have to move.

There was no chance she could fit anyone else into such a tiny home, it was way too small. It was with a sinking heart that I thought the same. My flat had one little bedroom. How could I possibly hope to fit a baby in there? I knew what Isaac would say, but I couldn't uproot my life without giving myself some sort of alternative. He might sound sure now, but we'd only known each other a month. He was making such a fast decision but, with a screaming baby, he might regret his offer to shoulder the burden, to take the responsibility. He'd not thought about it at all, which was why this time was just as important for him as it was for me. With a sad pang, I added looking for somewhere new to live to my mental list of things to do. There was a huge part of me that wanted to just allow Isaac to take care of me, of us, but I had to be realistic. He might change his mind and then where would I be?

Hiro pulled up outside Zara's. I hadn't even called her; she had no idea I was coming. I checked my watch to find she would probably still be at work. I'd turned my head to tell Hiro we might be waiting a while but, before I had a chance to open my mouth, Zara's mint green Fiat 500 pulled up behind us. She jumped out of the car and hurried over to my side, wrenching the door open. 'Isaac rang me at work, told me you were on your way over. Are you alright?' She was panicked. He can't have told her.

I nodded up at her, making to leave the car. Hiro reached out to place his hand gently on my arm. 'Anytime you need to go anywhere, you phone me. I'll be here.' I thanked him, resting my hand briefly on his before he released me and let me go. I stood before Zara, who enveloped me in her arms. I allowed myself to be comforted while we waited for Hiro to drive away.

'Have you fallen out?' she asked me, leading me across the pavement and through her front door. 'He just rang out of the blue, said I needed to get here, fast.'

How the hell was I going to tell her? I flopped down on her sofa, not knowing where to begin. 'Things between us seem to be moving so fast. We haven't fallen out, but I need some space, just to sort out my feelings.'

'He's not putting you under any sort of pressure?' she asked me from the kitchen. I could hear her rattling glasses. It wasn't long before she appeared in front of me with a big glass of wine.

Taking it from her, I took a gulp, enjoying the crisp taste sliding down my throat. Then I froze, glass halfway to my lips. I could feel the blood draining from my face. Reaching down, I popped the wine glass down on the floor. 'Rose, what's he done?'

'Nothing,' I croaked. 'Do you have any water?'

She looked at me strangely but headed back into the kitchen. She returned with a bottle of mineral water. She'd always avoided tap water, said it tasted funny. I opened it with shaky hands and took a sip, washing the taste of wine from my mouth. Zara perched next to me on the end of the sofa cushion, angling her legs towards me. 'What's really going on?' she asked me.

'I'm pregnant,' I whispered, eyes finally dry with the acknowledgement.

Silence. Stunned and shocked. In all our years of friendship, Zara had never been rendered mute. I looked across at her, finding a sad expression on her face. I wasn't sure what emotion I was expecting, but it wasn't that. 'Is this why you've left? Because he doesn't want the baby?' *Well, shit.* 'Did he ask you to go? Is that why he rang me?' Her sadness was quickly giving way to anger. Horrendously misplaced anger.

'Jesus, Zara, no!' I needed to stop her before she developed a full head of steam. 'It's me who wanted to go. I told you, everything's moving so fast. I need some headspace, and I won't get that with him.' I sighed and swigged more of my water. 'He consumes me. When I'm with him, I can't think about anything else. And I can't go home, not alone.' Looking over at her, I brushed my hair from my eyes. 'Is it alright if I stay?'

'What do you need to think about, though?' she asked me, ignoring my question. 'Do you not need to think about things together? Make decisions together?' She grabbed her wine glass and took a big mouthful. 'I get that it's fast and unexpected, but you can't exclude him from this.'

'Zara, you don't understand...it's not his-'

'Of course it's his decision to make!' she interrupted. She was misunderstanding in the biggest way. This conversation was running away from me. 'Yeah, ultimately it's your body and you have the final say, but he has the right to be part of that thought process, don't you think?' *Daddies have rights.* His words came back to me in a rush.

'Yes, you're right,' I muttered. *Fucking coward.* 'But I only found out this morning and my head's all over the place.'

'What did he say? When you told him?'

I thought back to his words in the bathroom. 'He was shocked.'

'Understandably,' Zara said, knocking back the rest of her wine.

'But he was kind. He said he would take care of me, and that he would love the baby.' My fingers were tapping away on my leg. 'He told me he would fight for me.'

'Because he loves you?' I nodded. 'And because he knows you're pulling away from him.' The last wasn't a question. Was I pulling away? Was I doing what Nana always feared I would? Pushing a good thing away? I had already planted the seed that the baby was Isaac's, thanks to my cowardice, and there was going to be no going back on that now. For all intent and purposes, Isaac was this baby's father. So, in effect, I had taken that decision away from him. Now, if he did come to the conclusion that I was too much work and he stepped away, everyone was going to think he was abandoning his flesh and blood. What a fucking nightmare. I was making everything worse.

The wine on the floor was looking more tempting by the second. But I passed it to Zara and watched her enjoy it, getting up to make a cup of tea instead. While the kettle boiled, I dumped my stuff in her spare room. I noticed I'd received a text. Opening it up, I saw it was from Isaac. **I called Zara, she should be on the way to you soon. If you need to talk, please get in touch. I won't bother you if you need the space, but I don't want you to distance yourself. I'm here.**

I sighed, feeling sadder than I ever had. I started to reply, then deleted the words. I brought up his number, ready to ring him, but found I couldn't press the button. In the end, I opened up the messaging app again. **Thank you. I'll call**

in a couple of days, I promise. I just need time. I hit send, then thought hard. I typed another message quickly and sent it before I could change my mind. **I told Zara about the baby. She misunderstood and assumed you are the father. I didn't correct her, either. I'm sorry.**

It wasn't long before the three dots appeared on the bottom of the screen. I stood in the bedroom and watched them. **Don't be. I'm glad.**

I waited for another minute or two, to see whether he would elaborate. He didn't. Every fibre in my being was urging me to call him. I wanted to hear his voice, to let him tell me everything was okay. I was so conflicted. I needed this time to marshal my thoughts and I was grateful to Isaac for giving it to me without any argument. But on the other hand, I wanted him. I needed him. I did need to let him have his time as well, to think everything over, even though I had pretty much forced his hand now, however unintentionally. So, instead of giving into my biggest desire, I sent him one final text. **I DO love you. Please don't give up on me.**

I waited just long enough to see his reply. **Never. You have my heart.** Then I turned my phone off, tears dripping onto the screen.

When I'd managed to rein in my emotions, I made my way back downstairs where Zara handed me my cuppa. I curled up in one corner of the sofa while she sprawled in the other. She asked me whether I wanted to talk about the pregnancy. I told her, firmly, that I didn't. Not right then. After I'd been to the cattery later on, for the evening clean and feed, I wanted nothing more than to eat crap food and watch a mindless movie. So, when Hiro dropped me back off at Zara's after I had taken care of business, we ordered Chinese food and sat down to watch *Dirty Dancing*. I thought it might have been a mistake when I watched the botched abortion and the aftereffect, but, by the end, we were up and dancing in her tiny living room to *Time of my Life*. It was just the lift I needed. The only thing I missed was getting as drunk as Zara. A night of no inhibitions would have helped me no end. By the time I put her in bed though, I felt quite grateful about the fact I would be missing the kind of raging hangover she would be facing in the morning.

Chapter Twenty Two

The next couple of days were weird. I kept my usual work routine, thanks to Hiro ferrying me back and forth. Zara swore off the booze for the duration of my stay; she told me it was in solidarity with my situation but I suspected it had more to do with the morning spent vomiting. My laughing at her through the toilet door certainly hadn't made her feel any better.

As Zara was a much better cook than me, she rustled up some lovely food so we didn't have to order any more takeaways. The second night I stayed with her, we were enjoying grilled salmon with chorizo and tomatoes when she began asking me questions about the pregnancy. How did I really feel about it? How did I find out? How did Isaac really react? Was I going to move in with him? When was I going to tell Mum and Dad? By the time she'd finished, I'd been grilled more thoroughly than the salmon.

I was exhausted by the end of the next day and even more panicked at the thought of telling Mum and Dad. They were so supportive but did hold fairly old fashioned values. Courtship, engagement, marriage, baby. They were hardly enthusiastic when they found out I was moving in with Isaac, no matter how temporarily it was going to be. Now, I would either be telling them that I was going to have a baby out of wedlock or was going to be a single mother. Mum was going to be apoplectic and Dad was going to retreat further into himself. I was just starting to repair the divide my assault had carved between us; this was likely to cause a chasm.

The morning of the third day with Zara saw me receiving a package through the post. I was by myself; Zara had popped out to do her shopping. I knew who it was from the moment I opened the door and saw the 'congratulations' balloon. My muscles seized, making it difficult to sign for the delivery. I dragged the box through to the living room, making sure I had locked the door securely. Heart pounding, I used a kitchen knife to slice through the sellotape. Inside the box were a stuffed bear, a rattle, a blanket and a sheaf of papers. Swallowing bile, I reached past the baby's things and pulled out the papers. They were titled 'Family Procedural Rules, 2010'.

Fucking bastard, I thought when I'd skimmed through them. The legalise was a bit over my head but I understood the gist. It was as he'd said. Daddies have rights. Even if I managed to get him convicted of my assault, he would be able to use the law to exert his parental rights. I was never going to be free of him. He was irrevocably tied to me.

There was only one person I wanted to speak to at this moment, so I pulled out my phone and dialled. 'Rose?' I was shocked into silence. I had been expecting his usual curt greeting and hearing his soft intonation of my name threw my thoughts off track. 'Rose, baby, are you okay?' Still soft and full of worry.

I gave myself a mental shake. 'I didn't know who else to call,' I started.

'Has something happened?' I could hear the rustle of sheets. I'd obviously woken him up. I should have thought about how late he would have been at the club last night.

'He's sent me something,' I said. 'Some things for the baby, and...well...a warning.'

'Are you still at Zara's?' Now I could hear him moving around, drawers opening and closing. I told him I was. 'I'll be there soon. Keep the door locked. Don't answer it again until you know it's me.' He hung up without a goodbye, clearly rushing to get going.

While I waited for him to arrive, I moved through the house, rechecking the front door, peering out the windows and making sure the back door was locked. I was as safe as I could be but I still jumped a mile when I heard the banging on the front door. I crept over, jumping even more when he shouted through the wood. In a hurry, I fumbled with the key in the lock before I could let him in.

Once through the door, he took me in his arms, crushing me to him. I returned his hug with feeling, melting into his embrace. It had only been a few nights, how was it possible to have missed him so much? When I felt him begin to pull away, I tightened my grip. 'I'm sorry," I muttered into his chest. 'I should never have left you.'

He bent his legs to look me in the eyes, hands gripping my face. 'Has it helped you get your thoughts in order?'

'I didn't think it had,' I told him. 'I felt as confused as ever going to bed last night. But now, hearing your voice on the phone, seeing your face? Feeling your arms wrapped around me? I can't do this without you, Isaac, if your offer still stands?' I asked him, tentative and suddenly shy.

His beautiful blue eyes shone. 'It's no offer, Rose. It's my calling. You and this baby are my purpose in life.' He dropped his hand to my belly, pressing it gently against me. 'I mean it, baby. In fact, I've never meant anything more. This baby is mine. No one else needs to know any different.'

My heart was pretty much full to bursting. I beamed up at him and launched myself into his arms, wrapping my legs around his waist and pressing my lips to his. I couldn't understand why I had been so uncertain before. How on earth could I have tried to distance myself from love and devotion as powerful as this?

'Well, isn't this fucking lovely?' The words were as cold as the draft I was feeling around me. I froze and slid slowly down Isaac's body until my feet were flat on the floor. Panic surged through me when I felt every muscle in his body tense. He was like a coiled spring. I gripped his arms in warning, scared of what he might be about to do. I peered my head around his body, coming face to face with my worst nightmare once again.

'Here I am, getting ready to iron out all the nitty-gritty so I can be an active part of this pregnancy, yet here you both are, ready to pretend I have no part to play.' He had to be deluded but he sounded so serious. Isaac bristled in front of me and I felt him turn round, using his body to shield me from view. 'Is there really any part of either of you that thinks I'm going to stand by and let you pretend to be my baby's father?' He leaned to the side, trying to look around Isaac. He puffed his chest up in response and moved further in front of me. 'I told you before, you're mine, Rosslyn.' I squeezed my fingernails into Isaac's arm when I felt him shift infinitesimally forward.

When Isaac spoke, his voice was like gravel. 'You have no business here.' I could feel the muscles in his arm swell and tighten as he clenched his fist. I had a bad feeling.

'I have more business here than you. And the sooner you realise that, the better.' He took a step towards us. A small whimper escaped my mouth. I clamped my lips together. 'We're a family now, Rosie. You must see that.'

'I will never let you near me and my baby,' I said from behind Isaac's back, still refusing to look at him.

'But you have no choice,' he sang, taking another step towards us. 'That. Is. My. Baby. Did you open the package? Did you see what I printed out for you? I have rights, as the biological father of that baby.'

'Rose?' Isaac asked, shifting subtly to the balls of his feet.

I tried to tighten my grip further, sensing he was maybe a minute away from exploding. 'He's right. English law protects his rights.'

'Like hell they do,' Isaac snarled.

'They do. He'll be able to take me to court for visitation rights.'

'From prison?'

'Yep,' he said, moving forward one more step, putting him within Isaac's reach. 'Even from prison. If I even end up there,' he finished on a shrug.

And that was it. Isaac launched forward, bending low and catching him around the waist, forcing him back against the wall. He brought his knee up, knocking the wind out of him. 'You'll be in the ground!' Isaac shouted, raining kicks and punches onto his slumped form.

'Isaac!' I screamed, lurching forward to try to pull him back. He was unhinged, spit flying from his mouth, eyes narrowed in pure hatred. I was seriously worried he was going to kill him. Placing my hands on Isaac's shoulder, I tried to tug him away but the momentum of his next punch pulled me off my feet. I landed on my knees with a jolt, bracing myself with my arms. 'Stop it!' I yelled, turning back to the action. 'Just stop it, please!' Isaac was grunting with the effort and my stalker was silent as he absorbed the pummelling blows.

'What the fuck?' Zara pushed through the front door, hands laden with shopping bags, too lazy to make multiple trips from the car. She dropped the bags and rushed around to me, helping me to my feet. When I was steady, she pulled her phone from her back pocket. 'I'm ringing the police,' she shouted over the cacophony.

'No!' I thrust my hands forward, grabbing for her phone. She looked at me like I was crazy. Maybe I was. 'Who are they going to arrest?' I indicated the melee on the floor in front of us. 'Help me, Zara, I need to stop him.'

She looked from me to the fight and back again. 'Right.' She nodded and ran to the kitchen. I heard water running and, before long, she reappeared with the washing up bowl full of water, which she proceeded to throw over them both. She passed me the empty bowl which I took, stunned. The shock of the freezing water paused Isaac's attack, which left Zara time to grab the back of his t-shirt and yank him over, so he fell back on his arse. She shoved her face into his. 'Get a grip, psycho,' she hissed.

Isaac gave his head a shake and flexed his fingers. They were bloody. I couldn't tell whether any of it was his own. He rose to his feet with a sudden gracefulness. Thankfully, he seemed to have regained control of himself, but he was still breathing heavily.

I felt livid. I looked over at my attacker, who was unsteadily getting to his own feet, using the wall for support. This could have been the perfect opportunity to apprehend him, but now he was beaten to a bloody pulp, that opportunity was lost. He knew it, too. Despite the blood and swelling, his look was smug. He wiped his nose and eyes with the back of his hand, smearing his blood across his face.

'Hug?' he asked me, holding his arms out and away from his body in invitation.

Shakes started wracking through my body, only this time they were in anger, not in fear. 'Get out of here.' I ground my words out through gritted teeth. 'You get out, right now, or I will let him beat you to death.' Isaac moved across to me and made to gather me in his arms. I stiffened in his hold. It was subtle but I know he felt it.

My attacker nodded his head once, eyes flicking between me and Isaac. 'Okay,' he said, walking backwards to the door. 'But we will be having a chat soon. Make no mistake about that.' On a wince, he turned on his heel and left the building, closing the door behind him.

I waited long enough that he must have left the vicinity of the house before I shrugged out of Isaac's hold. 'You fucking idiot,' I seethed at him. 'What possible hope do I have now of securing a conviction against him?' I got right in Isaac's face, my finger pointing between his eyes. I was close enough to poke him. 'If the police take one sniff near him, he'll be diverting them to you. Because you know he'll press charges, don't you. Just to fucking spite us.'

'Rose,' Isaac implored, trying to take hold of my arm. I wrenched away, slapping him on the shoulder instead.

'Actual bodily harm, Isaac. Did you see the state of him?' I shook my head and started pacing. 'I'll be surprised if he doesn't report you straightaway. He could be heading to the police station right now.'

'He won't.' Isaac sounded so sure of himself.

'No?' I narrowed my eyes to shoot him a dirty look before continuing with my pacing.

'He's not stupid, Rose. If he reports me, his name is in the system. The moment I'm arrested, both you and I identify him as the man who raped you. No matter how much he wants to hurt you, or me, he won't risk that.'

I opened my mouth to argue. 'I mean it,' he continued. 'He won't report me, because he doesn't want to go to prison himself.' Did he have a point?

'But his parental rights?' I indicated the box behind me, the papers resting on the top. I looked back over at Isaac; he didn't look so sure of himself now. 'He seems serious about that. The baby.' I pressed my hand to my abdomen, feeling a stirring of something unfamiliar within me. Something maternal?

'*His* parental rights?' Zara squeaked from the corner of the room. *Shit.* 'I thought you said-'

'No,' I interrupted her. 'You assumed.' I looked at Isaac, his eyes full of something. Love? Concern? I couldn't tell. 'I just didn't correct you.'

She moved from the corner of the room, walking towards us. 'How could it be his?' she asked, confused. 'They gave you the morning-after-pill in the hospital.'

'How could it be Isaac's?' I countered softly. 'We've used protection every time we've been together.'

'But contraception can fail.' There was a pleading note in her voice. I understood it. I didn't want my baby's father to be a rapist, either.

'So can the morning-after-pill,' I said. 'Especially when you throw up soon after taking it.' I looked at Zara, watching her face fall. 'I had an ultrasound. The size of the embryo pretty much confirms the timeline. Blood test results will be conclusive.' The final nail in the coffin, so to speak. I made a mental note to chase those results up if I hadn't heard anything by the beginning of the week.

'And he wants to be involved?' she asked, incredulous.

'It seems so,' I muttered. I looked back at Isaac and walked right into his arms, burying my face into his chest. 'You really are an idiot,' I spoke into his t-shirt. He wrapped his arms around me, stroking my back.

'I'm sorry,' he told me. 'I don't know what happened, where that came from.' He sighed. 'I wanted to kill him.'

'I was scared you were going to.' I looked up at him. His hair was a mess and his face was spattered with blood. He was impossibly handsome, my violent protector. 'I think he'd risk prison. If I don't allow his involvement, I think he will push for a DNA test in court. And then I think he'll fight the rape charge.'

'He couldn't. The evidence proves it wasn't consensual. And there was a witness.'

'Hmm. A witness whose testimony will be thrown out when they're accused of assault themselves.' Harsh, but true.

'You could wait until his bruises have healed,' Zara piped up from beside us.

I shook my head. 'Even if he was convicted, it still wouldn't stop him from taking me to court for visitation rights. I really won't be free of him.'

Zara chewed on her bottom lip, thinking hard. 'Have you considered other options?' she asked me.

'I won't have an abortion,' I told her, looking up at Isaac once more. 'I don't want to. This baby is part of me, too.' Isaac smiled and lowered his lips to mine in a tender gesture. I knew then, finally and totally, that I did have his support.

I pulled away and stepped out of Isaac's embrace. Isaac suddenly dropped to his knees by the wall. 'Isaac!' I exclaimed, dropping to my knees beside him. 'What's the matter?'

He swept his hand across the carpet. 'This blood is setting,' he said, rubbing his fingers together. 'Ladies, I can arrange someone to come and take care of this.' He stood in another smooth move, shoving both hands into the pockets of his jeans. 'Let me head back to the club and sort this out.'

I looked at him, anxious. He was acting weird. 'You should sort yourself out, too,' I told him, trying to read his expression. 'You're covered in blood.' I was noticing it now, the more I looked at him. Bigger droplets and a fine spray all over his face and his clothes.

Isaac looked down at himself. 'Yes,' he said. 'You're right. I'll head home and clean up. But Zara, I'll have a team out here, today, to clean up this mess.'

Zara looked slowly from me to him, her eyes wide. 'Thanks, Isaac,' she said. 'I'd really appreciate that.'

He nodded. 'Are you okay, Rose?' I nodded my reply. 'Good. Will I see you at the club later?'

'Yes, of course.' And with nothing further, he turned and walked from Zara's house, straight into his car. He didn't even glance back.

'Zara,' I asked, watching him pull away from the curb. 'What do you think is wrong with him?

'Honestly?' I looked at her, wrapping my arms around myself. 'I think his adrenaline's worn off.'

Chapter Twenty Three

The cleaning crew arrived within the hour. There were three of them, and they came armed with an array of liquids and machinery. None of them asked us what happened or commented at all, so we just sat in the kitchen and left them to it. I ordered us both a Starbucks to enjoy while they worked; my usual white chocolate mocha frappuccino and an iced matcha green tea latte for Zara. I wrinkled my nose when she pulled it from the bag. It looked like the green milk from *Star Wars.*

We talked in hushed whispers while we waited for the cleaners to finish up. The ferocity of Isaac's attack had surprised us both. I'd already seen him lash out at his brother, so I knew there was a violent streak of sorts lurking within him, but he'd *really* lost it then. Zara asked me whether it made me afraid of him, seeing him like that. With complete honesty, I told her no, I wasn't scared. Both times he had lashed out were in my defence. I knew with certainty that Isaac would never hurt me. Everything he'd done, right up until now, had been for my protection. I'd never felt safer.

As well as discussing Isaac's outburst, we also spent time talking through what the future may hold. It became abundantly clear I was going to have very little control over the situation. Probably none. Yes, for all intent and purposes, Isaac was going to be my baby's father. He was going to help me raise it and he would always treat it as his own. I knew that, but everything else was out of my hands. I would have no choice but to have a DNA test to prove my stalker was the biological father, if he pursued the matter, which I was sure he would. I'd have no choice but to go through the courts, fighting his demands for visitation, all the while knowing I would lose. We'd read through the papers properly while we waited for our drinks to arrive and Zara verified their legitimacy with a quick google search. If he was arrested and convicted as a result of his coming forward to claim parental responsibility, I would have the opportunity to file a restraining order against him. Which, considering he had threatened my safety multiple times since the actual attack, would probably be granted. That would mean, however, I would not be present during his visits with my child. Which could end up being in a prison setting. Good god, this was a minefield, and I wasn't sure what to do for the best. I would not be able to do what Isaac wanted and tell people he was the father. As soon as I was forced to complete a DNA test, everyone would know I'd been lying.

The only thing I couldn't decide was when to tell Mum and Dad. It was going to destroy them. Not so much the news of the pregnancy; I know they harboured a desire to be grandparents, even though they never badgered me to meet anyone and provide. It was what led to the pregnancy. Who they would also be irrevocably linked to. Would they look at their grandchild and see a monster? Would I?

There were still many shameful thoughts I couldn't let go of. One of the worst being walking into the registry office, to register the birth. I didn't even know his name, so what on earth was I going to put on the birth certificate? Yes, I could leave it blank but I also couldn't see that going down well with *daddy dearest.* I also couldn't stop thinking about people's questions, when they could find no family resemblance to Isaac. They might make a lighthearted, flippant comment but I wouldn't have an answer for them. Or they might ask outright, and I still wouldn't have an answer for them, not one that wouldn't upset me to discuss. I said as much to Zara. She asked me whether I'd considered any counselling, to help me truly come to terms with what had happened to me. In all honesty, I hadn't. I'd been so focused on making it through each day, just taking it one day at a time. I'd been thinking that if I didn't spend too much time dwelling on the events, I couldn't be affected by them. But now, I was wondering if bottling it all up was perhaps more toxic. I'd heard other women from the office saying how bad stress was for an unborn baby and how a mother's mood played a big part in the health of a pregnancy. At the moment, I figured I wasn't providing the most hospitable environment to nurture a baby.

'You know,' I told her, 'I think I'll make an appointment to speak to my GP. I'm going to have to go and see them to start all the prenatal stuff, so I'll try and get a referral.'

'And do you feel ready to start talking about everything?'

I shook my head. 'Not really, no, but I have to start somewhere, don't I?'

The cleaning crew finished up, one of them popping their head into the kitchen to let us know they were leaving. We followed them out, marvelling at the job they'd done. If it wasn't for the fragrance of industrial-strength cleaning product, you would never have been able to see any evidence of the fight. We looked at each other as they left, impressed. I don't think either of us was expecting their efforts to be so successful.

Once we were alone, Zara started picking up the bags and scattered shopping. I made to help her but she shooed me away. I should have known better than to offer. Heaven help the person who messed with her orderly cupboards. I was at a loose end, pottering about the living room when there was a quiet knock on the front door. 'Stay there!' Zara shouted, flying to the door ahead of me. 'Oh, hi,' she said, swinging it open, letting Hiro pop his head into the hallway.

'Miss Rose, how are you?' he asked.

I smiled warmly at him. 'I'm fine, Hiro, thank you. Did Isaac call you?'

Hiro stepped fully into the house. 'He did, but that's not why I'm here.'

'Oh?' I was confused.

'You have a client coming to pick up a cat this afternoon. I've come to take you over there.' Jesus, he was right. With everything going on, I'd completely forgotten. Grateful for his reminder, I grabbed my bag from the arm of the sofa and headed over to his car.

My cattery was empty when I had handed Binx over to his owners, one of whom was suffering from a severe case of travel sickness. I had never seen anyone so green. I gave the place a thorough clean and sorted out some paperwork in my office. Hiro was sitting quietly in the corner until he asked me whether it was safe for me to be around the cats in my condition. I was shocked and for a second didn't know what he meant. But then something clicked.

'Do you know, I hadn't even thought about that,' I told him, thinking about the potential risks. 'I have pretty stringent hygiene standards but I'll have to do a check and make sure I don't need to take even more precautions.' Hiro looked so concerned; he was such a sweetheart. 'It's not the cats, it's a parasite they can pass in their litter. It can be harmful to a pregnant woman, but I'm sure I'll still be able to run the business. I might just need to wear gloves and a mask, to stop me breathing the dust.' It was something I had to look at. It went onto the mental to-do list, which was growing arms and legs.

After shuffling papers around my desk for another few minutes, I took a deep breath, preparing to ask what had been on my mind the whole time I'd been at work.

'He was furious, but he's alright,' Hiro spoke quickly. The breath I'd taken hissed out of me in a rush. Had he read my mind? He smiled a sweet smile at me. 'It's just like you to worry about him when everyone else is worried about you.'

'I really thought he was going to kill him, Hiro.' I winced at the memory of his fists flying through the air, at the dull, repetitive thudding sounds as he made contact with his face and body, again and again. 'How long have you worked for him?' I wondered.

Hiro sat forward in his chair. 'A little over a year, but I've known him for several.' I tilted my head in question. 'My dad was very good friends with Isaac's parents. We've spent a lot of time together, particularly following their deaths.'

My heart hurt again at the thought of Isaac losing them both in such a tragic way. Hiro brushed his hair from his eyes before he continued. 'When Isaac opened the club, he approached my dad straight away to run the security side of the business. Dad drafted me to the team.' I looked at Hiro out of the corner of my eye. Hiro pressed his lips together. 'He's not a violent person, Rose.'

'I never thought he was. It just shocked me, that's all.'

'He would never have done that to anyone else.'

'No?'

Hiro shook his head. 'No one who hadn't hurt you.' It was as I'd thought. As I'd known. I don't know why I let those moments of doubt in. 'He's a good man.'

'I know that. I've never doubted that. I just can't see any way out of this,' I said on a sigh.

'Patience is a virtue,' he continued. I snorted. 'And I am a firm believer in Karma.'

I only wished I could believe the same. I'd never felt more hopeless.

It was knocking on quite late in the afternoon when Hiro was pulling up outside Zara's. I couldn't bring myself to leave the car. 'I need to see him, Hiro.'

'I know he's at the club if you want me to take you.'

I nodded, eager to feel the strength of his embrace once more. As Hiro pulled away from the curb and headed back into the city, I fired a quick text to Zara, letting her know I was heading off to see Isaac and wasn't sure when I'd be back. There was nothing I wanted more than to go back home with him.

Once Hiro pulled into the underground car park, I practically flew into the club. I ran straight into the bar proper, not expecting him to be there but wanting to pick him up a drink. I figured he might need it. 'Hey, Shaun.' I greeted the barman as I entered the space.

'Well, hello there, lady. I hope you're here to cheer the big man up.'

'I certainly hope so,' I replied, slipping onto a bar stool. 'Will you get him a drink, please? His usual.'

Shaun nodded. 'Of course.' He grabbed a tumbler and a bottle of Johnny Walker Blue Label from one of the shelves behind him. He poured a generous measure into the tumbler and slid it down the bar to me, western style. I giggled, catching the glass before it slid clear off the end. 'Anything for you?' he asked me.

'I shook my head. 'No thanks,' I told him. 'I'm not the one who needs cheering up.'

Whisky glass in hand, I left the bar and made my way through the labyrinth, until I found myself in front of his office door. Knocking softly, I could hear melancholy tones drifting through the wood. 'Yes?'

Gone was his usual brusque tone. I pushed my way through the door and stood, looking at his beautiful face. He had cleaned himself up; the blood was gone from his face and hair, and he had changed his clothes, slipping into a clean pair of jeans and another t-shirt, grey this time. Using my bum, I shut the door with a soft click, my heart wrenching at the look of utter despair in his bright blue eyes. The music was hauntingly beautiful, a lone male voice and a soft guitar. 'Alexa, stop.' Isaac spoke softly, plunging the room into an eerie silence. He lifted his head, his mouth a grim line.

'I haven't heard that song before,' I said, wanting to go to him, but the look on his face held me where I stood.

'Jeff Buckley.' He rose from his chair, arching an eyebrow. *Lover, You Should've Come Over.*

I smiled, his words and subtle grin putting me at ease in an instant. I walked right up to him, holding out the tumbler of whisky which he took and swallowed in one swift mouthful. He linked his hands behind my head, pulling me close before he lowered his head and consumed my mouth in a deep and passionate kiss. I could taste the whisky on his tongue and could feel the vibrations as he groaned into my mouth.

When he broke contact we were both breathing heavily and desire had pooled between my legs. Isaac was similarly affected; his erection was straining against the stiff denim of his jeans. 'I didn't realise how much I needed that,' he said, tracing my jawline with his knuckle.

'I thought as much,' I replied, reaching my arms around him, running them over his firm behind. On a little squeeze, I continued, 'that's why I asked Shaun to give me your favourite.'

Isaac chuckled, pressing his groin into my belly. 'Yeah, the whisky was definitely what I meant.' His voice was dripping with sarcasm, making me throw my head back and laugh. 'You're so beautiful,' he told me, causing my head to snap back up on my neck.

'I was thinking the same thing about you,' I told him. 'I just wish you didn't look so sad.'

On a sigh, Isaac sank back down into his office chair, pulling me with him. I curled up on his lap, legs draped over the arm of his chair. He circled my shoulders with one arm and ran his other hand up and down the top of my thigh. 'I want to be able to tell you that I don't know why I lost it like that,' he said, speaking into my hair. 'But I'd be lying. I didn't snap. There was no descending red mist. I didn't black out in rage. I watched him take those few steps towards me and I was desperate for him to take that last one because I wanted him close enough. I wanted to be able to reach out and touch him.' I stayed silent, knowing he needed to get this out, so we could move on together. No elephants in the room. 'I'm sorry if I scared you. I would never want you to feel afraid of me but I wanted to hurt him. Badly.'

'You may have succeeded.'

I felt Isaac shake his head. 'It kills me that there is a good chance he's going to be a near constant presence in your life. For one moment, I thought about taking him out of it. If Zara hadn't stopped me, I might have done.'

'That's what scared me the most.' I lifted my head so I could look at him, pressing my hand to his cheek. He leaned his face into my hand. I could feel his rough stubble. 'It wasn't seeing you acting so violently, because I understand where your anger came from. I've been feeling violent myself over the last month, but haven't got an outlet for it. But I was scared that you were going to go too far, and I was going to lose you.'

'I know. I'm sorry.' He was contrite.

I traced his lips with the tips of my fingers. 'We have to move on from this,' I told him, feeling an unfamiliar resolve settling into my bones. 'No matter what happens from now, we can't exist in this same level of torment. It's not going to be good for us, and it definitely isn't going to be good for this baby.'

Isaac smiled a tender smile, moving his hand from my thigh to my stomach. I placed my hand on top of his, gazing down at our unity. 'I'm going to do the best I can for you and this baby,' he told me. I looked back up, falling more in love with him as devotion poured from his eyes. 'I mean it.'

I knew he did. 'So, we *will* start to put this behind us?' I asked him.

He leaned forward and kissed me. 'Yes,' he said. 'I promise.'

'But?' I was starting to read him well.

He sighed and rested his forehead against mine. 'But nothing. We will.'

'You're not telling me something.' I was starting to get worried. I shuffled around in his lap, my muscles beginning to tense.

'I have to go away for a few days,' he said. 'On business,' he added, sensing my hysteria building. I deflated like a balloon, my breath leaving me in a rush. 'There's an old warehouse gone up for auction in Manchester that would make a great site for a new club. I've been thinking about expanding and it's a good opportunity, even though the timing couldn't be worse.'

I smiled. 'More shit timing, eh?' I teased.

Isaac's answering smile was lovely to see. 'Indeed. I won't be away long. Just a couple of nights while I view and participate in the auction if, it fits the criteria.'

'What's two days?' I asked on a shrug. I didn't want my disappointment to show. 'Shall I stay with Zara until you get back?'

Isaac pulled me into a bear hug, nearly squeezing the oxygen from my lungs. 'Would you mind?'

'Of course not. She's a great roommate.'

'Hiro will be close, too.'

I would have expected nothing less.

Chapter Twenty Four

The thought of Isaac leaving, even if only for a couple of days filled me with dread. There was a part of my mind that was convinced something was going to happen, something terrible. I had no plans to do much of anything while he was away because I was so sure my stalker was going to do something to try and hurt me. I didn't trust him not to take advantage of my isolation. Thankfully, I had no real reason to go anywhere or do anything, seeing as I had no residents in the cattery for the next few weeks. And I knew Hiro was probably going to be camped out in the car, on Isaac's instruction, until he returned from Manchester. I would be able to keep all doors locked and keep myself safe inside Zara's for a couple of days but I still couldn't shake the feeling that something bad was just around the corner.

It was clear that Isaac didn't want to leave. He looked so troubled when he told me he had to go. I had never seen him look so sad, was more used to the mischievous twinkle in his eye. I wanted to comfort him but, after giving me a fierce squeeze, he urged me to uncurl myself from his lap and stand. He told me he had to leave straight away, that he wanted to check the location as soon as he could, so he could have a talk with his architect before the auction. I tried to hide my disappointment.

'I really am sorry,' he told me, kissing me softly. 'Hiro will take you back to Zara's.' And just like that, I was dismissed. He'd never been so abrupt with me before. I was walked back through the underbelly of the club and escorted to the bar, where Hiro was chatting to Shaun. They were obviously good friends, for I had never seen Hiro so animated before.

Before Isaac left me, he placed a gentle, lingering kiss on the top of my head, completely at odds with his curt, dismissive tone. He shook Hiro's hand and said something so softly, I couldn't make it out. With a last look at me, he started walking back towards his office. A loud bang halted his progress and we all turned to face the front door, watching Jack slither his way into the building. An unexpected fury rose in my belly at the sight of him, which I had to swallow down as he approached. Of course, he was making a beeline for me. I don't think I could hide my look of disgust because he threw his head back and laughed. There was still the same sour smell to him, like curdled milk.

'I almost didn't recognise you, girlie,' he drawled when he was in front of me, reaching out for a strand of my shorter hair. The smell grew stronger as he lifted his arm; I instinctively drew back, leaning away from his touch. 'We could have some fun together,' he began.

'Jack.' Isaac's voice was low with warning. I stiffened and Jack slid his eyes over my shoulder to look at his brother, eyebrow raised in question. 'Leave her alone, and get in here.' The words were whispered with frightening menace. I never wanted to be on the receiving end of that tone.

Jack gave me a last look, lips curling upwards in a sick smile before stalking over to his brother. Isaac offered no further goodbye or even a glance in my direction. I couldn't help but feel slighted but I shoved the feelings away. His relationship with his brother was a complicated one. I wouldn't take anything personally.

'Right then,' I said, giving my head a mental shake. 'Shaun, it's been lovely to see you again, but I have to go home.' I saw Hiro's eyes widen. 'Zara's,' I clarified. 'Would you mind, Hiro?'

He shook his head, rising from his stool. 'Not at all,' he said. I waved goodbye to Shaun and exited the club into the car park, where I jumped straight into the passenger seat. There was no point fighting Isaac's wishes. They would keep me safe.

'Have you been given any specific instructions for the next couple of days?' I asked, already having a fairly good idea of what they might have been.

Hiro gave me the side eye from the driver's seat, pulling out of the car park. 'I believe I'm to watch the house until his return, to make sure you're not bothered again.'

'Oh, Jesus christ,' I muttered under my breath, my eyes rolling so far back, I think I saw the inside of my skull. 'He can't be serious.' I wasn't asking.

Hiro chuckled. 'He most certainly is. Your safety means more to him than anything. And now he knows where you're staying, you're at the most risk.'

'I don't think he would dare come back,' I mused. 'Not after the beating he took. It may have scared him off for good.'

'Maybe,' Hiro replied, quietly. 'He still doesn't want to take that risk, not while he's away for work.'

We sat in silence for several minutes. I was thinking hard. 'He can't expect you to sit in your car and wait for trouble that might not even be coming.'

'Yes, he can,' he said on a shrug.

I chewed the inside of my cheek. 'Well, I can't expect that of you,' I told him. 'Zara only has the two bedrooms but the sofa is comfortable enough to get your head down.'

Hiro was shaking his head before I'd even finished. 'I wouldn't want to be an imposition.'

'You won't be.' I knew this. Zara would be more than happy to let him sleep on the sofa. 'I can't have you sleeping in here.' I indicated the limited space in the car, still seeing Hiro shaking his head. Growing frustrated, I folded my arms across my chest in a huff. 'I don't like the thought of you out in the car,' I began, ready to play a game. 'What if he comes in through the back door and you don't see him? He could have snuck in and done something before I even woke up.' I glanced out of the corner of my eye, feeling sick with myself. The scared victim card is not one I ever wanted or felt remotely comfortable playing. Not in such a calculated way. I could see it was working; Hiro had paled and was pursing his lips together in thought. 'If you were in the living room, I'd feel so much safer.' Good god, I just needed to flutter my eyelashes and swoon to complete the damsel in distress routine.

'You're right, it will be safer for me to be in the house,' he said, concreting my feelings of both guilt and relief in my gut. At least I knew he would be comfortable now. He drove with purpose to Zara's, seemingly in a rush to get us there. It wasn't long before we pulled up outside. Ever the gentleman, Hiro swept around to my side of the car and opened my door, holding his hand out for me. I took it gratefully, feeling bone-weary all of a sudden. Everything was catching up with me. I couldn't wait for this all to be over, whenever that ending may be.

I hauled myself to my feet on a groan, ungraceful and not caring in the slightest. An early night was on the cards tonight. I dragged my feet through Zara's front door, Hiro following close behind. A quick glance behind me showed me he was scanning the street around us. It was like having my very own, unassuming bodyguard. I hoped Isaac was paying him well for putting his own life on hold while he pretty much stuck to me like glue.

'Zara!' I shouted, the moment we had cleared the threshold, Hiro closing and locking the door behind him. The air still smelled of the fresh tang of the cleaning chemicals. 'Zara!' I shouted again, realising I could hear her vacuuming the upstairs. I shook my head. I should have expected her to try to match the rest of the house with the stellar job the cleaning crew did. A third shout, growing more shrill, finally made her shut off the vacuum. She popped her head around the corner, hair dishevelled and face red from her exertions.

'Alright?' Was she panting?

'We have company for the next couple of nights,' I told her. Hiro joined me at the bottom of the stairs with a polite nod. 'Is that okay?'

Zara nodded. 'Course. Is the sofa alright?' she asked.

Hiro cast his eyes into the living room, which now resembled a show home. 'It's perfect, thank you,' he replied quietly.

'Great.' Her head disappeared back around the corner. 'Just make yourselves at home, I'm just finishing up here.' A second later and the vacuum started back up again.

On a smile, I urged Hiro into the living room who just stood, staring down at the immaculate array of scatter cushions, all of which had been freshly plumped. 'People sit in here?' he asked me, uncharacteristic worry in his tone. I couldn't help the little laugh that escaped. I knew how he felt. I'd felt the same the first few times I came to her house.

'She's house proud but isn't as bad as you'd think,' I tried to reassure him.

Hiro raised his eyebrow. 'She's not going to be rearranging the cushions around me?' He sounded like he was aiming for sarcasm, but I wasn't fooled.

'I promise,' I told him on a laugh, 'she won't even look at you funny if you chuck a cushion on the floor.'

After about an hour, Hiro started to relax. Probably when he saw Zara spill a large glass of white wine and didn't run around like a madwoman trying to clean it up. They got on well, which wasn't a surprise; Zara got on well with everyone. Despite his unwavering politeness, Hiro even started to wind her up about her obvious attraction to Shaun the bartender. I was pleased to hear they had arranged a date for a night in the week when Shaun didn't have to work at the club. Knowing Zara, it was likely to just be a few dates of fun, but I hoped it would lead to something more. Shaun was a lovely guy from what I'd seen and Zara really did deserve the best. She had so much to offer someone and no matter how casual she was, every time a string of dates ended abruptly without the possibility of becoming anything more, I could tell how sad she was. She tried to hide it, but I knew her too well to be taken in by her bravado.

The three of us spent that night playing card games and watching rubbish on tv. At some point, I must have nodded off in my chair, because Zara shook me awake and guided me to my bedroom. I was desperate to speak to Isaac but didn't want to disturb him, not knowing whether he might be asleep himself. So I settled instead for sending him a quick text. **Hope all is well with work. See you soon. Rose x.** Still utterly exhausted, I put my phone down and promptly sank into a deep sleep.

I woke late the next morning, sleeping almost until lunchtime. I was halfway between annoyed that neither of them had woken me up and grateful that I'd been allowed to catch up on some much-needed sleep. I settled on grateful because I felt better than I had done in days. I was pleased to see a reply from Isaac when I picked up my phone. **The warehouse is perfect for expansion. Needs work but should get it for a good price. Things are moving quickly. Auction is today so will be home tomorrow. Looking forward to getting back to you. x**

I was inordinately pleased, not only to see his reply but to know that he would be back tomorrow. My attachment had developed in such a short space of time. Some would say it was too quickly, or it was unhealthy, but I didn't feel that way. I could not and would not allow myself to question my feelings for Isaac, or how our relationship was blossoming. I would take nothing for granted and just enjoy every minute of it. He had my heart and he was my strength.

Once I pulled my lazy self from the bed, I had a quick shower and blasted my hair with the dryer, slipping into a pair of leggings and an old hoodie. I couldn't be bothered making any sort of effort today, not when I had no plans to leave the house. Downstairs, I could hear Zara and Hiro chatting in the kitchen.

'Well, well,' Zara started the moment I walked in. 'I didn't know whether to chuck water on you to get you out of that bed.'

I stretched, unable to hide my smile. 'I'm not even sorry,' I told her. I took a deep breath, smelling something beautiful. 'What's cooking?' I asked, my stomach already growling.

'I thought I'd channel your mum and do a nice roast. I was going to offer you breakfast, but as you're up so bloody late, the dinner will have to do.'

'Smells gorgeous.' I walked over to the oven and bent at the waist to peer inside. 'Ooh, lovely,' I said, my mouth practically drooling at the sight of the pork roasting, crackling already crisping on the top.

Zara bumped me out of the way with her hip. 'Sit down, then,' she said. I joined Hiro at the table, smiling warmly at him.

'Sleep alright?' I asked.

A mug of coffee appeared in front of me. 'Decaf,' she said. 'For your condition.'

I rolled my eyes and looked over the top of my mug at Hiro, blowing some of the steam away.

'I slept fine, thank you,' he told me, sipping from his mug of tea. 'I heard from Isaac this morning,' he said.

Nodding, I took a mouthful that near scalded the whole of my mouth. 'Me too.' I stood and grabbed a glass, filling it with cold water from the tap and gulping it down to soothe my burning tastebuds. 'Say's he's coming back tomorrow.'

'He did. Sounds like things are going well.'

'Did you speak to him?' I asked, trying another mouthful of coffee. What a truly pointless drink it was, without the caffeine.

Hiro nodded, draining the last of his tea and rising to place the mug in the sink. 'I did, early on this morning.' He looked at me, confused. 'Did you not?'

I shook my head. 'No, I just text him before I fell asleep last night. He'd replied while I was still sleeping.' I pulled my lower lip into my mouth, worrying at it. 'How did he sound?' I asked, still a little worried about how he'd seemed when he dismissed me yesterday.

'He was fine,' Hiro said. 'Very positive, and upbeat.'

'Good,' I muttered, mostly to myself. The sooner he got back and I could see that for myself, the better.

Dinner was a massive success, Zara pulling out all the stops. The pork was delicious and tender, her crackling was spot on. She really had channelled my mum and made far too much, which led to me eating far too much. My stomach hurt by the time I'd finished and I was thankful for an elastic waistband. I made sure Zara sat down while Hiro and I did the washing up, despite all her protests, then the three of us went for a walk to try to burn off some of the colossal dinner. The weather was still holding. It might have been getting cooler but the sun was sticking around. Once back inside, we sat about, lazy and replete, while we watched a film. I was nodding on and off throughout, so didn't see much of it. Is this what pregnancy was like? I wondered to myself between naps. Tired all the time and a massive appetite?

As the evening drew on, I decided to excuse myself and head to bed. I kept thinking that the sooner I went to sleep, the sooner I would be seeing Isaac again. So I left the two of them arguing good-naturedly about which *Indiana Jones* movie was the best and fell into bed, quickly falling into a deep sleep.

I startled awake at some point in the night when I felt the bed shift beneath me. My heart leapt into my throat and my stomach dropped in panic. But then I felt Isaac's arm circle my waist, his hand pressing against my stomach. My heart rate slowed under his touch and I stirred in the bed, trying to turn and face him. He just scooped me closer to his chest, tucking his legs in tight behind mine, not allowing even a millimetre of space between our bodies.

'Shh,' he whispered in my ear. 'Go back to sleep. I just needed to be near you.'

I tried to argue, to protest even a little, but with Isaac rubbing soothing circles onto my belly, I soon slipped back into sleep.

When the morning light woke me, I was convinced I'd imagined it. I'd been so desperate to see him again, my subconscious had conjured him up in my dreams. I felt a pang of sadness, which I chased away with the thought of him returning later on today. But then I took a breath and smelled his aftershave and his unique masculine scent. I realised I could also hear his deep breaths as he slept beside me.

I turned myself over as gently as I could so I didn't jostle him. Once I was laying on my other side, I was free to admire him. He had flipped over onto his back while he slept, one arm still beneath my body and the other curled inwards, his hand resting lightly on his chest. His mouth was slightly parted and his lashes were fanning out against the tops of his cheeks. His hair was a dishevelled mess, waves falling onto his forehead and into his eyes. I reached up to brush a stray lock away, causing him to stir. His eyelashes fluttered for several moments before his eyes opened. He blinked in confusion a couple of times as if trying to work out where he was but then he flicked his eyes to me with a smile. I returned it with a beam of my own and snuggled closer to him, propping myself up on my elbow so I could continue gazing down at him.

'Morning, gorgeous,' he said, his voice thick with sleep.

'Good morning, yourself,' I replied, stroking my fingertips up and down his chest. I held back a giggle when I felt him twitch beneath me. So, he was ticklish too? I was going to have to remember that. 'This is a lovely surprise,' I told him, leaning in to press my lips to his.

Isaac took my head in both of his hands, holding me close while he deepened our kiss. I moaned into his mouth, allowing him to slip his tongue inside. I let him devour me, enjoying the taste of him and the feel of his hands all over me. Hooking my leg over his waist, I could feel his erection growing large, laying across his taut stomach. I delighted in the fact that he'd slipped into bed naked.

Breaking our kiss, Isaac started tugging at the bottom of the t-shirt I'd slipped on the night before. 'You're not nearly naked enough for my liking,' he grunted. I lifted my arms straight over my head, letting him whip the t-shirt off and then shuffled out of my undies before he took hold of me and lifted me above him. He lowered me straight back down onto his waiting erection. Good god, the feel of him bare, skin on skin. We both paused, marvelling at the new sensation. Isaac's breaths were coming heavy and his eyes were hooded as he looked up at me.

I shifted a little, desperate for some friction. Isaac had an iron grip on my hips and the steely twinkle in his eye told me he wasn't about to let go. 'Isaac, please.' I spoke through gritted teeth, trying to circle my hips. 'Please, let me move.' Sweat was blossoming all over my skin with the effort of trying to contain my lust.

'Rose,' he began, his gaze piercing me. I was held captive under his eyes. I stilled in an instant, falling deeper into his beautiful blue pools. 'You are a warrior. I'm in complete awe of you and how strong you are.' I placed my hands on his chest to support myself, feeling every beat of his strong and steady heart beneath my fingers. 'You're so beautiful,' he said, tracing the curves of my breasts with his fingertips before lightly circling the tight buds of my nipples. 'My heart just about stops every time I see you.' I shuddered beneath his gentle touch. 'I love you so much, Rose. I can't imagine my life without you in it.'

'I'm not going anywhere,' I told him, keeping his eyes so he could see how much I meant it. 'My heart and soul belong to you, and I feel so incredibly lucky to have you in my life.' Lifting my hand from his chest, I placed it on my tummy. His eyes dropped briefly before looking back to my face. 'My baby is going to have the most wonderful father.'

Isaac's breath caught in his throat. 'I don't care what biology says,' he said with passion, covering my hand with his. 'I know I've said this before, but I need you to know. I will be the best father to your baby.'

'Our baby,' I whispered, tears spilling out of my eyes.

Isaac swept his thumbs across my cheeks, wiping my emotion away. 'Live with me?' he asked. I could only nod my wholehearted agreement. I didn't trust my voice to hold steady, I was so in danger of breaking down completely.

My response was enough for Isaac, who then took hold of my hips again and lifted me, before lowering me back down, maddeningly slowly. My head dropped back on a sigh, the friction was so delicious. I placed my hands back on his chest and tensed my thighs, helping him lift me up and control my descent back down, grinding my hips in a circle, taking maximum pleasure from him.

He met every one of my descents with a forceful thrust of his own, impaling me so deeply, stretching me to the fullest. It wasn't long before I felt the familiar stirrings and I began to shake on top of him. Isaac used his strength to maintain a steady pace, muscles tight in his forearms, his stomach muscles flexing. I could feel myself reaching the top of a cliff, my breaths coming harder and faster. I squeezed my eyes closed, trying to absorb the pleasure rippling through my core.

'Look at me, Rose,' he ground out. I could feel him swelling inside me; he was close too. I opened my eyes and he caught my attention again, once more holding me captive with just a look. 'I love you,' he mouthed. I cried out as his words and one last deep thrust catapulted me from the edge of the cliff, sending me into a tailspin of delirious pleasure. I rocked against him as he found his release, taking everything he had to give me. He wrapped me in his strong arms as we rode the waves together.

Chapter Twenty Five

I snuggled closer to Isaac, enjoying his body heat. It was much chillier that morning, the temperature seemingly having broken in the night. He pulled the duvet up around us, trapping the heat in. If I could wake up this way every morning, I'd be very happy, indeed. 'Did you win?' I muttered into his chest.

'Hmm?'

'The auction,' I clarified. 'How did it go?'

'It was intense and there were several bidders, but I managed to secure the top bid.' He sucked his teeth in annoyance. 'I paid more than I wanted to. A property developer was there and I think he was driving the price up.'

'But you're happy?'

'Very.' Isaac stretched before turning on his side to face me. 'As much as I hated leaving you, it was a great couple of days.'

I smiled, pleased to hear it. He sounded more like the Isaac I'd come to know and love, not the wound up ball of tension he'd been before he went away. 'Would you mind taking me back to mine later on this morning?' I asked, running my hand over his chest, tugging gently on his chest hair.

'What for?' He jolted when I pulled a little too hard. He reached up and captured my hand in his own.

'I didn't pack very much when you moved me in before, so I could do with stocking up.'

'We could just arrange for the whole lot to be brought over,' he said. 'Saves you trekking back and forth.'

I laughed lightly, rolling over and out of the bed. 'It's hardly a trek, is it?' I slipped back into my underwear and dressed quickly. 'And it's not as easy as having the *whole lot* shipped over. I'll need to sort stuff out.' I paused, running my hands through my hair and tying it in a messy bun on top of my head. I was mentally running through the sheer amount of sorting I was going to have to do. 'I'm going to have to sell my flat. Furniture. I really will need to go through my things and work out what I'm keeping and what I'm not.'

Rolling onto his back, Isaac sighed and stared at the ceiling. 'Of course, but do you need to start this now? I just got back.'

I knelt on the edge of the bed, leaning over to kiss his grumpy face. 'I don't want to start it now, but I do need to pick up a few things. Will you take me, please?'

Isaac narrowed his eyes and gave me some side eye. 'After breakfast?'

As if on cue, my stomach growled. I rolled my eyes. 'Definitely,' I said. 'I feel hungry all the time.'

Isaac jumped out of bed in a rush. 'Right then, come on. If you're hungry, you're eating.' I watched him, bewildered, as he threw his clothes on, darting around the room like the Tasmanian devil.

Downstairs, Zara and Hiro were both up. I greeted them and took a seat at the table. Zara prepared coffees for both of us, placing them on the table. 'Good morning,' she said, heavy emphasis on the *good.* I could feel my face flame, even more so when Isaac pulled me close, smiling, and kissed my cheek.

'Yes, it is,' he said on a wink, making it worse.

We ate eggs, bacon and toast for breakfast, the four of us enjoying our time together before Zara had to head off to work. I walked her to the door and hugged her, thanking her for letting me stay.

'You know you're always welcome,' she told me, returning my hug and squeezing me tightly. 'Although I get the feeling you won't need to anymore.'

I shook my head with a smile. 'No, I don't think I will.'

'Right then,' Isaac said from behind me, making us both jump. 'Let's get you over to yours.'

'Thanks, Hiro,' I told him as he walked past us, heading to his car.

He inclined his head. 'Always a pleasure, Miss Rose. Sir,' he added, giving Isaac a head bob too.

And then it was just the two of us, comfortable and warm in Isaac's car. He drove with only one hand, holding onto mine with the other, letting go only when he needed to change gear. All too soon, we were pulling up outside my flat. I felt another stirring of anxiety at the thought of being in there again, which made me even more glad that I'd agreed to move in with Isaac. It no longer felt like home. I wanted to get this over with as quickly as possible, so I rummaged through my bag, pulling the keys from the bottom and unlocking the door. Once up the stairs and into the living room. I was so focused on getting to my bedroom to grab some things, I almost didn't notice the body sprawled across my sofa.

I froze, coming to an abrupt halt in the middle of the room. Isaac bumped into my back, not expecting me to come to a complete standstill. The jolt pushed me forward, closer to the body. It was him. My attacker. Dead. In my flat.

'Jesus,' Isaac pulled on my arm, moving me away. 'Get back.'

I couldn't believe what I was seeing. The horror of it, the inconceivability of it. Just the other day I was standing face to face with this man. Now I was here, in my living room, staring at his grotesque corpse.

'Rose, come away.' Isaac stood in front of me, trying to shield my view. I was struck dumb. I was unable to move, seeing nothing and seeing everything, all at once. 'Come on, you don't need to see this.' He steered me through the living room and into my small kitchen. It was freezing in there. The window over the sink was broken and glass was all over the floor. 'Fucks sake.' Isaac tugged me from the kitchen and took me to my bedroom. Everything in there had been rifled through. My clothes were all over the floor, my bed covers were pulled back as though someone had been lying in the bed. Some of my perfume bottles had been smashed, leaving a pervasive, overpowering smell in the room. I coughed, trying to clear my throat.

'Isaac?' My voice came out in a croak. I turned my head to look at him; he was stood, taking in the mess. He looked back at me when he registered my voice, his eyes wide in shock, mouth hanging open.

'You should wait in the car,' he said, taking hold of my elbow again.

I pulled my arm from his grasp. 'What is this?' I asked him. 'What's going on?'

I watched him run his hand through his hair. 'Please, let me take you outside. I don't want you seeing this.'

My head was turning of its own accord, back in the direction of the living room. 'Is he really dead?' My body followed my head, my feet starting to walk back toward the doorway.

Isaac moved his large body in front of me, arms gripping my shoulders. 'Rose, do not look at him,' he said, his tone growing firmer. It had the opposite effect.

'Let me go,' I yelled, wrenching free from his hold and darting back into the living room, stopping short once more at the sight of him. I could vaguely hear Isaac swearing behind me, footsteps thudding along as he followed me back in. He joined me in front of the sofa, hands on the tops of my arms. I could feel the gentlest of pressures as he tried to pull me back, but I remained rock steady as I took him in.

I'd seen a dead body before. Before Nana's funeral, I'd visited with her in the chapel of rest. She'd looked peaceful and beautiful. There was something very calming about being in her presence. It was nothing at all like being there, looking at him.

His eyes were half-open for a start, gazing off to the side, sightless. His mouth was drooped open, rigid. It looked as though a line of drool had, at some point, fallen from his mouth, drying in a crusty rivulet. His chin and the front of his shirt were covered in vomit. His face was a mess, the bruises from his earlier beating having bloomed marvellously. His lips had turned a blue-black colour, as had his fingernails, I noticed.

The smell was like nothing I had ever smelled. Like rotten eggs but with a sickly sweet undertone, almost like a foul cheese. I stopped breathing through my nose and started taking shorter, shallower breaths through my mouth instead. What the hell was I going to do? My rapist was here, dead, in my flat. My door was locked when I came through it, so he must have broken my kitchen window to come in. But how did he end up dead on my settee? That was when I noticed a thin rubber tube beside him on the sofa. 'What's that?' I asked, pointing.

Isaac took a hesitant step forward, leaning in a little to get a better look. He was mouth breathing, too. He narrowed his eyes as he took it all in. 'What?' I asked again, not liking the hard glint in his eyes.

He moved another step closer, pointing out a syringe and needle. 'Looks like drugs,' he said. The syringe had a brown and pink-tinged residue remaining inside. He shook his head, straightening up. 'Don't touch anything. We need to call the police.' This time, when Isaac took hold of my arm, I allowed him to lead me from the room, back down the stairs and onto the street.

I sat in the car, watching him pace up and down the street with his phone pressed to his ear. I'd closed the door to keep the cooler air out but I was still shivering. I wanted to turn the heat up but Isaac had the car keys in his pocket. He seemed to speak for ages but, eventually, he hung up and jumped in the car next to me. 'They're on their way,' he said, turning to look at me. 'Fuck, Rose, are you alright?' He shifted round in his seat and tried to gather me in his arms. 'You're shaking.'

'Is everything okay?' I recognised the voice over the sound of my teeth knocking together. It was the owner of the bakery beneath my flat. Barbara. I didn't want to look at her, I just buried my head beneath Isaac's chin. 'Rose, honey?'

'I think she's in shock,' I heard Isaac say.

'Has something happened?' Nosy, nosy Barbara. She'd always been the same, ever since I'd moved in. Always gossiping with her customers.

'There's been a break-in, upstairs. We're waiting for the police.'

'Ooh, a break-in. Must have been during the night, I've never heard anything during the day.' Her voice grew fainter. 'I've got just the thing for her,' she said. 'I'll be right back.'

While we waited for Barbara to return, Isaac rubbed my back and stroked my hair, muttering calming words in my ear. I was comforted, but I still couldn't get my shaking under control.

'Here we are, then.' The passenger side door opened, letting the cold air in. Isaac released me from his grip, letting me fall back into my seat. 'A weak tea and a little cake,' Barbara said, handing me a polystyrene cup of something that looked like tainted milk and a paper towel wrapped slice. 'They'll make you feel better.'

Thankfully, a customer demanded her attention back in the shop, otherwise she would have carried on hanging around. I took a hesitant sip of the milky monstrosity, finding it so sugary I pulled a face. But, after a few more sips, I found my shaking was beginning to subside. I looked across at Isaac, finding nothing but concern on his handsome features. 'I'm sorry,' I told him, having another sip.

He screwed his face up in consternation. 'What for?'

'I don't know why I reacted like that.'

'No?' he asked. 'I do. That's why I wanted you out of there.'

I leaned forward and placed the stodgy cake on the dashboard. There was so much sugar in my tea, there was no way I was going to be able to stomach that as well. 'Why would he do that?' I asked in despair. Isaac cocked his head in question. 'Why would he kill himself, in my home?'

'I don't think he did it on purpose,' he replied, leaving me confused. Seeing that, Isaac continued. 'I've seen that sort of paraphernalia before, at Jack's. It can be easy to accidentally overdose on those kinds of drugs.'

'But why my home?' I asked again.

'Why not?' he shrugged. 'He's been following you around for weeks. He might have even been intending to wait for you to turn up.' I looked at him, aghast. 'He's crazy, Rose. Nothing he's done surprises me.'

We sat in silence while we waited for the police, me feeling better and better with every mouthful of tea. Isaac sat with his head back against the headrest, fingers tapping on the bottom of the steering wheel. Every now and again, I could see Barbara walking to the shop doorway from the corner of my eye. I was glad she didn't come over to try and chat. I didn't have the strength. Eventually, though, we could see the flashing blue lights of a police car, followed by an ambulance.

'An ambulance?' I scoffed.

'It's just protocol, baby.'

When the police car pulled up behind Isaac's Merc, he exited the car to speak to the officers. They all spoke quietly, so I couldn't make out what they were saying but, periodically, one of the officers would glance in my direction. It made me think Isaac was giving them chapter and verse. Wonderful. At this point, I just wanted them to get in there and get him out of my flat.

Eventually, the two officers and two paramedics made their way through the door and up the stairs. I could see Barbara rubbernecking through the bakery window, mouth hanging open in wonder. I made a point of locking the car from the inside, so she couldn't pop out and ask me questions. Isaac loitered on the pavement, hands in his pockets. After ten minutes or so, one of the officers popped their head through the door, calling for Isaac. With a quick glance at me, he turned and headed up the stairs.

This was killing me, not knowing what was going on. I unlocked and left the car and, steeling myself mentally, made my way into my flat. The two paramedics were on their way back down, so I stood to the side to let them pass. Neither made eye contact with me. I could see Isaac at the top of the stairs, hands still in his pockets. He startled when he heard me approach. 'Please go back out,' he pleaded. 'They're going to bring him down.'

I shook my head in frustration. 'What's going on?' I asked him. 'Why have they asked you up here?'

'DC Neil is on her way to take a look.' He ignored my question, which made me feel so angry. I wanted to lash out at him but managed to swallow my fury and try again.

'What have they found that they wanted you to see?'

I could see he didn't want to tell me; his indecision was evident. I nearly stamped my foot in frustration. On a sigh, he practically pushed me back down the stairs and onto the street, moving me far enough away that the paramedics had room to manoeuvre the stretcher up the stairs. 'It may not have been an accidental death,' he told me. 'They've found a note.'

'What kind of note?' My voice rose, making Isaac shush me, nodding his head in the direction of Barbara, who was pretty much pressed up against the glass, her nose squished to the side. I made sure to lower my voice. 'A suicide note?'

Isaac shrugged. 'I don't know, I didn't get chance to read it. You were practically nipping at my heels.'

Affronted, I pulled away from him, getting more pissed off. I was getting close to flipping my lid but had enough control of myself to realise it wasn't Isaac's fault. I took a few steps away to gather myself, hearing the sound of footsteps coming slowly down the stairs.

Chapter Twenty Six

At the sound of the paramedics coming back down, Isaac moved to my side, circling his arm around my shoulders and pulled me in tight to his body. As the first paramedic walked backwards onto the street, carefully carrying the stretcher, I leaned my head onto his chest, absorbing his comfort. Atop the stretcher was a black body bag, which somehow felt more sombre than seeing his body. We stood in silence, watching him being loaded into the ambulance. My tears started falling when they started to pull away from the curb, blue lights eerily absent this time.

Isaac heard my sniffling and took my chin in his hand, raising my head so I was unable to hide from him. 'What's this for?' he asked me gently.

'Fucking guilt,' I spat out between sobs.

'Guilt?'

I nodded, more tears tumbling down my cheeks. 'For being glad he's dead.'

'Oh, sweetheart.' He pulled me back into his body, resting his chin on the top of my head. I threw my arms around him, squeezing him tight. 'No one will think less of you for feeling that.'

'What sort of terrible person wishes another dead?'

'You haven't wished him dead. But you're human. I feel a sense of relief too. Relief that he won't be able to hurt you anymore. Relief that he won't be a factor in our lives anymore.' He was echoing my thoughts perfectly. 'Come on, let's get back in the car and get warm. DC Neil will be here soon and we'll know more then.'

Isaac got me settled in the car before walking around the front to join me. I had a brief flashback to the first morning we'd woken up together, when he was ripping a parking ticket from under the windscreen wiper. I don't know what made me think of that. It wasn't too long before DC Neil arrived, looking quite lovely in a navy-blue trouser suit. She nodded to us as she passed in front of the car and went straight up to my flat to talk to the officers. Twenty minutes later, she came back to the street with a folded piece of paper inside a clear evidence bag. Isaac lowered the passenger window as she approached the car.

'Follow me to the station. We'll talk there.' No greeting, no please or thank you and absolutely no friendliness in her tone. Isaac and I exchanged a look before he pulled away from the curb and followed behind her. I knew I would never set foot in that flat again. What once was my home was now a nightmare. The sight of his bloated, beaten body would be forever burned into my memory. I wouldn't even be able to go back in to pack up my belongings. I'd have to organise a removal company to pack it up for me, maybe take it to a self-storage facility for me to sort through later. The sofa was destined for an incinerator. I was already thinking of a few estate agents who could be contacted to sell the place. As long as it was a quick sale, I didn't care. I had no love for it now, and never would again. It was tainted.

Once we arrived at the police station, we were escorted through the building until we reached the most disorganised office environment I'd ever seen. DC Neil sat behind her desk, indicating we should sit opposite. I sat, surveying the scattered files and stationery all across the desk. 'It's not normally like this,' she said, noting the mess. 'We're having an office shuffle round. Half of this isn't even mine.' Neil huffed out a sigh and leaned back, looking at both of us in turn. 'Do you want a drink?'

We both shook our heads, I think just wanting to get this over and done with. It must have been evident for her to see. 'His name was Billy Vincenza.' *Billy.* So normal. 'Preliminary findings indicate he most likely suffered a heroin overdose.'

'On purpose?' I asked her.

She sighed again and placed the clear evidence bag on the table in front of her. She pulled on a pair of latex gloves and opened the bag, removing the folded note, gently placing it in front of us. 'Please don't touch it,' she warned, before sitting back in her chair. Isaac and I both leaned forward to see it better. It was poorly written and the handwriting was untidy, making it difficult to read in parts.

Rosslyn Rosie Rose

You might never know what you meant to me

Not only were the screams you made the sweetest Ive ever heard

But you gave me something I never knew I wanted
Family
You were mine from that moment
But you fought me too much
I like my women sentient and meek
After the first screams of course
And him
Your fucking hero
Making it far too fucking difficult to get near you
So Im doing the only thing I can
The only thing that will make sure I never truly leave you
I go now knowing that you will always look at that baby and see me
And you will always wonder
How much of it is like its dad
Will it have my eyes
My temperament
Im inside you now
You will never be rid of me
I hope your the one who finds me sweet girl
I want to be all you think about when you close your eyes at night

I squeezed my eyes closed when I finished reading, the words burned into my mind's eye, like when you've stared too long at a light bulb. So he did it to torture me, in one final act. I swallowed, feeling bile trying to escape my throat. He was right; I was going to be thinking about him when I closed my eyes at night. Probably at many points throughout the day, too. I don't think there was a part of me that was going to forget walking into my living room and seeing him. But he was wrong about one thing. I was never going to worry about whether my baby was going to be like him. He or she might have got half of its DNA from *Billy Vincenza,* but half was from me. And I knew about the *nature versus nurture* theory. Billy's nature was not going to play a part in mine and Isaac's nurturing of our child.

I opened my eyes, feeling resolute, and found both Isaac and DC Neil staring at me. Isaac with worry; the detective with a calculation I didn't like. I took hold of Isaac's hand in a tight grip and focused my gaze her, silently inviting her to ask her question.

It didn't take her long. 'You're pregnant?'

'Yes.' I was ready. 'But not with his baby.' I indicated the suicide note and looked instead at Isaac. 'With his,' I finished in a soft tone. I watched his eyes fill with love.

'Really?'

DC Neil's tone made my head snap back around, anger flaring in my stomach. 'Yes, really,' I responded, perhaps a little harshly. Her eyebrows jumped up to her hairline. 'I was given the morning-after-pill after the assault. And it's a very early pregnancy. The blood tests confirmed it can't possibly have been his.' I indicated the note again, unwilling to say his name.

'So you wouldn't feel the need to make sure with a DNA test?'

'Why would I?' I was practically snarling. 'The other tests are conclusive enough.'

Isaac coughed softly and squeezed my hand, trying to rein me in. 'What happens now?' he asked, shifting in his seat.

Her gaze lingered on me for a moment longer. 'We notify his family. They have to come and identify his body. Then he will be released to them for burial.' She paused, thinking. 'I can't help noting the bruises on your hands, Mr Yates.' I followed her gaze, mentally wincing when I saw the state of them.

'Can you blame me?' he asked.

DC Neil studied Isaac for several moments. 'Did you go looking for him?'

My anger flashed again. 'No, *he* came looking for me - again. Isaac reacted, to protect me.' I was actually seeing red. 'You can't tell me Isaac could be in trouble for that?' I was exasperated by her.

DC Neil kept her eyes on Isaac. 'Without Mr Vincenza here to make a statement…' She drifted off, leaving the sentence unfinished.

'So what are we doing here, then?' I asked, desperate to leave and get away from the claustrophobic box room.

'I need to make you aware, Miss Carter, that I'm unable to arrest and prosecute a deceased individual.'

It took everything I had not to roll my eyes. 'Yes,' I said slowly. 'I understand that.' I looked at Isaac, pleading with my eyes. 'Can we go now?' I asked him.

'Is there anything else you need from us?' he asked DC Neil.

She rolled her tongue across her top teeth. 'No,' she eventually said. I shot up, needing to leave fast before I started spouting about how justice had already been done, no thanks to them. I didn't trust my brain or my mouth at that moment not to say or do something stupid. We were halfway out of the door when she called out to us. 'How did he know you were pregnant, Miss Carter? Just out of curiosity.'

I stopped, feeling Isaac placing a warning hand on the small of my back. I took a deep breath before turning around to face her. 'He's been following me for weeks and saw me buy a pregnancy test. He followed me to the doctor. He jumped to the wrong conclusion and thought he was the father. Thank you, Detective Neil, for all your help.' Isaac propelled me through the door before I could say something I might regret and ushered me from the police station.

Back outside, Isaac took my hand and started walking away from his car. I hung back, confused. He just tugged me harder until I fell into step with him. 'Let's walk a while,' he said, leading me into the dappled shade of the tree-lined street. 'We'll get the car in a bit.'

The street was practically empty, with the majority of people being at work. We were also too far outside of the city walls to be surrounded by tourists. It was just us. Our meander was slow, taking us to one of the many side streets that lead to the river path. With a hitch in my chest and a falter of my footsteps, I allowed Isaac to lead me down the stone steps, onto the river bank.

He didn't acknowledge my obvious hesitation and I didn't say anything to draw attention to it. I just concentrated on the feel of my hand in his and put one foot in front of the other. 'You know, you might as well have just given her the finger and a big fuck you,' he said as we walked.

I wanted to laugh. 'Well, what did you expect? What could *she* have expected?' My voice dripped with sarcasm as I imitated her. 'I cannot arrest a deceased individual.' I shook my head, still annoyed. 'I can't believe she felt she had to tell me that.'

'Perhaps she has to be clear in the event someone is suffering from shock.'

I scoffed. 'It would have been nice if she didn't insult my intelligence.' I fumed for a few minutes, my rolling boil settling down to a simmer. I couldn't keep allowing myself to get so annoyed and angry. Especially not now it really was all over. I looked at Isaac while we walked. He looked deep in thought. 'Are you okay?' I asked him.

He returned my look, smiling at me. I was thankful to see it reach his eyes. 'I'm feeling similar to how you did earlier,' he told me. 'It doesn't feel right to feel so happy and relieved, not at the expense of another person's life.'

I did know what he meant. For the first time in weeks, I felt light and truly hopeful. My life was stretching out in front of me, completely unencumbered. I'd become so prepared to be forced to allow Billy into my life, and now I knew I would never have to. Given time, I would be able to dismiss him from my thoughts completely. It wasn't going to be easy, but I was going to make sure that no aspect of my life would be overshadowed by memories of my assault. I was also hoping that enough time would pass so I would no longer remember the horror of finding his dead body with such vivid clarity. It was like it was burned into my retinas at the moment. Thankfully I wouldn't have to do any of it alone. Not only did I have Isaac now, but my family and friends were always going to be there to prop me up. To make me laugh and let me cry. To help me heal.

Inhaling deep, filling my lungs, shoulders lifting high, I let it all go in one long lungful. All of my anxiety, all of my stress. Every negative thought. All of my tension left me, giving me a spring in my step. Isaac looked across, amusement teasing his lips into a smile. 'Things are going to be good now,' he told me, stopping our walking and taking me in his arms.

'I have no doubt.' I stepped onto my tiptoes so I could kiss him. He returned my kiss with passion, neither of us wanting to break away. At least, not until we attracted a cheer or two from a couple of young lads. We came up for air, laughing and completely unembarrassed. I don't know what it was with us and public displays of affection. It was then that I realised where we were. The riverbank behind Shiver. I gazed around, taking in the area, seeing and reliving my memories on a sharp intake of breath.

Isaac smoothed my hair from my eyes before gripping my face in his hands. 'Any painful memory you have, I'm going to fill it with light.' He placed a gentle kiss on my forehead. 'I'll never be able to undo what was done to you but I can make it all easier to bear. I promise. I'll spend the rest of my life trying.'

Tears welled in my eyes. 'You already are,' I told him, placing my hands on top of his. 'You've been my beacon of hope through the darkest point of my life. I don't know how to repay you.'

He shook his head, gracing me with the most beautiful smile. My favourite smile. 'You owe me nothing. It's me who owes you everything. You know already how empty my life was before I met you. I never thought I could have fallen so hard and so fast. I never thought I wanted to. It wasn't something I needed. But then there you were. Beguiling and beautiful, trying to hide how hurt you were, there in the hospital. It surprised me how frustrated that made me, that you thought your injuries made you somehow...' he struggled to find the words.

I jumped in to help him. To at least justify my actions. 'I didn't want you to identify me with what you'd seen. As the woman you first saw, here, by the river.' I indicated around us with a sweep of my hand.

'But, Rose,' he stroked his thumb over my cheek, soothing me. 'That wasn't the first time I saw you.'

I cocked my head in question. Isaac laughed softly. 'No, I saw you in the club, laughing with my staff and your friends. I'd been following you around the club on my CCTV all night.' He appeared bashful for a second. 'Granted, my first thoughts weren't completely pure, as I've already said. But you captured me right then, Rose. I just didn't fully realise until later.'

My heart was full to bursting; I had never felt so cherished. 'You know,' I began, taking his hand in mine and starting our walk back along the river for the car. 'My Nana would have loved you. I'm so sorry she's not around to have met you.'

‘I’m sorry, too. Although I think I may have always been wondering if I was living up to her expectations.’

I looked up at him, narrowing my eyes playfully. ‘If you met Nana, you’d know you had already surpassed them.’ I smiled at his confusion. ‘She was a naughty little minx,’ I deadpanned, making him laugh out loud, startling a passing cyclist. We were still laughing together when we got back to the car.

I knew there were still going to be some trying times ahead - telling my parents about the baby, for one thing - but I knew with a certainty that was almost frightening in its ferocity that everything was going to be just fine, as long as I had Isaac by my side. My heart. My soulmate. My hope.

Epilogue

ISAAC

I could be an old man on my death bed and would still never forget the first moment I saw Rose. Actually, I heard her first. I'd just arrived at Shiver and had decided to walk through the front door instead of the staff entrance. I'd had a trying week and needed to blow off some steam. Walking through the front door gave me chance to scope out the clientele, to see who I could invite back to my office. I was halfway to the bar when a laugh stopped me in my tracks. It was a gorgeous sound, louder than the subtle music in the quieter bar area. It was like wind chimes. Nodding to my bar and wait staff, I threaded my way through the throngs of people. It was packed early on a Friday, just what I liked to see.

There she was, surrounded by a group of friends. Her head was still thrown back in a laugh. She was curvy, gorgeous, with minimal makeup, if any at all. Black dress hugging her plentiful curves in all the right places. Her hair was astounding. The lightest blond, hanging straight down to her waist. It caught the dim lighting of the club, shimmering like gold every time she turned her head. I couldn't take my eyes off her.

Sidling up to my floor manager, I asked her, 'that party?' indicating her group with a nod of my head.

As on it as ever, Vivienne flicked her eyes over in a cursory glance. 'Party of six under the name Zara Benson. Leaving party for the blond.'

'Have a bottle of champagne sent,' I demanded before heading straight to my office. There was no further need to cast my eye anywhere else. She was the one I wanted.

Later on in the evening, Vivienne buzzed through. 'I've called through to security.' She spoke without preamble. 'A patron has been inappropriate with Carla.'

I gritted my teeth. The safety of my staff was paramount. I rose from my desk. 'Send her to the security suite.' I left my office immediately, striding down the corridor and into the security suite, which housed a wall of CCTV cameras, covering practically every inch of the club. I nodded to Charles, my head of security who was already scanning the bank of monitors, walkie-talkie raised to his face, murmuring to the bouncers. I joined him in scanning the screens; of course, she captured my attention straight away. She'd done just that every time I'd popped my head in there, all evening. She was on the dance floor with a couple of her friends, surrounded by other dancers who were trying to crowd her and her group. Jesus, she could move. Her arms were up in the air, her hips pumping to the music. I could feel my cock twitching behind my zip as I watched her.

A quiet knock pulled me from my observations with a shake of my head. There would be time for her later. I opened the door to see Carla, head bowed, eyes rimmed red. Anger pulsed through me as I ushered her into the room. 'Tell me,' I commanded.

On a sniffle, she told me about a man who appeared to be alone in the club, who kept brushing up against her as she delivered drinks. She didn't think much of it at first because it was crowded but then he grabbed her arm and dragged her to him. He cupped her breast and slid his hand between her legs before she managed to pull free of his grasp and ran straight to Vivienne. I was livid. I'd never stood for any inappropriate overtures against any of my staff, but it made me even more furious that it had happened to Carla. She was my youngest staff member; just turned eighteen but appeared younger than that. She was quiet and shy but was a hard worker. I liked her a lot.

I told her we would take care of it, that I wanted her to take the rest of the night off, but I first needed her to find him on the monitors and tell us who he was. She moved close to the screen and studied for several minutes, eyes narrowed as she searched. Eventually, she pointed out an average looking man with a shaven head. I snarled when I realised he was pushing his groin in close behind *her.* I could see he was bothering her, too. Every time he pressed in close, she moved away, trying to put other people between her and him. 'Get home, Carla,' I told her, before touching Charles's elbow as a signal we needed to leave.

Bodies were everywhere around me and by the time I made it to the dance floor, she had gone. She wasn't at her table either. In fact, she wasn't anywhere. And neither was he. I had a sick feeling in my stomach as I made my way outside. Most of my bouncers were wading into a scrap that had broken out in the street. As long as it wasn't inside my club, I didn't give a shit. I was growing frustrated and turned to rest my elbows on the wall to gaze down at the river, thinking hard. And then I saw them.

He was on top of her, pressing her into the ground, spreading her legs wide. Her dress was shoved up to her waist and one of his hands was fisted in her hair, yanking cruelly. I shouted and started running. He leapt up as I reached the bottom of the stone steps, running away from her. I made to chase and tackle the bastard to the ground but stopped short when I saw her laying there. She was unconscious. I couldn't leave her there alone, so I called an ambulance and the police and stayed with her, growing more horrified at her injuries the more I examined her.

The next weeks were a whirlwind. I hadn't intended on seeing her again, despite my earlier attraction to her. I just wanted to return her belongings and make sure she was okay. Or, as okay as she could be expected to be, considering. After handing her things to her father, I wanted only to pop my head in to check up on her.

I don't know what happened to me when I walked into the curtained area. I couldn't explain what I was feeling as I took her in, dwarfed in the bed by all the hospital equipment. I knew then that I wouldn't be able to stay away. When I'd been shooed out by the police, I scribbled a quick note for her and, whilst giving my regards to her father once more, slipped it into her bag.

The relief I felt when she called the next day was unexpected and palpable. She utterly captivated me when we met for coffee. I think my heart nearly broke when I saw her looking so lost and afraid, stood in the middle of the room. But I could see her spirit, could feel the fight radiating from her. I wanted nothing more than to know her. To just be near her. It was an alien feeling for me, but one I was keen to explore. My desires warred with the knowledge that I needed to be cautious with her, to tread lightly. I couldn't treat her as roughly as all the others.

She changed all that on the night of our first date. I'd been so desperate to see her, I couldn't wait until the time we'd agreed and I was also keen to see the business she'd been working so hard to get off the ground. So I headed straight there and was greeted by the most wonderful sight. Paint spattered and dancing to whatever she was listening to in her earphones. I could only stand there and admire her, and experience how joyful she was. She moved with abandon, as though she had no care in the world. Her dancing was wonderful to watch but her singing was dreadful. Bless her, she didn't give a shit. Her embarrassment when she caught me watching made me want to tease her all the more.

Back at hers, she took me by surprise. The fire in her eyes and the passion in her voice. I did not and would never have intended in pushing her into bed, not after what she'd been through, but she showed me what she wanted with such decision and clarity. I meant it when I told her I couldn't deny her. I'd wanted her since the moment I saw her, but I first realised I was falling for her when I pulled her tight into me and soothed her into sleep after her breakdown. I had never felt such peace and sense of purpose as I had right then. I wanted only to be with her, to love her, to make things right for her. For the first time in my life, I felt whole. It was too soon to tell her, not wanting to overwhelm her and scare her away, but I recognised the things I was feeling. I may never have felt them before but I'd seen that pure love, in my parents. No matter what, I wasn't going to let Rose go. She became my reason for living.

Despite the near-constant presence of her now stalker, I could see Rose slowly coming to terms with what had happened to her, finding ways to move forward. I was sure our path was set until I walked into my bathroom and found her there, knife to her wrist. My whole world shook and I didn't know whether to despair or be angry with her. I'd seen her upset, seen her fall to pieces before but this was something else, something I felt wholly unequipped for. And then I saw the pregnancy test. Everything I was witnessing made sense in an instant. But I still couldn't understand. I don't know how she couldn't see things as clearly as me. Even when I told her, that I would love her and the baby as if it were my own, she still wanted to run. I almost begged her to stop, to stay, but I knew she needed to feel in control. I couldn't take that away from her. Not like *him.* When she left, I could hear her crying in the stairwell. My heart shattered into a million pieces and it took everything I had not to go running down there and scoop her up, carry her back to mine, to protect her and love her. But she didn't know I could hear her. She'd been saving those tears, those heart wrenching sobs for when I was out of earshot. I needed to give her that privacy, as much as it killed me.

Everything changed the day I beat the bastard half to death. I'd been so happy to take her phone call, no matter how serious the circumstances. I was grateful to hear her voice, to know that she needed me. And my happiness turned into pure elation when she told me she wanted us to be a family together. Then there he was, taunting, teasing. He was never going to let her go. I would have happily pounded his face into a bloody pulp, but I'm glad Zara managed to stop me. It wasn't good for Rose to see me like that. And it led me to spot his driving licence, right there on the floor, in plain sight. I dropped like a stone to pick it up before Rose saw it. I didn't want to frighten her but I needed it. I needed to find out who he was. The police had been useless. Two lots of DNA left, fingerprints all over the fucking place. He'd been following her around for weeks but they still hadn't been able to find him. Now, though, his name and address were in my hand.

Billy Vincenza. He lived close to the city, in a small village just on the outskirts. I had him now. I could make it so he never bothered Rose again. And I know who I needed to help me. Jack. Surprisingly, he came without question. I didn't trust him around Rose, probably never would, but he was there when I needed him, to his credit.

Saying goodbye to Rose was the hardest thing I've ever done. She could never know what I had planned. My alibi was secure; I really was going to view an abandoned warehouse in Manchester and was going to take part in the auction the next day. I was going to check into a hotel that night. Jack lived so far off the radar, he would be able to move between cities without notice. He also had access to the drugs. He knew exactly where to get them. As much as it sickened me, the only way Rose would be safe and free was for Billy to die. So Jack drove to Manchester to pick me up from the hotel and took us to Billy's local pub. He dropped several drops of GHB in his pint when he was using the toilet and then we waited in the car for it to take effect. Jack grabbed him when he was leaving the pub, weaving all over the place, already halfway there to passing out. He got him secured in the car and drove the three of us to Rose's flat. I'd already taken her key from her bag before urging her to spend the next couple of nights at Zara's.

Once we had him laid out on the sofa, Jack took care of the rest. He prepared the excess amount of heroin and tied the tourniquet around Billy's arm. He found his vein and injected the drug. Billy never woke up from the GHB, but I still sat and watched the effects of the overdose. His breathing slowed and his skin turned grey. His body went limp and his face became clammy. He vomited in his unconsciousness, his chin practically resting on his chest. I listened to his last choking breath before his heart stopped and his chest stilled. Then I waited until he'd gone cold, just to make sure he really was gone. I was mortified with myself. I'd engineered the death of another human being, but I knew now that Rose would be safe. It was worth it.

Jack wrote the suicide note. I told him what to write, having heard the things he'd said to Rose, how he spoke to her. I only hoped she or the police wouldn't notice the change in his handwriting from his first note. If they did, I hoped they would just put it down to his nerves or trepidation about what he was about to do. I left Jack to trash her bedroom, too. I needed to be as surprised as she would be when we got in there. Once we had left her flat and locked up, I went around the back and dragged one of the industrial bins up against her kitchen wall, throwing a loose brick from the floor through the window. I pulled myself up and cleared the window of glass shards, making enough room for a person to climb through.

I knew Rose would have to be the one to find him. It couldn't work any other way, no matter how much I wanted to protect her from the grizzly sight. She took it better than I thought she would, if I'm honest. In shock, obviously. But by the time the police had spoken to her, shown her the note, she'd begun to calm down. The fact that she was as relieved by his death as I was made me feel like I could cope with having orchestrated the whole thing. In the long run, providing she was going to be okay, everything I'd done was worth it.

A few months later, I was able to take her away to Cape Verde. I needed to get her away. Her business had started booming in the weeks after Billy's death and I was starting to worry that she wasn't taking the time for herself. I didn't want her bottling her thoughts up. I booked us a villa on the beach, a private beach, just for the two of us. We'd been there a few days when I woke early. She looked so peaceful and beautiful, sleeping beside me beneath the crisp white sheets. I grabbed my camera from the suitcase and padded out to our beach. I'd centred the shot and snapped my picture of the crystal clear sea before I heard her, chuckling to herself. Her voice was like a magnet. I turned without thought, operating on pure instinct, finding her wrapped only in the bedsheet.

'So it's you,' she said, tilting her head to take me in, naked on the sand before her, camera around my neck. I just shrugged, not knowing what to say. 'Your pictures are beautiful,' she breathed. Her eyes moved lazily up and down my frame, taking all of me in.

I tossed my camera onto the sand and walked up to her in two strides. 'Nowhere near as beautiful as you,' I told her, unwrapping her from the sheet to reveal her stunning beauty. I took her right there in the sand, revelling in the feel of her around me and beneath me and loving the sounds she made.

Everything I've done is for her, including the ring box I've put under her napkin while she's been using the restroom. I can see her now, coming back across the beach. She looks effortlessly beautiful, as always; her skin sun kissed, her chestnut hair blowing in the breeze, her maxi dress clinging to her growing belly. They are the two most important people in my life and one hasn't even been born yet. In the background, the restaurant speakers are playing Nothing But Thieves *Impossible.* There isn't a more appropriate song to capture how I feel at this moment, to encapsulate how I've felt since the moment I first met her. I'd been drowning in her from that very moment. As she approaches the table, she looks right at me from beneath her lashes. Her stunning, cornflower blue eyes are glittering in the setting sun. She blesses me with that smile of hers, the one that makes my heart ache at the very sight. I close my eyes briefly to steady myself. My heart starts pounding as she joins me at the table and my hands are sweating as she reaches for her napkin. God, I hope she says yes.

A Note From The Author

Thank you, reader for coming with me on Rose and Isaac's journey. I hope you have loved reading it as much as I loved writing it.

The journey as an indie author can be a tough one, and I would love it if you could help me by leaving a review or a rating on Amazon or Goodreads. Share my book with your friends and family, let more people fall in love with Rose and Isaac.

I love to connect with other reader and writers, so please feel free to come and chat to me. You can reach me via…

Email: rlstokesauthor@gmail.com
Facebook: facebook.com/RLStokesAuthor
Twitter: @R_L_Stokes
Instagram: @R_L_Stokes

I can't wait to get to know you as readers and friends. Until next time…

R L Stokes x

Printed in Great Britain
by Amazon

65343908R00137